THE JONES FILES

BOOK TWO: BRAIDY

ADAM C. JONES

Gotham Books

30 N Gould St.
Ste. 20820, Sheridan, WY 82801
https://gothambooksinc.com/

Phone: 1 (307) 464-7800

© 2025 *Adam C. Jones*. All rights reserved.

No part of this book may be reproduced, stored in a retrieval system, or transmitted by any means without the written permission of the author.

Published by Gotham Books (March 19, 2025)

ISBN: 979-8-3485-8115-2 (P)
ISBN: 979-8-3485-8116-9 (E)

Because of the dynamic nature of the Internet, any web addresses or links contained in this book may have changed since publication and may no longer be valid.

The views expressed in this work are solely those of the author and do not necessarily reflect the views of the publisher, and the publisher hereby disclaims any responsibility for them

CHAPTERS

1	1
2	5
3	9
4	11
5	13
6	17
7	20
8	23
9	26
10	30
11	33
12	35
13	37
14	40
15	45
16	51
17	54
18	56
19	59
20	61
21	63
22	66
23	71
24	74
25	77
26	80
27	87
28	92
29	97
30	101

31	104
32	106
33	110
34	116
35	119
36	122
37	126
38	132
39	137
40	140
41	145
42	147
43	150
44	153
45	157
46	160
47	163
48	166
49	170
50	173
51	177
52	180
53	187
54	189
55	192
56	194
57	196
58	200
59	202
60	205
61	208
62	211
63	216

64	218
65	222
66	224
67	227
68	230
69	232

1

Roger Braidy works for Big Lift Salvage Shipping and Lumber Company, Inc. He flies fixed and rotary wing aircraft and has thirty-five years of experience. He is an integral part of the upper management of the company.

Braidy is a big guy and is, what some folks would call a string bean. He hates using his first name and avoids using it whenever possible. He prefers simply, Braidy.

Jones represents the company's good will ambassador, public relations and human resources. Jones has a huge black dog, and he's no ordinary kind of mutt. When it's at all possible, Jack travels with him. Jones was the owner and operator of a dairy farm in Nebraska.

Nancy is in charge of security. She and Jones are sharing a romantic relationship. The fact that she is a beautiful black woman doesn't matter one bit to either of them. Her job keeps her busy doing research on the internet and any other source out there, seeking more information on techniques and updates for the security system.

Rose is the President and CEO of Big Lift Salvage. She inherited the company when her father died unexpectedly. Rose is thirty-three years old and is very beautiful according to most men. She is a compassionate woman who cares intensely about people. Her working days are as long as twelve hours and at times grueling. Since she lives in the headquarters building in the apartment she and her father used to occupy, it's possible simply because she has no travel time from her residence to the office. She eats and sleeps business, and her company is involved in shipping, lumber and salvage all over the world. There are thousands of employees in the various departments. She is very close to Jones, Nancy, Braidy, Carmen and of course Jack.

Braidy keeps models of the aircraft he has flown in his home office. He owns a fixed wing float plane that he keeps in the company hanger. The plane can land on water or land.

Braidy while instructing warns, "Jonesy, don't get so tense, relax, feel the plane in your hands, let the yoke talk to you. The plane wants to fly level and straight just let it help you fly."

Braidy has taught Jones to fly the company single and multi-engine aircraft and is instructing him to fly the helicopter too.

Braidy is as excited as a kid on Christmas Eve waiting for the new aircraft. The colors Rose decided on takes a little longer to complete. Both Braidy and Jones enjoy short hops flying to other cities to gain more flying hours for Jones. Sometimes Nancy and Rose go along too just for lunch. The two women enjoy each other's company very much.

Nancy learned to fly from Braidy years earlier and is now an old hand at flying. She can fly every aircraft the company owns and some they do not. She is confident in flying, driving and most everything else she does.

Rose has never learned to fly. Her father thought it was too dangerous for his only child. The young woman never understood the over protectiveness of Ken, but she never complained. Now she is more interested in people and communicates effectively with nearly everyone.

She attends service club meetings and gives generously to charities if she thinks the cause is worthwhile.

The newest member of the office staff is Carmen. Sadly, she was struck on the back of her head during the kidnapping of Rose. She was kidnapped by her Uncle George and rescued by Jack and Jones after being held in a nearby warehouse. Uncle George died of an apparent massive stroke after the kidnapping. Oddly enough this is the same cause of death as his brother Ken. Carmen has been recovering in a nearby hospital, she is a slight woman. She has recovered enough to know where she is and what's happened to her. The office staff and others visit her often, but her recovery has a complication. Unfortunately, she is now permanently and completely blind. A blunt force trauma to the back of some one's head can sometimes result in blindness. Carmen is feeling so sad for herself as would anyone.

BOOK TWO: BRAIDY

Jones who once was blind himself encourages her and she is hopeful. He is careful not to offer any hope that she will ever see again with her natural eyes, but does offer the possibility that she too, can obtain some prosthetic eyes similar to the ones he has.

Rose has made arrangements for Carmen to have regular visits from social workers and Carmen tells Jones about one of the visits.

"The woman sounded nice enough, but after all was said and done, she really didn't say anything about my sight." Carmen paused, thinking carefully before she continued. "Jonesy, one of the nurses told me she heard the Social Worker asking very personal questions about me, and I guess that's to be expected, but why would she be asking about the company?"

Jones becomes very attentive.

Carmen continues, "The guy from the State office came by. I think he said he was from Vocational Rehabilitation. Any way he said there were many services that he could offer me for getting me back on my feet."

Jones nodding his head, "That's good to hear Carmen. I think that's really good news."

He doesn't tell her he thinks they weren't much help for him in his time of need. However, he doesn't want to stop her from investigating all possibilities. Carmen starts to cry, and Jones moves from a chair to sit beside her. He takes her hands gently in his. He knows how she is feeling better than most. He thinks this sweet young woman is as innocent as everyone else that has been damaged by the madness.

Jones trying to sound sure of himself offers, "Carmen, remember I too once was blind and felt completely lost and helpless, maybe the same as you're feeling now." He squeezes her hand. "You know you've got all of us behind you and we'll be here to help you recover as much as possible."

The young woman sits up and wraps her slim arms around Jones'. He feels her pain as she shakes with grief. Jones wishes Jack were here to do what Jack is best at, comforting people at times like this. Carmen begins to pour out her heart and soul. She tells Jones she doesn't have any family who even care what happens to her.

"What am I going to do now that I'm blind?"

"I know what you mean. That's the way I felt, but there are ways of doing what you need to do using alternative techniques."

She wipes her eyes on the sheet and asks, "What do you mean?"

"We can get you a computer that talks when you type. You can surf the Internet and compose documents too." Jones says in a cheery voice.

"You think I can do this and still do some sort of job?" Carmen looks doubtful.

"Yes of course, and besides that none of us is ever going to leave you hanging out to dry on your own. Rose cares very much about you and all the rest of us too." Jones smiles into her sad face.

He looks into her eyes knowing she can't see him, "I feel responsible for what happened to you, Carmen, and you will never have to worry about how you will live. You'll do much more than just survive. Your part of who we are and we need you."

Carmen starts to cry again, and this time Jones pulls her onto his lap like a little girl and rocks her gently. She slows her crying and Jones is surprised to find that she has fallen asleep. He thinks to himself, *'well what the hell does this mean? Is it my charm, or am I just that boring a human being I'm able to put women to sleep?'* He lays her softly onto her bed. He leans down and gently kisses her.

He whispers softly, "I promise you Carmen, I will get the bastards responsible for hurting you."

2

Rose decides to do some major redecorating in the office. She has the rosewood table removed. It was one of her father's favorite pieces of furniture. She replaces it with a huge slab of stone with highly polished chrome legs. The chairs have been replaced too, with ones that still swivel and tilt back, but they are made with leather and chrome to match the table. She has had; the model rail road, the huge aquarium, the ridiculous desk taken away as well.

Rose has gotten rid of the wipe board and instead uses computer graphics using the big monitor to demonstrate what she shares with her people.

Nancy discreetly asks Jones, "Is it just me, or has Rose disposed of any piece of furniture and office equipment that Ken used? I'm guessing she is still dealing with her anger at him and doesn't want any reminders."

Jones waving her comments away with his hand, "Yeah, that's what I've been thinking, too. It's her company though she's in charge."

Braidy whispers from the other side of Jones. Nancy and Jones look at each other and Jones chuckling.

"He's got the hearing of a dog, doesn't he?"

Nancy smiles and all three re-focus on the meeting.

Rose has borrowed one of the young women from the secretarial pool and keeps her busy with correspondence and other duties. Rose continues to make the coffee for everyone. It's just not a duty she is willing to pass on and believes this particular task needs to be kept within the original crew. This is silly of course. What does it really matter who grinds coffee beans anymore, but it just feels right to her?

Rose is hesitant saying, "Carmen will be discharged from the hospital tomorrow and I think we should have some sort of a welcome home party."

"We could set up a surprise party for her at her place." Braidy suggests.

"No!" Rose quickly states. She's not going back to her place for now. I've invited her to move into my apartment here at headquarters."

Braidy, Jones and Nancy are surprised by this decision.

Carefully Nancy asks, "Rose, have you spoken to Carmen about this decision?"

Rose looking disappointed with her security specialist says, "You don't have to walk on egg shells with me, Nancy, I'm not a fool. Of course, I spoke with her about it and Carmen is all for it."

The three sit quietly and say nothing. Rose realizes that her words may have come out to abrupt, she rubs her face with both hands looking overwhelmed.

"I'm so sorry guys. I didn't mean for that to be short."

She sits down on the chair at the head of the table. She turns her chair and looks out at the harbor with her delicate hands folded politely in her lap.

"It's OK, Rosie," Braidy says, "we understand. Things haven't been easy for you, and we're here for you always. Right guys!"

"Of course, we are." Nancy answers for everyone in her no-it-all-way.

After taking a minute to compose herself, Rose turns her chair back to face her people.

"I feel so guilty because this awful thing happened to Carmen. I feel like it's all my fault," tears of frustration fill her eyes, "if Daddy, I mean Ken and Uncle George had been able to work out their differences Carmen wouldn't be blind, and no one would have been killed."

"Oh Rose, you can't keep carrying this around on your shoulders," Jones offers, "if you don't let it go it will drive you nuts!" He waits for his words to sink in. "We all wish things were different, but they are the way they are, and we can't change the past. All we can do is try to keep going, watching out for each other and doing the best we can."

BOOK TWO: BRAIDY

"You're not responsible for what happened to Carmen," Nancy states absolutely in her Know it all way, "and you're not alone in caring for her either. We're all a part of this because we are a team and that's what team members do for each other."

Rose looks from one face to another seeing the sincerity in each one, "I don't know what I'd do without all of you." She smiles just enough for them to tell it's there. "I just want Carmen to have the best after what she has sacrificed for us and the company, and I don't know exactly how to care for her. We have several employees who are blind, but they have been blind for a long while. Someone who is newly blinded is different." She takes a deep breath and quickly stands gazing out the windows.

Jones reassures them all, "Just act normal around her. She doesn't want to be treated like an invalid. Being blind is going to present new and different challenges for Carmen, that's true, but the worst thing we can do is treat her like she is handicapped. There's a big difference between being handicapped and being challenged. The last thing we want Carmen to feel is helpless or a burden," his words are strong and definite, "she's lost her sight, that's true; all the rest of her is just fine. Yes, she will need our help and the help of experts to get her used to the new world she has to live in, but it's all possible and we have to hold onto that for Carmen's sake."

"That's right." Nancy chimes in.

"You've walked in Carmen's shoes? Now that I want to see," Braidy jokes, "let me know Jonesy when you're going to put them on so I can take pictures."

Jones playfully taps Braidy on his nose and they all chuckle. Jack woofs!

Jones says, "See, just act normal like Jack here." As he reaches down to ruffle the dog's ears. Jack woofs again.

Braidy with a look of wonder on his happy mug states, "I still think that mutt can understand English."

Rose smiles, then moves on to other business. "Back to the business at hand. Some of the problems we need to work on are with maintenance issues on the heavy freighters. These ships have specialized equipment and not just anyone is qualified to work on them."

Jones putting down his cup asks, "Is there a particular problem right now with some equipment?"

"Yes, we have one of our bulk carriers tied up in Brazil in South America. The ship cannot be sailed anywhere until someone repairs the huge diesel engine. In the condition the ship is in we were fortunate the captain was able to get her to a port of any kind. As it is our ship arrived using limited power that was available."

"They were lucky right?" Braidy says.

"Yes, now the captain is calling daily wanting to know what to do. Some of the crew have jumped ship, after collecting their pay. My concern is with the cargo. It's not perishable, however sitting in one-hundred degree or more temperature is not doing it any good either." Rose brushes her hair off of her pretty face.

Braidy looking hungry as usual informs, "We're already shorthanded because of losses due to the bombings. We got plenty of ships, but not so many crew members"

Rose agreeing completely sighs, "We need to get some more want-ads going in the local papers, but of course that all takes time."

Braidy from out of the blue intrudes with, "The new plane will arrive early next week."

"And just what does that have to do with hiring new crew members?" Rose asks in a playful tone. She already knows where Braidy is going with this.

Braidy looks from Rose to Nancy and then to Jones. He looks down to find Jack is staring at him too.

He is hesitant and stutters a little, "I just thought you might have forgotten that it's being delivered."

"And this has nothing to do with how anxious you are to see the new company colors, does it?" She is still kidding.

He has convinced Rose to have the new plane painted in colors other than the old red and white. She chose a soft pastel sky blue and a deep royal blue. These colors are so very different from the old ones. They all believe it's like a new beginning.

3

The new secretary who presides at the desk outside the main office is April. She has been recruited by Rose to fill in for Carmen. Carmen has been working very hard and is getting better and better at using the computer. Carmen has a sweet voice that everyone likes. She is regaining some of her old self and really can take charge. She spends hours and hours practicing her computer skills. She has surpassed Rose and Nancy too. She can find information faster and easier using a screen reader than Rose or Nancy using mice.

Carmen feels as if she's not holding her own in Rose's company, however she's doing much more than holding her own.

Rose playing with Carmen's long dark hair, "Carmen, I am so proud of you, you're doing very well. I want to ask you please if you're interested in talking with shippers and selling services? I can help you get going but I don't think you will need much help from anyone."

Carmen looking up in surprise, "Oh I'm not ready for anything like that, besides I have that accent that people can hear."

Braidy who has been listening while munching pizza, "Oh Carmen, you have a lovely accident, oops I mean accent."

Carmen grabs Brady's empty huge paw, "Do you really think so?""

Braidy kneeling down to her level says, "Yes of course you do, I like to listen to you talk and your laughter is absolutely beautiful. When you laugh that bubbly laugh it's like the sun is shining and that's not so often around here, you know because of the rain."

Carmen blessing them with her bright smile, "Ok Rose, if you think I can, of course I'll try. You are so good to me, more than I deserve."

Jack wanders over following the pizza slice as much as Braidy, provides Carmen's bare knee a giant car washing lick.

Carmen with a yip, "Oh Jack, yuck, you're a big dummy."

Carmen does well at selling services and catches on right away. She tries not to think about how many millions she is playing with on a daily basis. Rose stays close at first and soon realizes that it isn't necessary. Carmen is a real people person and shippers ask for her when ordering shipments.

Jones comes wandering in the office looking for Rose. He has been traveling out to lumber camps and ships to spread good will. He looks at Brady's pizza slice nearly gone and decides he's hungry. He heads for the kitchen and finds not much. He looks in the cupboards in the fridge but nope nothing. He strolls back into the big office and ruffles Jack's ears.

Jones rubbing his flat belly, "So is anyone else hungry?"

Braidy licking his empty fingers, "Well now that you mention it, I could use a little nourishment."

Carmen standing up and reaching out for Jones hand, "Hello my friend, I'm sort of hungry."

Rose smiling big as a sunny day says, "Oh well who cares about running a shipping company, let's all go to lunch."

Rose and company passing by the outer office says, "Ok April, you got the con, right!"

April peeling off her headset shrugs and says, "Right!"

April looking starved, "Say do you think you could bring something back for me if I give you money

Rose admiring April's new ring says, "Oh I got it honey, you're good, we'll be back in an hour or so. I have my phone in case you need something, ok?"

4

Good old Kenny Hamilton is alive and well, but he has to find another hideout. While driving around Kenny starts talking to himself, not realizing of course this is the same habit old Doc developed from spending so much time alone.

"The warehouse where that stupid George tried to hold Rose captive was too obvious, and he always thought I was the dumb one. Ha! He was so dumb he never thought I had the smarts or the guts to do him in. I showed him." Kenny sneers into the mirror. He finds an empty warehouse about a mile away and still close to the water. As he stops in front to write the phone number, he notices that the building looks like all the others and is off the beaten track. Once he has made arrangements to lease the warehouse, he hires some bad guys who like hurting people.

"Have you guys ever killed anyone?"

The men look at Kenny glaring, "Why would you ask us that?"

They are now face to face with each other and for the first time Kenny is a little intimidated"

"I just want to make sure you're not the squeamish type."

Kenny is sure the men have killed many times before, but it's safer not to assume. After all, George assumed Kenny was harmless when it came to the bottom line.

"You just make sure we get paid and you won't have to find out how easy it is for us to put your pathetic ass on a bar-b-que spit and roast you slowly like a big fat pig."

Kenny nods his head, swallows hard and the men leave. He is still hoping to find Don Hamilton to steal another revised nasty beaming device, but so far, he's had no luck. It appears to Kenny that

Dr. Don must know where he is hiding and is working hard at avoiding him.

Kenny settles into the living quarters with his girlfriend Barbra. The apartment is above the warehouse's main floor. It has all the comforts of home including a bathroom and everything they need to get by quite nicely. Kenny gets busy plotting a new attack on Rose's company. He gathers his gang of low-lives, he informs his collection of bad guys.

"You know this broad is worth millions."

He dangles the bait, their faces light up with just plain greed, and since they are all greedy it doesn't take much to get these animals interested in lots of money and even more violence.

"Are we gonna get to hurt some of these folks?" One thug asks.

Kenny looking well satisfied smirking, "Of course, otherwise you won't have any fun at all, will yeah?" Kenny assures.

Since he can see he won't have much control over this crew he doesn't even try. He does, however know how to lead them by the nose using their own greed. He's good at manipulating and has had lots of practice using this technique on Doc. For a split second, he wonders where slobby Doc has gotten off to, then shakes the thought out of his head and returns to planning the next attack.

Kenny likes these warehouses because they're so anonymous and they're all over the neighborhood. They are also big enough his gang can bring their various vehicles inside and out of sight. This building doesn't have a landing pad on the roof like the first one, but he will manage without one.

5

Rose is talking with the others about the problem with the needed repairs on the huge Diesel engine on board the Maria. They will need to send someone down there to make repairs. Carmen is using her new device that she can type on, record with and transfer information from it to other devices.

Rose watching Jack settle onto a comfortable spot on the floor, "We need to fly some mechanics down to Brazil and get the Maria going again. I contacted a couple of guys who are willing from the Augusta."

Jones looking at Carmen, "Ok we can fly them down there, and get the Maria goin again sure thing."

Carmen isn't ready for Jones to go anywhere without her. She is still very dependent on his help. She doesn't say anything but looks so sad. Jones really cares for this darling girl and has an idea.

Jones smiling big and bright at Rose, "Say Rose, don't you think we need Carmen to keep a record of what goes on away down there in South America?"

Rose looks puzzled and stares into Jones smiling face. Then it dawns on her and she smiles big and broad back at him.

Rose smoothing her hair like Jones does, asks, "Say Carmen, would you be willing to travel on our new plane to Brazil and keep track of what these rogues are doing with my new plane?"

Carmen lighting up like Christmas yips, "Oh yes, yes, yes, and thank you Jones."

Rose and Carmen are in their apartment and Carmen is excited over the upcoming trip. She is bubbly and almost like her old self.

"I've got a really nice hand-tooled leather suitcase. Would you like to use it for the trip?" Rose offers.

"Oh, that's very nice of you Rose. Thank you, and I'll take very good care of it. I promise."

"I know you will Carmen."

Rose goes to her room and pulls the case out of the back of her closet and returns to Carmen's room. The two women lay it out on the bed. Carmen begins filling it up with more clothes than she will ever need for this short trip.

"Would it be all right if I help you with some choices that are appropriate for this trip?"

Carmen blushes a little and says, "Thank you, I would appreciate that."

Rose selects several outfits and includes dresses that are not <u>too</u> short. She moves again to Carmen's closet.

"Now I think we should include some slacks. I want you to be comfortable but you're still there for business so you also have to look professional."

Rose slides some hangers to one side, "Oh, this would be perfect and you look wonderful in it."

"Which one are you talking about?" Carmen asks excited that Rose is so enthusiastic about her choices.

"The black slacks with the white lace inset button up top with the yoke collar, Plus, this light weight jacket makes a perfect outfit. Now for something casual, after all, it's not business all the time."

"I think that should do nicely. I'll leave you to pack your personal things."

"I can't thank you enough for your help Rose."

"Well, I have to admit I've never been to Brazil so I hope all these outfits work for you."

Carmen touching the suitcase with her left hand, "I've never flown on a plane before." Carmen bubbles out.

Both women are facing each other as they begin to giggle like school girls going to their first slumber party.

"I've never helped pack a suit case for someone else either. It does feel kind of like being someone's mother and that's something I've never thought about. I'm excited for you. I sort of wish it were me going with the guys, but as the boss around here it's just not possible for me to drop everything when I get the urge to fly off somewhere."

Carmen looking so small shyly whispers, "I'm kind of nervous."

BOOK TWO: BRAIDY

"Yes, this is going to be a new experience for you, you'll be OK, you're traveling with two very distinguished escorts." Rose smiles.

"Don't forget Jack." Carmen chimes in feeling comforted by her friend's words.

"Of course, we can never forget our Jack." Secretly Rose was hoping the boys wouldn't take Jack. After he found her locked in that warehouse of George's his presence makes her feel safer.

"So, how about some ice-cream?" Rose suggests.

"That sounds great," and Carmen reaches for her cane and the two go to the kitchen.

"Ah ha, I've found some rocky road. Does that sound OK?" Rose remembers this ice cream was her father's favorite.

"That sounds wonderful, but since we are sort of celebrating how about adding some hot fudge and whip cream?" Carmen says while smacking her lips.

"Why not." Rose says with enthusiasm and proceeds to put the jar of hot fudge into the microwave. Both women sit at the kitchen table and talk about girl things and enjoy their special treat.

Next morning, while they talk about what Rose expects from Carmen on this trip, they hear Braidy flying in with the helicopter. Carmen grabs the suit case and takes Rose's elbow, they make a bee line to the elevator. In moments, they are on the roof. Carmen was too excited to eat anything for breakfast so she shares a cup of coffee with Rose and Nancy.

Nancy is feeling left out and desperately wants to ask for permission to go, but not only go along Nancy wants to fly the new plane. She decides it's better to keep her desires to herself. As she watches the elevator doors close in front of her, she wonders if her desire is more because she is feeling uncertain about Jones lately.

Carmen finds the steps to the helicopter with her cane and some help from Jack. She takes hold of the short leash on his collar and tells him where she wants to go. She gets settled into a seat and Jack lays on the floor at her feet. The others say their goodbyes and climb aboard. Rose gazes until the chopper is out of sight feeling misty eyed. They fly out to the company hanger where the mechanics are standing around the new plane. Braidy sets the chopper down close to the hanger and greets the mechanics.

Jim comes ambling over and says, "I sure hope you don't wreck this new plane like you did the old one."

Braidy is the only pilot that has crash landed any of the company planes. He looks a little sheepish but takes it all in good stride. Jim and Braidy have known each other for at least thirty years and are comfortable with this dialog.

Jones chips in with, "Hey it was the most successful crash landing in history. I don't think anyone could have done a better job setting that plane down without getting both of us killed except Braidy."

Braidy lays his big paw on Jones shoulder, "Thanks, and besides, if it weren't for that crash, we wouldn't be flying this shiny new plane here!"

6

Bill and Marvin are directed to load the luggage into the King Air's rear compartment and look in before climbing aboard. They are taken aback at first when they see Carmen's white cane with the red tip. They look at each other speechless. However, they can see how very beautiful she is and begin to change their minds.

"Gentlemen, time to get aboard please and take your seats." Jones urges from behind.

He has seen in their faces the doubt about Carmen's blindness and he's not about to put up with any of their bull. Bill and Marvin nod their heads and climb aboard. They take seats as far from Carmen as they can. Jones wants to confront them but knows it would only make Carmen feel uncomfortable and self-conscious. He climbs in and steps over Jack. Jack is much too large to slide under the seat and has to lay on the floor in front of Carmen. The big dog is eyeing the other two passengers then looks up at Jones. His owner nods and without hesitation, Jack places a paw on her foot and lays his head on top.

Carmen smiles and reaches to pat his head, "Hey Jack, you holding me down so I don't fall out or something?" and she giggles.

"He makes a great anchor."

Jones says as he walks forward looking over his shoulder back at Bill and Marvin glancing from one to the other. Jones holds their attention without blinking and the two men understand they had better watch their step on this trip.

Braidy doesn't have to shout or use headsets to talk. His voice sounds normal since this new plane is much quieter than the old one. Jones joins him on the flight deck and the two go down the check list. It feels comfortable for both friends being pilot and copilot.

Braidy lines them up at the end of the strip and says, "Are we all ready?"

Everyone says, "Yes."

He advances the throttles and they roar off. The new King Air is bigger and takes more runway, but when he pulls back on the yoke they lift smoothly into a partly cloudy sky. This plane is such a joy to fly Braidy never wants to let it go.

The two engineers settle in. They turn out to be fun guys after all and are bidding for Carmen's attentions. She is flattered and gives as much as she gets. The two men have talked to the captain of the stranded freighter and are feeling confident they can fix the problem. They have worked with these ships all their adult lives and know their jobs.

Jones and Braidy take turns flying. Once Jones takes the controls Braidy stretches his arms toward the ceiling and casually says,

"I think I need a snack."

He is delighted there is a refreshment station on board. Jones for once is glad his friend has a feeding problem because while Braidy finds something to eat, he gets to fly the new plane. Most people can move around the cabin without major issues; however, they cannot stand up straight because of the low ceiling, but they manage. Jack is the only one who doesn't have to bend over so he moves about easily. Of course, the biggest problem with Jack is when he sprawls out on the floor there's almost no place to walk and everyone has to carefully step over or around him. Braidy has stocked the galley with all kinds of goodies and helps himself. The plane has a restroom too and everyone appreciates this feature.

Flying time is much longer and with an altitude of five thousand feet, you just can't pull into the corner gas station for a pit stop. They have to stop for fuel about every fifteen-hundred-miles, and the landings and takeoffs are what Carmen likes best. She quickly finds she loves flying; She is feeling important and hopes maybe, she can be useful and live the good life once again with these wonderful people. She couldn't help what happened to her and she certainly didn't ask for it, but she can make the best of everything from now on.

Jones comes back to check on everyone and use the restroom. He stops and touches Carmen's hand.

BOOK TWO: BRAIDY

"How are you liking air plane rides?" Jones smiles at her loveliness.

She looks up and smiles with a big grin. That about says it all, Jones thinks. Carmen takes his big hand between her two small ones and says.

"Thank you so very much my dear friend. You are the best."

Jones has to look away before saying, "Oh yes I know," he takes a quick breath before saying, "and so are you, my good friend."

7

Rose and Nancy are working at the headquarters building. Nancy misses having Jack along on security rounds. She knows all the shadowy places and is cautious, but still, the extra security she feels when her partner good old Jack is with her is just not there. She is on the lower level of the garage area and is thinking about Jones.

From behind, from out of nowhere, much too late, she hears quick footsteps. She reaches for her 9MM but before she can pull it from the holster, someone from behind her has their hand clasped tight on top of hers.

In an instant, she is surrounded by guys she doesn't know and one of them has a gun to her head.

"Hello little lady, we've been waitin' for yeah," he says.

Another creep pulls her arms behind her back binding her wrists with a zip tie. She is gagged, blindfolded and shoved to the floor of a van. Nancy is thinking *'what a fool I am for letting these creeps grabbed me like this'*.

Nancy realizes she is her own worst enemy for letting her guard down and promises herself she will never let anything like this happen again if she lives.

Someone covers her with a tarp that smells like new plastic.

Nancy is more angry than afraid and hopes they don't decide to frisk her or they might just find the hidden weapons she has secreted in private places. She's thinking; *'When I get the chance, I'll get free of these bad guys and then we shall see what happens'*.

The van with the name of a local plumbing company painted on its side drives up the ramp and is stopped by security. The van has no windows in the back and the four extra guys hide behind a hanging tarp between the front and back of the vehicle.

BOOK TWO: BRAIDY

"Did you get that leak taken care of?" The guard wonders.

"Sure did, and thanks for pointing out where the main valve was. It sure saved us a lot of time."

"Glad to be of help and you have a nice day."

The driver waves and pulls out onto the street. Nancy is pissed at the shabby and haphazard way her security guard checked these guys out. To herself she says, *"I'm going to fire that man's ass when I get out of this mess."*

Nancy feels the van turn left and left again at the corner. She's making an effort to remember details of the journey. They drive for about a mile mostly south she thinks. In a short while she knows the van has entered a building, she hears the difference in the way the engine sounds.

The enclosed structure sounds completely different compared to engine sounds on the open street. Thinking back to her capture she believes there are at least five big guys and she has not heard all of them speak yet. In fact, they haven't said a word so far except for the driver at headquarters building.

Her training in security teaches her to listen carefully to voices because sometimes an accent, drawl or a stutter can help identify a culprit. With most of them keeping quiet so far, she has nothing to go on except the one man who spoke that drove the van.

She hears the side door slide open. They grab her by the ankles and roughly pull her out plopping her on the cold cement floor. Once she is standing on her feet, they push her from behind in the direction they want her to go. She is shoved into a room that smells like old dirt and something else she doesn't want to think about. Someone cuts the wrist restraints and leaves her alone. She pulls off the blindfold as the door is slammed behind her followed by the distinct sound of a slide bolt shot home. She gags after pulling out the dirty rag they used for her silence. She finds that it is so totally dark she can't see her hand in front of her face.

Talking softly to herself she says, "This must be what it's like for pore Carmen now. Knowing even when there is light it's still dark. How terrifying it must be for that poor girl."

She puts her hands out in front of her feeling her way around. She shudders and reminds herself,

"It's just as well, better not to think about Carmen now it won't help."

21

Nancy takes stock of what has happened and what she can do about it. She is no coward and if given half a chance, will kill whoever these creeps are. Her hands feel for the two knives she carries and finds comfort in the knowledge she knows how to use each. She explores the room and finds it is about fifteen feet square. There's no furniture, tools, work bench, or anything else. She begins to feel her way around walls looking for a light switch but there is none to be found.

"Dam, dam, and double dam!"

8

Rose calls Jones, "Nancy is missing. We can't find her anywhere in the building and she's not answering her secure phone. I've sent guys to her places and she's not there either. I don't know what to do."

Jones softening his voice says to her, "Slow down Rose. What do you mean Nancy is missing?"

Brady's ears prick up and he moves next to Jones leaning his ear closer to the phone so he can listen to both sides of this conversation.

Rose is in a panic her breaths are coming much too fast, "She left to go do her usual rounds and hasn't come back."

Braidy looks at his watch cringing, "It's been several hours ago Jonesy."

Jones and Braidy look at each other. "Did anyone see her leave the building?"

"No and I've checked with every security guard on duty and they have reviewed the recordings. She's nowhere." Rose plops down into her chair and adds, "If anything has happened to Nancy because of what my Dad and George started I will never forgive myself." The sound of defeat and guilt weighs heavy on her and comes through all too clear in their boss's voice.

"We're on our way back Rose. Calm down. We'll find her."

Jones turns to Braidy with a look of frustration, "We've really gotta Hussle with this one, if you know what I mean. How fast can this new plane get us home?"

"As fast as I can make her fly." Braidy wondering himself.

"Carmen, we have to get back to the office? Something has come up. For some reason Jones wants to ask her, if she will be OK staying here with Bill and Marvin?

Carmen shakes her head in disapproval, "What's going on, and besides I don't know either of these guys"

Jones and Braidy look at each other and question if they should tell her the truth.

Carmen feels their hesitation, "Come on guys, if something has happened that's bad, I'm part of the company and you're my family now. Please don't leave me out."

Braidy lets out a sigh and nods to Jones.

He gathers his feelings, "OK Kiddo, you're right," He takes a deep breath and says, "Nancy is missing and Rose can't find her anywhere."

Carmen calls for Jack, "What are you waiting for? We're wasting flying time." She demands.

Once back in Seattle Jones tells Rose, "I need to find Dr. Don Hamilton to get information concerning his cousin Kenny."

"Why?"

Jones brushing back his short hair, "Because a little voice is telling me Kenny has something to do with Nancy missing and Dr. Don being Kenny's cousin is the best place I can think of to start."

"Do you want me to go with you?" Braidy offers.

"Thanks, I appreciate the support."

They drive to the cab dispatcher's office where Joni told Jones and Nancy she works. The two men walk up to the reception desk. A young brunet with rings on all her fingers, smiles and says, "Can I help you?"

"Yes, we need to speak to Joni please."

The young woman excuses herself and disappears through a closed door at the back of the reception office. A few minutes later she returns followed by Joni.

"Hi Joni, remember me?"

Joni with a brilliant smile says, "Yes of course you're Mr. Jones, right?"

He smiles back at her, "Well most folks just call me Jones." He notices Braidy trying to slide behind him. Jones looks at him with a question, then notices the young receptionist is flirting with Braidy.

Jones turns to his friend and whispers, "With your size, you're trying to hide behind me from that tiny little girl?"

Braidy looks away, and says nothing, he is pretending to be reading the posters on the walls.

BOOK TWO: BRAIDY

Jones turning back to Joni still smiling at her, "I'm sorry about this Joni. I'm trying to get in touch with Dr. Don. Do you by chance know where I can reach him?"

Joni lights up with her knowing, "I know exactly where he is. If you like I can take you there."

Jones explains, he doesn't want to take her away from her job but she assures him it is alright.

"I live about ten blocks from here and it's an easy walk, it's really no problem."

"We have a company car parked outside if you don't mind riding with us." Jones offers.

Joni shrugs shaking her pretty head, "That would be wonderful. Just let me get my purse."

9

When Joni comes back, seeing her white cane reminds Braidy and Jones both of Carmen.

Jones reminding himself, "Oh, by the way, this is my friend Braidy. Braidy this is Joni, Don Hamilton's friend."

She reaches her hand out, "Hi Braidy, it's a pleasure to meet you."

Braidy gently shakes her hand as if it might break and bashfully says, "Yes Ma'am. Thank you."

Jones parks the car at the curb and Braidy, being the gentleman, he is, opens the back door for Joni. She unlocks her front door and invites them in, "Don, are you home?" From one of the back rooms Don calls out, "You're home early. Is everything all right?"

Joni closing her front door, "Yes, everything is fine. I have someone who wants to speak with you."

As Don comes to the living room, he is surprised to find Jones and Braidy with her.

With a surprised look on his face, "Hello Mr. Jones, how are you doing?"

Jones reaches out to shake Don's hand firmly. He looks right into Hamilton's eyes with that 'we've got to talk stare'.

Hamilton nods his head slightly so as not to be too obvious in front of Joni.

"Hey Doc. How yeah doin'?"

"I'm good Braidy, and you?"

"Been better, but we can talk about that later."

Joni invites them to sit down and they all take seats around a glass topped coffee table.

BOOK TWO: BRAIDY

"Would anyone like coffee? It won't take but a few minutes for me to make a fresh pot."

Braidy nods his head, then Jones speaks up. "That would be great Joni, Braidy and I could use a strong cup about now."

"Thank you, Joni." Hamilton adds his thanks too. Joni excuses herself and goes to the kitchen.

Once they have the room to themselves, Jones doesn't mess around with small talk and gets right to the subject at hand.

"Nancy has been kidnapped and I believe Kenny Hamilton is behind it."

"Well I'm not surprised at that, Kenny is capable of anything, including murder."

Jones agrees and asks, "Do you know where he is living now?"

"Actually, I do and I have a camera on the warehouse he hangs out in. I believe it's where he lives now, and I know some of what he is doing."

Jones looking relieved, "Good, that maybe where he has Nancy. Where is this place and how far from here?"

"Not far, about a mile or so."

There's a pause before Jones gets impatient. "OK, would you be willing to tell us where?"

Don looking away, "I wasn't sure I want to share that information, however since Nancy maybe there against her will that changes everything."

Joni brings coffee in with cookies, and muffins. Chow hound Braidy comes to life and smiles big as life itself at this unexpected treat. Joni has good taste and pours coffee all around. She uses a liquid level indicator that beeps when the coffee is near the top of the cup. She passes cups on saucers around to everyone with ease. Watching her Jones is thinking one day Carmen will be that comfortable with little tasks like this.

"Thank you, Joni, it looks delicious!" Jones compliments.

Joni sits beside Don and says, "Thank you and you're very welcome."

Don begins the conversation with, "Nancy is in charge of security for your company, isn't she?"

"Yes, she is. I think she has been with the company for what, Braidy, about fifteen years or so?"

Braidy with a bite of muffin says, "Yup, that's about right."

Don says, "Kenny is living in a warehouse. I can show you on the TV screen."

Jones is amazed at the way people use technology. Don is using what looks to be an ordinary TV to display the front of a warehouse. As they're watching, some nasty looking characters come out of a walk-in door and move off down the street.

Don wiping his lips with a paper napkin, "Those guys have been working with Kenny for about a month now and I found out they are some really bad dudes. All five of them have criminal records and are wanted by various law enforcement agencies for doing some very nasty things to people."

Jones setting his cup down, "So if they're so wanted why are they running around loose."

Don sighs with a frown, "They're just that devious and are very good at avoiding the law."

Braidy takes a turn, "So how do we go about finding out if that's where they are holding Nancy?"

"Say Don, do you know how many people are in that building or do I need to go there to determine if there are additional sources of heat?"

Don looking over at Joni, "To the best of my knowledge there are the five guys you see and Kenny plus a woman, apparently she lives with Kenny."

Jones, "Ok, if I detect eight heat sources from outside the building, then that's probably where Nancy is being held."

Don exclaims, "I'd forgotten you can detect life forms with those prostheses."

Jones says, "Yes and that ability gets stronger and better all the time." With Doc opening the door to this subject Jones is hoping to ask Don about his own situation. He wants to know as much as possible about the prosthetic eyes he uses and the possibility of other implants that might have been placed in his head. *Now is as good a time as any, I guess.*

He asks, "Say Don, just exactly what did you guys do to me after the explosion that blinded me?"

"Sorry Jones, there were others working on the project, so I don't know everything concerning your prosthetics, but I do know the other doctors were doing something to do with your brain."

Jones is alarmed and it shows on his face, "What do you mean?"

"I mean I believe they put some implants inside your head as well."

"Oh shit, how long has it been, two or three years since the implants were installed and I'm just finding out now?"

Don shrinking back from Jones frustrating outburst, "Yes that's about right." Trying to calm the situation Don asks as casually as he can, "What else have you discovered about yourself?"

Jones looks at him suspiciously. Finally, he says, "Well I seem to have incredible strength at times especially when I get mad or frustrated or when friends are in danger. And I see GPS numbers anywhere in the world. I can run much faster than I ever could before and for a lot longer."

Braidy with pride for his friend, "Yeah, I believe that Jones here can run two or three times faster than anyone else I've ever seen. "Don," "I don't know about that. Like I said some of the docs were messing around with other devices." Don continues, "We could x-ray your head and find out what shows up."

"How do we do that without everyone knowing what we're doing?"

Joni jumping right in, "We ask Dr. Howard, he is discreet and is good at keeping secrets."

Don with a look of surprise, "Doesn't he work for some gangsters or something like that?"

Joni, "There are no gangsters around here that I know of, but he does patch up bad guys sometimes when they get shot up."

Don is shocked that his gentle Joni would know things like these. "How do you know about a doctor, like that?"

"I'm not just another pretty face you know. I get around." She smiles and lifts her shoulders in a modest shrug. "Besides, whenever someone sees my white cane, they automatically think I can't hear either and they pretty much ignore me. As you know Don, when one's eye sight grows weaker their other senses become more aware, so, I can hear things most others don't."

Don looks at her and touches her hand, and now he's wondering what else she has heard about his secrets.

Jones, looking anxious, "Well I don't care how we do it as long as it gets done and I find some answers."

10

Rose is pacing back and forth in her office. She hasn't heard from Jones or Braidy but she has heard from Kenny. Now Kenny is waiting for a response from Rose on his demands. Kenny's last words resonate in her mind.

"Remember Rose, I got no problem with killing this black bitch." A shiver runs down Rose's spine.

Nancy has been without food or drink for an entire day and night, she complains loudly but no one cares. She is moving around in the locked room and not being quiet about what she is doing. Since there is nothing in the room Kenny is wondering what she is up to.

He will have to feed her some time. What a pain in the ass keeping someone captive surely is. He complains to his thugs. He decides to send a couple of the guys out for some fast food crap.

He is surprised when they all decide to go. They are back after about an hour with a bag of some kind of greasy mess. The food, if that's what it is, smells dreadful.

Kenny goes over to the room and unlocks the door being careful to open it just enough to stuff the bag in. He quickly sets the food inside and slams the door.

Nancy calls out. "Hey who's there?"

Kenny offers no answer until he's half way across the warehouse.

"I really hate this black witch."

Nancy heard something hit the floor and after a short while goes over to investigate. She smells the burgers before she finds

BOOK TWO: BRAIDY

them. She doesn't usually eat any fast food but in this instance, she will make an exception. Taking large bites, she is eating much too fast, eating as fast as possible, she realizes how hungry she is. She finds a couple of giant burgers and a cold drink with ice, in a bag and the grease from the burgers has gotten slimy.

"If only I had a micro wave oven. Oh well what the hell." She says out loud and the sound of hearing her own voice is comforting.

She thinks of when Rose was taken which reminds her of Jones.

"I hope Jones and Jack can somehow find me like they did Rose." Nancy misses Jones and Jack too, and she wonders what's this all about!

When they found George's body, she thought everything would be alright, but not now. After feeling her way around the entire room, she discovers it has nothing except the door where she was pushed in. The walls are metal and very solid and from her experience she can tell the construction is old but very well built. There's not even a little give to any part she has pushed on. She pounded on the walls with her fists, and she knows the bad guys are out there and can hear her but she doesn't care. She begins to sing to herself softly, then gets louder. The guys outside hear her and are curious and move closer to the door. Nancy has a beautiful singing voice and it is loud and clear. She puts her heart into it and really begins to belt out the gospels. Her favorite hymn is Shall We Gather at the River and she puts every bit of her spirit into it.

Back in the office Jones and Braidy tell Rose and Carmen what they have discovered.

Rose brushing back her hair like Jones does, "You say there are at least seven bad guys and one of them is a woman?"

Carmen's face is red from anger, "I'm so mad I could take on that dirty gang by myself."

Rose petting Carmen on her pretty hair, "Down girl, your turn will come I think?"

"I think we can round up more than enough guys to do the job. After all, everyone who knows Nancy really cares about her."

Braidy points out, then asks. "However, how do we keep Nancy safe?"

"Yeah, that is the main problem alright. Let me think about this for a while." Jones sits down in one of the soft chairs.

Rose looking resigned to her fate, "What about the ransom?"

Jones looking at Rose. "What were the directions?"

"He didn't say yet, only that they would tell us later how to get the money to them."

"That means we have a little time." Jones observes, putting his finger to his chin in thought.

Braidy crossing his long legs, "You know this stinks like a bunch of rotten fish. It's too easy and I believe there's more to this than meets the eye."

Carmen reaching out for Jack, "What do you mean Mr. Braidy?"

Braidy asks, "What if they have Nancy loaded down with a bunch of explosives or something?"

Rose gasps. "Oh, dear God, you don't mean it, do you?"

Jones responds, "These are nasty people we're dealing with and I believe they will do anything to get what they want. I can't say for sure who murdered George, but we do know they are not hesitant about killing. According to Don Hamilton, the bad guys all have very extensive criminal records."

Carmen, "So why don't the police catch them?"

"The cops are reluctant to charge these guys without definite proof, and they are armed and dangerous. They also are very good at staying out of the line of fire so to speak. They are here, but not here, if you get my drift? Kenny hides them in an old ware house out of sight but handy for what he needs them for."

II

The Maria is out on the open ocean. She left South America heading for Africa with a load of wheat. The ship travels at her usual nine knots. The engineer Marvin is satisfied with the engines performance and relaxes with the rest of the crew.

In the mess, Marvin can be a fun guy and tells off colored jokes, but rather badly and half the time he forgets the punch lines. The crew has time on their hands, and they listen politely. Marvin is a new crew member and they enjoy spending time with him.

The ship is loaded down and sits low in the water. The holds are fully loaded and this trip will take weeks to get to Africa.

After three days and nights of sailing the ship blows up in a spectacular fireball that lights the night sky. She sinks in a few short minutes taking all aboard down to the bottom three-thousand feet below.

One moment she was there and then she was gone, little did anyone know that the spare parts crate contained one hundred pounds of high explosives, with a timer set for three days.

Dispatch at headquarters was talking with the Maria Captain and then only silence. On the fifteenth floor of headquarters is the communication center.

Ma'am, "I was just on the radio with the Maria and suddenly everything was gone." Janice reports to Rose.

Rose is very quiet and her blood runs cold and all the color drains out of her face.

Janice continues speaking with a lump in her throat, "I notified the coast guard and they had a plane in the area but by the time they reached the Maria's last coordinates there was nothing there." Janice is tearful.

Carmen comes to the door way of the living room in the apartment she and Rose share. "Rose, what's the matter?"

Rose sighs and in a very defeated sounding voice says. "I think another company ship has been blasted into nothingness."

Carmen makes her way over to Rose and sits beside her on the sofa. The younger woman puts her arms around her boss and friend.

"I'm so sorry." Carmen tries to comfort.

"If this keeps up, I think I may need to start drinking soon!"

Rose leans her head against her loving friend and they rock back and forth in their misery. Rose has come to depend on Carmen for expressing personal and quiet comments and thoughts. Carmen has a way of understanding that surpasses any of Rose's other friends. Carmen understands frustration and pain and can help Rose through these difficult times.

They can't always resort to ice-cream whenever feeling down, Carmen can give her friend a boost.

Rose wiping her streaming eyes, "Oh Carmen, what would I do without you?"

Carmen smiling sweetly at her. "Oh, Rosy Posy, you'd be ok, just not as good."

Rose ruffles her hair, "Oh you're such a brat."

12

Marvin doesn't go down with the ship. He placed the explosives under a fuel tank so when the bomb went off the fuel's ignition added to the destruction of the Maria. Marvin has his own plans for the shipping company and doesn't need Kenny Hamilton telling him what to do.

Marvin slips on a life jacket and unnoticed by the rest of the crew, goes to a lower deck and down a ladder that is welded to the side of the ship. The ladder is used by harbor pilots when boarding the ship from a harbor launch. He floats around in the ocean and the ship sails away at nine knots and he is soon alone.

Marvin has some help. He has friends who have been shadowing the ship and they come and fish him out of the water.

The boat is a Chris Craft 50-foot cabin cruiser that is made from wood. It's white with a sea green stripe painted all the way around just under the main deck.

Even if the crew on the Maria knew of the boat following them, it wouldn't have mattered.

There are many small craft on the ocean and no one really cares what they do as long as they stay out of the way of big ships.

Marvin has been involved for some time with Kenny's plan to take over the company, only as long as what Kenny does helps Marvin's plan. Marvin knows the intricate details of the shipping industry, especially this company and moves about freely within the ranks. He will possess the giant company and run it like it ought to be run. No more of that stupid lumbering or salvage. This company is shipping and should be kept that way. That's where the money is. All those other divisions just cost too much and drag the real money makers down.

Some of the nasty destruction has not been all Kenny's idea or even George's. Marvin is perfectly capable of planning and implementing his own schemes.

He watched with the others when the Maria turned into a fireball and, man oh man, did that baby go down fast.

Casually he states. "I wish I had some video of the sinking of one of Rose's finest ships with tons of cargo on board."

Marvin doesn't even think about all the crew members he's just killed.

"There will be a bunch of starving Africans in the near future but who in the hell cares."

He turns toward the bridge and yells, "Let's head for home!"

As the cabin cruiser makes a wide slow turn Marvin goes below and pulls a cold beer from the bar refrigerator. He stretches out on the couch and spends time thinking about how proud he is of himself for what he considers 'his achievements.'

The captain of the boat has no idea what crazy Marvin is up to, he only knows if he doesn't get paid, he will have to kill this lazy bastard. The boat is old but still sea-worthy. He only steels from boat owners who are responsible and take good care of their craft. Marvin has no idea where he comes from and it's better that way. The captain scratches his back against the bridge doorway and looks towards the compass for a heading back to shore. The other crew members will get something but not much. If they give him any trouble, he will throw them overboard.

Captain holding his hands around his mouth shouts, "Hey your lazy assholes look alive down there, pull in the damned anchor, will you? How do you expect me to get us to shore with the stupid anchor down?"

13

Back at headquarters building the friends have gathered for a strategy meeting. The police have been there gathering information concerning Nancy's abduction. They will not say if they think Rose should pay or not so they aren't much help. They also aren't offering any suggestions for a positive ending.

Jones looking pissed. "I'm so sick of the police. I hate the pompous bastards. They think they are so superior and act like they know everything. In my opinion and from what I've seen so far they are pretty much useless."

Rose is a wreck. Sitting on the couch she is physically shaking and can't seem to stop.

Jones goes over to her and puts his arm around her, "Rosie, I'm here and we'll get through this too."

She looks into his eyes with tears in her own and asks in an exhausted voice. "When will this ever end?"

"I don't know, but whatever it takes I will find all of the creeps and kill them." Jones is adamant.

His voice is full of anger and revenge.

Rose shudders at his violence and pulls away slightly.

Jones holding her hand, "When rats have invaded your house you have to get out the big traps. You want the trouble to be gone for good, don't you? He doesn't wait for an answer. "So, we must get tough with our resolutions."

She considers the look in his eyes and now also sees the compassion this man has. She moves back to the circle of his strong arms wanting him to hold her and says, "Of course you're right. I just don't think I'm cut out for this job."

Jones reminds her, "You're not alone in this Rose. All of us will work together and find the answers."

Jack is nosing all around the room sniffing and whining in frustration.

Braidy isn't even munching any food and now he is watching Jack.

Braidy following the dog with his eyes, "Say Jones have you been watching Jack lately?"

Jones standing up, "Yup, I see he is bothered by something."

Carmen brushing hair off her pretty face says, "He is vibrating. He is really bothered by something or someone."

Rose lifting her head out of her hands and looking up, "What do you mean Carmen?"

"He's vibrating; when he comes to me, he is shaking all over, but then he goes away like he is distracted as if he knows Nancy is missing and is in danger."

Jones watching Jack more closely, "Of course he knows Nancy is gone and he feels all of our stress which he senses is danger. Jack come here boy!"

Jack comes to Jones and leans up against him. Jones lays his hand on Jack's head and tries to understand using telepathy. Braidy gives him a strange look.

"It's no good, Jones despairs. Jack and I can't make sharing thoughts happen."

Rose and Braidy look at each other and both see the surprised expression on Carmen's face.

", Jonesy, are you telling us you can read that dog's mind?"

Braidy says thinking his friend is losing his marbles. Jones doesn't even flinch when he replies, "Whenever Jack and I share a thought it's when there's some action that needs an immediate response, and there is no thought process involved."

"Uh huh." Braidy says and they all exchange disbelieving looks again.

Marvin pays the pirates for picking him up. The boat belongs to guys who, rumor has it, are drug dealers, but Marvin has seen no evidence of that. He thinks they're small time pirates stealing penny-ante stuff that most people don't even bother reporting to the police. These guys live off the land and sleep on the boat. Marvin runs with them because they have no ties to anyone or any place. He does wonder if they have enough fuel to make the nearest land fall. He is sure they are not using their real names, and he isn't sure if they are American citizens. He doesn't know where they're from. Maybe from Florida or Cuba. Anyway, where they're from doesn't matter as long as they do what he pays them to do.

Marvin pays them each one hundred dollars and that pisses off the captain after they dock.

He probably may not ever see them again and it doesn't matter. They're like throw-away pirates.

Marvin has a more important decision to make. He has a choice to either pretend he was thrown off the ship when the blast occurred or fell off during an earlier watch. In either case, he will have some explaining to do if he wants to keep his place within the company. For now, he decides to lay low and see what shakes loose. He has time so he will wait and see what that crazy Kenny does with the black woman they kidnapped.

Marvin and Kenny are not pals and Marvin thinks Kenny is stupid and cannot be trusted. Kenny hardly knows Marvin exists but the two nasty guys are going in the same direction. They both want Rose's wealth but are going about it in different ways. Marvin will use any method to get what he wants including blowing up company ships and Kenny chooses to kidnap people. So, Marvin will drive the company out of business eventually using his method but it will take longer and is more permanent. Kenny wants everything faster and takes more risks. In the end, the result is the same. Whatever the method, they will try their best to ruin Rose.

14

Jones decides to take Jack outside for a walk about. He wants to find out why Jack is anxious. Jack doesn't need any kind of leash because he follows Jones directions faithfully.

Jones and Jack and at the last moment Braidy, go down to street level and out into a lite mist, the two men don't mind. It is lite and they're used to being damp. Jack of course has a fur coat to keep him comfortable. He stands on the sidewalk sniffing not just the ground but the air as well. He looks and listens all around, finally without hesitation he heads north, in the opposite direction from the warehouse where George died after kidnapping Rose.

Jack walks slowly exploring, taking his time moving carefully. Jones has never seen his dog track in this manner before. Jones feels Jack is learning something new as he puzzles out details. He starts down one street then comes back to the corner. He reverses direction and goes the other way.

Braidy with a curious look at Jones asks. "Say Jonesy have you ever seen Jack act like that?"

"Nope never. He seems to be learning a new technique of exploring the world." Jones is curious too.

Jack hears them but pays them no mind. He is sniffing everywhere. Not passing up any smell he moves slowly checking out any new smells and every bit of litter too. He isn't interested in finding something to scrounge on, but rather seeking information.

The two men follow along watching and waiting for Jack to show them what he is doing. Jones and Braidy simply try not to influence the big dog in any way. Jack moves along steadily and thoroughly not missing anything that might help him to track Nancy. Most objects don't matter so he disregards those items that are meaningless but once in a while something grabs his attention. He looks over his shoulder at his partner, Jones and Jack are in silent agreement and Jones encourages Jack with a hand wave. Braidy has never seen anything like the team work of Jones and Jack communicating this way and quietly watches in fascination.

The three are out in the mist for hours when Braidy gets a call on his phone.

Rose sounding concerned wants to know, "Are you two alright?"

Braidy tells her what's happening with Jack and she is interested.

Rose clearing her throat, "Do you mean Jack is following some sort of sent, moving down the street to the north?"

"Yes, that's right. He's definitely a dog with a purpose on a mission." Braidy agrees.

Rose trying not to beg shyly asks, "Well stay in touch and please be careful."

Braidy and Jones are both armed all the time. After Nancy had been kidnapped, they will not hesitate to shoot the bad guys and there won't be a warning shot fired first. The two men have talked about that and finally Braidy agrees with Jones that taking the offensive is the only way to keep people safe.

Jack stops and cocks his ears listening to something. Jones sees the alert and motions to Brady to watch. Braidy observes Jack and looks in the direction that big nose is pointing.

Jones gazing down the street, "Any idea what's down that street?"

Braidy wiping the rain off his face answers, "More warehouses I think."

Jones walks over to Jack and once again lays his hand on Jacks head trying to hear what Jack hears. Jones hears a woman singing *Amazing Grace How Great Thou Art*. He knows that singing voice as well as his own. He recognizes Nancy's contralto voice clear and rich.

Jones swelling up with pride, "Good, good boy Jack. Man, oh man you are the best my friend."

Braidy feeling left out wants to know, "What is it Jones?"

"Jack has found where Nancy is and she's right down the street there in the third building on the left side."

Braidy stunned and almost afraid to ask, "You mean Jack heard her singing?"

"Yup and I just got a line of a gospel song. I am sure that was Nancy singing," he looks at Braidy and says with a smile, "She was singing Amazing Grace."

Something was telling Nancy to belt the song out at the top of her voice.

Braidy smiling down at good old Jack, "Well I'll be damned, what an amazing mutt."

Jack grins up at Braidy showing all of his front teeth as if to say, 'See I told you so.'

Braidy looks down and agrees, "Yes, you did my friend and you're a brilliant dog."

Jones and Braidy slide over to the sidewalk across the street, to a nearby building and into a doorway. They don't know if this is the building Don Hamilton is watching or not but they decide to just watch for a while.

Nothing is happening at the building, and the street is quiet. Jack is watching the building like a hawk daring anyone or anything to move but, nothing does. Jones isn't totally sure about Dr. Hamilton and thinks Hamilton has his own agenda for his cousin.

Jones quietly speculates, "It could be that Kenny hasn't got Nancy in the same building he uses for his main place. I think I'm going to move closer to get a better look."

Braidy embarrassed states, "I'm not experienced in this kind of work, tell me what to do?"

Jones smiling at his friend, "You and Jack stay here and keep watch. I want to try and get a sense of how many there are inside."

"Right, we'll stay right here and if you need us, you'll call out, right?"

"You'll hear me." Jones moves off.

Marvin decides to contact Kenny and confront him on his trying to horn in on the action. Marvin has the address for the warehouse and drives there. Jones, Jack and Braidy are still watching when Marvin drives up in his old Ford pickup. He Parks in front of the building and gets out. He looks at the building and wonders how to get in or even get someone's attention. He is armed and thinks of shooting his way in but decides to just bang on the little door beside the big wide one.

Jones doesn't recognize Marvin right away since he hasn't been with the company all that long, but Braidy does.

"Hey, that's Marvin at the door."

Jones says looking blank, "So what about him?"

"He was the engineer who flew with us to South America to fix the Maria," a shocked expression on Brady's face, "oh, shit he's not dead."

"I can see that Braidy," Jones being a smart ass, "What's your point?"

Braidy ignores his friends' tone and says, "Didn't Rose tell us he got transferred to the Maria?"

"Are you sure Braidy?" Jones questions.

"Yup he is the one."

"Alright," Jones says, his usual statement, "Oh well, what the hell."

Right then one of Kenny's nasty thugs comes to the door and asks Marvin, "What do you want?"

Marvin pulls out a 45 automatic and says, "Let me in or I'll ventilate your innards."

Of course, the punk decides to comply. "Not his problem, mate."

Marvin disappears inside the building and the bad guy looks up and down the street before closing the door with a bang. Braidy is quick and before he can enter, takes a picture of Marvin, with his cellphone not using the flash. He pulls up the photo and looks at it with curiosity. He calls Rose.

"I've just sent you and email with a picture of a guy I think is Marvin off the Maria. Can you verify that I've got the right guy?"

Rose, "Indeed that's Marvin."

She pauses. "I don't understand Braidy, what does this mean?"

"It means the bastard didn't go down with the ship and he is somehow here to see Kenny." Braidy is fuming mad.

"What on earth is he doing there?"

Braidy explains, "I don't think Marvin not going down with the ship explains some of the other bombings."

"I don't understand." Rose is nearly in shock.

"It means Rosie, Marvin is our ship bomber!" Braidy is almost yelling and Jones and Jack spin around on him.

Jones is waving his hand to shut Braidy up and Jack is staring at Braidy, showing every tooth in his mouth but without making a sound. Braidy quickly gets the message.

Rose is getting mad, "I want him and want answers Braidy. You and Jones have to bring me Marvin." She demands.

Braidy doesn't like tempers, they rarely resolve problems but, in this case, he thinks it's a good thing. Rose needs to get tougher.

"I don't mean to try to tell you how to run this company, Rose but I think you need to look through the entire company directory and evaluate each person, especially the ones with opportunities to make decisions." Braidy suggests.

"I agree Braidy and I'll start right now."

Jones and Jack are watching and waiting and cannot hear Nancy singing now, however they are both convinced that she is there. Jones waves his hand and Braidy goes around the corner to the end of the other block. He wants to know what's behind the building. He finds there's only an alley and another big door. Otherwise just solid walls without even a single window. He guesses that the bad guys have the vehicles inside the warehouse out of sight out of mind, a good deal for bad guys.

15

Kenny and Marvin face each other and both are ready to draw like killers in an old western movie. Neither one wants to die so they just glare daggers at each other.

Finally, Marvin says, "Say Kenny, there's no point in killing each other, there's enough for everyone don't you think?"

"Yeah, you're probably right. You can have what you want and I get the rest. I just want the money."

Marvin relaxing visibly stands up straight saying, "I want to own the shipping parts of the company and don't care what happens to the rest."

Looking around the warehouse, "I heard you have that black woman from the company. Is that true?"

"Sure do. She is inside that little room over there. She is quite a singer. Not bad really, if she weren't black. Her singing reminds me of my mother's when I was still a good boy." Kenny sneers.

Marvin says sarcastically, "That must have been a while ago."

Kenny glares at him. After a moment, he invites Marvin over to the kitchen table they use for nearly everything. He offers him an untouched soda. The drink has ice in it and is still cold.

"Take a seat anywhere." Kenny waves his arm all around.

Marvin takes the wobbly chair farthest from Kenny. He eyes the remains of a bag of French fries, but decides no.

Kenny shrugging looks like he couldn't care less where the fat boy sits, "So what kind of deal suits you the best?"

"Like I said, I want the shipping, you can have the rest." Marvin slurping loudly.

Kenny rubs his chin with his hand contemplating, "That includes lots of the company's worth, right?"

"Yup you're right so we will have to compromise."

Kenny is thinking to himself *'I never compromise with anyone for anything.'* He feels the forty-five tucked in his belt and wonders how fast he can get it out and up. He isn't much of a gun fighter and wisely decides not to try right now. Kenny's way is to get the thugs to do his dirty work for him. He looks at the five big bad bruisers and decides that killing Marvin will be OK for later.

Braidy comes back to Jones and tells him there's only an alley behind the building.

"That is usually the case. It's a security thing to protect any customer's storing cargos. If cops can drive around properties it tends to discourage thieves some times. Makes it harder to break in and steal stuff." Jones pets Jack.

Jack is becoming bored and lays down beside the doorway they are hiding in. Jones goes off to peek around in order to get a look at the license plate on Marvin's truck. He calls Rose providing license numbers from Marvin's old Ford.

"Do you know anything about Marvin's personal vehicle?" Jones asks her.

"I have a friend in the police department. I'll call and ask." Rose offers.

Jones wonders if anyone ever really has a friend in the police department, but lets it go for now.

Rose is quick, "Yes, indeed the truck does belong to Marvin, why?"

Jones sighing loudly answers, "Either he is a really convincing ghost or he didn't go down with the Maria."

Rose exclaims loudly with feeling, "What in the world are you talking about? All hands went down with that ship, didn't they?"

Jones shaking his head, "Nope not this guy. He is here and in with Kenny right now and they are holding Nancy."

BOOK TWO: BRAIDY

"You mean you found Nancy for sure?" Rose excitedly says loudly.

"Yup! Jack heard her singing Amazing Grace loud and clear and there's no other voice I know like Nancy's."

Rose smiling at the memory of Nancy's beautiful voice allows, "Yes your right Jones. She is unique and not in just that way." Rose continues, "She could be a professional singer any time."

"Yup you are right Rose!" Jones tells her.

Carmen, who has been sitting quietly listening to Rose's side of the conversation gets excited and whispers, "Did they really find Nancy?"

Rose nods her head and realizes Carmen can't see her nod, "Yes, they have found Nancy. Now hush until I'm off the phone and I'll tell you everything."

Braidy doesn't have the patience Jones and Jack have and is becoming restless, "So what do we do now?"

"Well my son, you just settle down here beside Jack and me, and we wait." Jones makes calming motions with his hands.

Braidy resigning to his fate settles down, "Ok that's not much fun and I'm not known for having patience, but I'll do it for Nancy's sake."

"At a boy, that's the ticket. Don't worry my friend we'll get her back." Jones assures.

When the three are sitting down on the sidewalk they are hidden behind a parked truck and some cars which puts them out of sight of the people using the building. They can see legs when they are looking underneath the truck and cars and know when guys come and go from Kenny's place. After an hour, they see the same pair of shoes leaving; the shoes belong to Marvin. They are workman's foot ware that lace halfway up to his knees.

Jones turns to Brady and warns, "Don't move. Just stay still and watch."

Braidy sighs but remains still. Jack lifts his head and tracks Marvin like he is ready to fire a missile. Marvin opens up the driver's door of his old truck and it protests with a loud crackle and squeal. Rust is a big problem in the Northwest and oil cans are never in the right place when you need them.

Jones and Braidy are thinking of doing something although they aren't sure what.

Jack leaps up and stares at the door. He hears something and is alarmed.

Jones hears Nancy screaming through the building walls, he knows she is in pain. He is at the door before he knows it and bashes right on through blowing it off its hinges.

There are five bad guys and Kenny and they have Nancy tied down on the table spread eagled. Kenny is touching her bare skin with a lighted cigarette.

Jones piles the five guys into a mess in front of Kenny. Kenny runs out the back of the building before Jones can catch him. Jones is off balance after using his body like a bowling ball and the five thugs are a bloody mess but all quite dead.

Braidy comes in with Jack, he just stares from Jones to the bloody pile of bodies. Braidy doesn't know what to think about the look on his friend's face. He looks very dangerous and a little disoriented.

Braidy with a shaky voice speaks softly, "Man, I'm so glad you're on our side. Man, oh man, what raw power!"

Jones isn't even winded as he moves to stand next to the table.

Calmly he looks down at Nancy, "Hey baby, are you all right?"

Nancy is crying but through her tears says only, "Yes."

Jones releases her from the table and helps her to her feet. She falls into his arms and holds on for all she is worth.

Jones comforts her saying, "You're OK, I got you now and your OK."

Braidy with trepidation says, "What about these guys, what do we do, call the police?"

Jones nods his head slowly saying, "Well I guess we'd better."

BOOK TWO: BRAIDY

Nancy looks around holding up a hand and says, "No way, even though you were defending me, the cops wouldn't necessarily understand and how exactly do we explain how you were able to do this alone?"

Jones shakes his head, he wonders How did he do this smash job? He doesn't even remember smashing down the door. But there it is hanging off to one side.

Braidy calls Rose, "We've got Nancy and she is OK."

"Are you sure?" Rose questions.

"Well of course I'm sure, I'm looking right at her." He grins into the phone.

"No, I mean are you sure she's, all right?" Rose clarifies.

"Yes, Rosie, she's all right and she's safe."

Rose heaves a big sigh of relief and says, "Is there something we need to clean up?"

Brady looking down at what used to be five big bad jerks, "How did you know that?"

Rose with a private smile tugging gently on Carmen's long hair, "I'm getting smarter in my old age don't you know!"

Braidy tells her there are five this time"

Rose gasps, "You mean Jones took care of five of those creeps?"

"Yup, all in less than a second too. He rolled a perfect strike."

Rose thinking to herself, *what kind of man is this, I'm so glad he's on our side*. "Does anyone know you were there?"

"Nope no one, that guy Marvin was here, but he left before he saw us," Braidy tells her "There's no one just the four of us." He continues, "Kenny Hamilton was here, he got away before we could catch him, I don't think he will tell anyone anything."

Rose agrees then suggests, "Say Braidy, do you think we could fly the dead guys out over the ocean for a big swim?"

"Well I guess we would need to be discreet of course, good news is this warehouse is off the beaten track and no one else is around here."

Rose smoothing Carmen's long dark hair, "Just tell me what you need and I will get it for you right away," Rose's voice clouds up, "I am so glad that Nancy is OK."

"It's OK boss lady." Braidy comforts.

Wiping the tears off her cheeks with a tissue Carmen has handed her, Rose pulls herself together and suggests, "This evening we can all get together to make our next plan."

Braidy suggests, "Jones wants to go active and hunt for Kenny and Marvin. He also wants to find everyone else involved in this bad stuff."

Rose wishing Jack were with her and Carmen sighs and says, "I know that's what he wants, but I think we need to be more careful about that now."

Jack comes in through the broken door.

Jones looks down and says, "Hey, where you been big dog?"

Jack is a little winded as he looks up at Jones and thinks, *'I been chasing after that scumbag Kenny. Where else do you think I would be? Humph!'* He circles around the dead guys then barks into Jones face. He is saying in his doggy way, *'You didn't wait for me. Why don't you ever leave any of the bad guys for me to take care of?'*

"Sorry Jack I lost my head." Jones chuckles at his bad humor.

Nancy is still being held by Jones with her face tucked tightly against his shoulder. She once again feels safe in the arms of this good strong man.

16

Kenny looks back before he stops to catch his breath. He is shaking with fright and rubbing his rear end. Even though he had his electric motor bike flat out that bastard dog nearly got him. His index finger feels the ragged tear in his sweatpants. He felt the big dog's teeth scratch the skin of his but.

Boy, he has never seen anyone or anything move that fast and with so much power as Jones. Those weren't little guys either. All over six-foot and more than two-hundred pounds each.

Looking around to be sure he is alone he says out loud, "If Jones would have gotten hold of me, I would be like cream cheese on the floor."

He doesn't know what to do about the ware house, although he believes he can eventually go back after a while. For an instant he wonders what about that island girl than moves on. He finds a quiet little café and steps inside for a cup of coffee. A few of the patrons notice the rip in his pants and snicker. Kenny's cheeks get warm and slightly pink. His hands are still shaking as he picks up the mug to take a sip. Looking out the front window he knows if Jones finds him, he probably won't attack with others around.

The café is about half full of seamen from all around the world and he can hear the various languages being spoken.

Kenny thinks to himself, *'I better find somewhere to hide for a while in case Jones is still on the rampage. And I sure as hell don't want to end up as a dog treat.'*

After a few more sips of coffee he calms down and decides to rethink some.

He pulls his cell phone from his pocket and calls Marvin. He is glad they had at least shared cell phone numbers. The phone rings twice and Marvin answers.

"Yeah what do you want?"

Kenny putting down the coffee cup, "Do you know who Jones is?"

Marvin scratching under his arm pit, "Yeah, so what about that slime ball?"

"You wouldn't say he's a slime ball after what he did to my men."

"What are you talking about?"

"He came to my place just after you left and smashed the five of them into a pile of goo, and they're all dead."

Marvin lifts his but cheek off the table, "No shit and you couldn't stop him?"

"It happened in less than an eye blink and he just mowed them all down like a bowling ball knocking down pins."

Marvin is shaken by what Kenny is saying. He doesn't like Kenny, but he can hear in his voice that he is telling the truth.

Marvin asks, "Where are you?"

Kenny tells him the name of the café.

"I'll come right over."

After Marvin gets there and finds Kenny's table, they both are somewhat calmer, not by much.

Kenny stirring a fresh cup of coffee with creamer, "I've never seen anyone, or anything move that fast with that much power. He became something other than human."

Marvin still isn't convinced and doubts Kenny, "What kind of fish story are you trying to feed me here?"

Kenny, "No shit man, I'm not kidding, not one little bit. He killed those guys quicker than you can blink your eyes."

"So how did you get away?"

"I ran for my life out the back door with that huge dog chasing me. That dog wanted to bite my ass off."

Kenny absently rubs his sore bottom. He thinks no one see's but a weirdo at the next table snickers right out loud. Kenny thinks he will have to just kill that bad boy.

Marvin is gaging looking green.

Kenny asking, "Hey man what's the matter with you?"

BOOK TWO: BRAIDY

Marvin looking for a trash can or something to hurl into, "Oh hell it's some of that old food I been chowing down lately, it must be bad."

Secretly Kenny is laughing inside, he really doesn't like this asshole. Maybe Marvin will die and he won't have to do anything after all. Like killing George, killing Marvin means nothing, if Marvin's gone than there's more for him.

17

In the office, the friends are celebrating Nancy's return. The burns are painful, and Jones treats the wounds with salve and just for Nancy, some tender words too.

Nancy lifts her hand to draw attention to herself, "OK, I have to ask. Why am I always the one who gets damaged?"

Braidy is munching a piece of pepperoni pizza they ordered and in typical Braidy fashion—his mouth partially full, he mumbles, "Ah hell Nancy, I guess you're just lucky."

"Thanks a lot, you're a big gorilla and oh hell whatever." She snarls.

Rose and Carmen are sitting on the floor under the windows. Rose has taken over some of Jones job helping Carmen with her recovery. Carmen is becoming more independent and everyone praises her for the way she is handling little problems for herself. The two enjoy each other's company and have gone out for dinner and on short trips to Vancouver B.C.

Carmen doesn't even think about not using her cane any longer. She uses canes like tools as Jones explained and the use of them has become natural for her. She now has a small collection of canes in various colors and chooses the correct color to match her shoes or other apparel. She and Rose are similar in size and can wear each other's clothes if they like

Carmen's hair is very long and reaches her very slim waist. It's shiny, lush and a dark rich brown with a slight curl. She is a very attractive woman and some of the younger guys around the company have definitely noticed. Some of the older ones too. Every chance the young men get they offer her their opinions.

BOOK TWO: BRAIDY

Jones notices too and says, "It looks like my favorite girl is in high demand these days."

Carmen swats him on his hard belly playfully and whispers, "You'll always be my best friend and I will always love you for believing in me."

Jones just can't take a compliment and hides his shyness with an imitation of John Wayne, "Well shucks little lady, it wasn't nothing. It's the cowboy way don't you know!"

Carmen pulls on his big hand and shyly asks, "Come dance with me!"

Even though there's no music they prance around the office for a while moving with some grace in spite of Jones big feet.

After what Nancy has just gone through, she doesn't mind, because she knows they're only having a little fun.

Braidy and Jack are looking at the empty pizza box with regret wishing there was one more slice. Braidy has eaten half the pizza himself and of course good old Jack got the crusts

Jack declares the empty box a lost cause and joins Rose under the windows. She pets his big block head and dreams about a beautiful island where there's no danger or troubles.

18

Braidy gets a phone call from his Mother. She tells him that his old friend Allen has passed. She informs him that Allen died in his sleep at the age of ninety. Braidy learned to fly from Allen Cartwright and remembers his kindness to a boy who was trouble by a father who was abusive and just plain mean.

Jones can see that his friend is troubled and waits until they are alone before asking.

"Hey man, what's wrong?"

Braidy looks at Jones after staring out of the big windows at the harbor.

"Oh well I guess it's to be expected, my old friend Allen died. He was the one who taught me to fly when I was still a kid. Things were kind of tough back then; my father was a real tyrant and my poor mother really caught the abuse. She tried to protect us and got beat up for that."

Jones looking over at Jack waving his finger. Jack is so good at understanding the feelings of people comes over and stands close to Braidy.

Braidy is so un-Braidy like that Jones is worried. He moves them into the kitchen and settles him down at the little table. He pores Braidy a hot cup of coffee fixing it just the way that he likes it. Braidy mumbles his thanks and tells Jones some about his early life.

"My father had a construction business, digging basements, pushing down trees, digging pits, anything he could to make a living. He must not have been a happy man, he was always yelling at someone or something. The equipment we used was old and needed fixing nearly all the time. The machines all used pony motors to start the Diesel engines, we had to crank them by hand. Those little motors could back fire and crack your knuckles or brake an arm. My mother was very talented at running those big bad boys and often finished the job in spite of my Old Man's cussing."

One summer in Nebraska we were digging pits at the end of big fields to catch the runoff water to be used over again. Water management was just beginning and my father got a contract digging big pits art the lowest end of fields. Each pit had very specific dimensions and when completed were inspected before the Old Man got his pay. We had nearly finished and all that was needed was for the bottom of the pit to be smoothed flat using the Cat. Well Pops drove our D8 down into the hole and began smoothing out the bottom. The Cat came a crossed a sink hole and got stuck. The old bastard started blaming my mother, the dog and all of us brothers. It got dark and we had to stop for the night. When we came back to the job sight in the morning, the Cat wasn't there.

Well it was there of course, only thing was, it had sunk. The only part of the Cat that was visible was the top of the exhaust. The county came out with bigger heavier equipment and tried but no way was the stuck Cat coming lose.

They documented the sinking and actually tied some line on the exhaust and over the years the discovered the Cat sank over fifty feet.

We had to go back to using the D4 Cat, in some ways it was better, it had a front-end loader with a bucket. We used that one for digging basements mostly and it work well enough for pushing down trees. We raised the bucket up about ten feet or so and pushed down trees with ease. If the tree was so big the D4 couldn't push it down, we just dug all around the tree, exposing the roots, cutting them off with a chain saw and over it went.

After my father was killed when the scraper fell on him off a jack, we sort of went our different ways. My brothers joined the army or something military. My Mom and I lived together until I finished high school. I went to work for Allen and learned to fly from him. After several flying jobs hauling car parts, I got a job working for Ken.

Jones listening to his friends asks, "What happen to your mother?"

Braidy looking up into Jones eyes, "Oh hell she's doing just great, she remarried and got a job at the public library. She buys herself pretty dresses, goes to the hair dresser and lives the life she missed. She has never said, but really, I think she was relieved that Dad was killed. She lives well and from what I can tell is happy."

Jones offering a doughnut says, "Oh that's good, and at least your friend Allen lived a good life. He taught you well and you are a good teacher too. So, although I'm sorry for your loss I'm glad he lived for a good long time."

Braidy taking a big bite, "Oh hell of course you're right, and I'll be alright, thanks."

Jack is looking forgotten and utters a short sharp bark followed by a growl. Jones relents and offers a crawler to his dog. It doesn't take Jack long to decide, the pastry is gone in a split second.

Jones smiling down at his friend offers, "Jack, did you even chew that thing?"

19

Kenny Hamilton realizes that the current plan for grabbing what he so desperately wants, Rose's company, isn't working. Also, he has to come up with another place to hang out. He thinks he and Marvin need to bury the hatchet.

Kenny has never gotten along with others. As a kid, he always fought with his brothers and as far as the old man, not a chance. He does remember his mother with fondness and she was always good to him.

He remembers her singing those sappy gospel songs and when he heard that black woman singing <u>Amazing Grace</u> it took him back to another time. Kenny's mother was a small woman with a beautiful and very strong voice. She was always in demand by folks wanting her for funerals, weddings and Sunday morning worship services.

Kenny hardly ever went to church, and when he did, he usually helped himself to money from the collection plate. Once he got caught by some old bag with an eagle eye. Man, oh man, did his old man beat him for that one. Kenny wanted to kill the old bastard, but never got the chance. Someone else got there first. His father had a gambling problem that got into the thousands, and when he couldn't pay one time, they literally got their pound of flesh. Kenny didn't even feel bad about losing his father, he thought, *'good riddance.*

Kenny calls Marvin and they agree to meet in another greasy spoon café they both like. Marvin doesn't like Kenny either, but the two realized they can help each other out anyway.

Since the last attempt to force her hand, Rose's company has gotten more and more difficult to attack. The security is almost like Fort Knox. They can still blow up ships, but what good is that? They need to come up with another way.

Kenny is thinking and says to Marvin, "It's too bad about Don Hamilton. That beaming device worked well. You could be anywhere in the world and just zap anyone. Ah hell, someone got it from the first warehouse and no one knows who."

Marvin has no idea what Kenny is talking about. He thinks Kenny is a couple of fries short of a happy meal, and sometimes Kenny thinks someone else may be driving Marvin's mind. Kenny figures that Marvin is good for performing nasty jobs he can't do or simply doesn't want to do himself.

Marvin thinks Kenny is just stupid and doesn't have any balls. Both men know they have problems with the other guy, but right now the benefits outweigh the shortfalls

Kenny sucking on a toothpick nods and then says, "So Marvin, did you ever wonder what really happened to that George?"

Marvin looking annoyed, "No who in the hell was George again?"

Kenny looking all around before answering, "Oh hell you dummy, he was Ken's brother you know."

Marvin remembering, Oh yeah, that's right, so what about him?"

Kenny looking oh so smug, "Well it was me that done him in."

Marvin looking more than surprised, "No shit!"

20

He is a man who tells everyone he is from Ireland; however, he keeps his true home of origin secret. He isn't from Ireland at all, he wants everyone to think he is from the Emerald Isle. He tells folks his name is Seamus, but who really knows what his name may be. He is a small guy about five-foot-four, weighing about one-hundred-thirty-five pounds. He looks completely innocent with white hair and blue eyes. He never seems to make much of an impression. He's got everyone fooled, this little guy is a genius at making nasty things work for him.

One might say he is the way he is because he was always picked on when he was younger. Not true, this isn't so. He was actually treated well enough as a youngster. He suffers from a different kind of problem. He was never accepted by his mother, and now hates all women.

He doesn't really know anyone at the Big Lift Shipping Company, it's simply a nice fat target. He likes power, and the fact that this very large company is run by a woman just makes him furious.

He reads about Rose in business magazines. She is considered to be the richest, most eligible single woman anywhere. Rose looks very beautiful in the magazine photograph and even though she is wearing jeans and a sweatshirt her natural beauty is apparent.

Seamus knows Marvin. They met in a bar in Barcelona Spain and enjoyed each other's company. Marvin and Seamus have kept in touch over the years, so he's not surprised to hear from his old pal again.

Marvin looking in a little black book for the number, "Hey old man how you doing?"

Seamus sipping on some tea, "Oh, I can't complain."

"I got something that you might be interested in. You've probably heard of Big Lift Salvage and Shipping Company?"

"Yes, I have. As a matter of fact, I'm just reading about it now." Seamus puts down his tea cup.

Marvin, tells him all about the company and the little witch that manages it.

"You know Seamus, you can get in on the action too if you want." Marvin is so generous with someone else's money.

"What do you mean?"

"I used to work for that company on some of the heavy freighters and I know where the bodies are buried. He is so smug.

Seamus raising his bushy eyebrows, "What exactly does that mean, and what bodies are buried where?"

"It's kind of a long story and we really need to discuss it in person." Marvin advises.

"I'll be over the pond next week. When and where can we meet?"

The two men set up a time and place and each think to themselves. 'This is a lucky break.'

After ending their call Marvin thinks, 'meeting up with good old Seamus is great timing for all of us.

Marvin is hungry for something he doesn't know what. He feels a little better but not much. He sometimes wonders about some of the really old cans of food he has been gobbling down. He doesn't know what it means when the side of the can is bulging out. The stuff inside all smells the same to him so how can he know. Marvin decides to not worry about it, as long as he can barf once in a while, he's ok.'

21

Rose and the others are talking about the disposal of the five bodies in Kenny's warehouse.

"Braidy and Jonesy did a good job for us."

Jones and Nancy are talking about her kidnapping and she shares more details.

She looks at her healing burns and shakes her head, "I can't tell you much since I was blind folded and then locked in that dark little room. I can tell you however, there was a woman who I think, lives with Kenny in the apartment above the warehouse's main floor."

Jones waving her hands away from the burns," How do you know that?" Jones wants to know.

"I got only a brief sound of her voice when she gasped unfortunately, but I think the woman is from Jamaica or somewhere like that."

Nancy closes her eyes trying to remember what she heard.

"The woman may have peered over the railing just for an instant when they took me out of the van, then disappeared. Nancy frowns in concentration."

Jones gently asks, "Did the woman see you, Nancy?"

"Yes, I am certain she saw me. She got a good look when I was tied up on the table. I saw her watching for an instant and then she backed away."

"Why did they torcher you like that?"

"Kenny wanted you all to be convinced he meant business. If I screamed in pain and Kenny recorded it, you would believe he would have killed me."

Jones takes her hand looking into her brown eyes, "Well he's right about that one. I think Kenny is capable of murder without any remorse."

Nancy continues, "He had a motor cycle stashed between the warehouses the one I was in and the one next door.

He kept it out of sight for fast getaways."

Jones looking puzzled, "I don't remember hearing any engine sound, how did he keep it quiet?"

"It had an electric motor. I heard him talking about it when I was tied to the table. He was bragging he could jump on it and off he goes."

"That would explain how he got away from Jack."

Jones reaches over and touches Nancy's face gently. "I am glad you're alright, it seems you are always getting in harm's way."

Nancy moving her hands all around, "You're telling me. First, I'm shot in the leg, then shot in the chest, and thank goodness for my bullet proof vest. Now I'm kidnapped and burned."

Jones, "I think we need to protect you and everyone else better."

Nancy looking frustrated wants to know, "How are you planning on doing that? We already have vests, cameras, better radios, bigger guns, what else can we do?"

Jones making calming motions with his hands, "Well your right of course, still there has to be a way to make everything safer."

"One way would be to increase the training of our security team." Carmen suggests.

"The guard at the garage entrance isn't worth a plug nickel. Letting that phony van in without checking with his supervisor to verify we called a plumber. Then the idiot let them just drive out of here with Nancy in the back. I'd like to see him fired." Carmen's voice is strong and assertive.

"Already taken care of. I handed him his final paycheck myself." Rose informs them.

She comes over where Jones and Nancy are sitting on the floor under the windows.

"Is it OK if I join you?" Rose is polite in her asking.

"Yes, of course." Nancy pats the floor beside her as an invitation.

Carmen and Jack move too making room for her, and soon they have a little pow wow circle of people sitting on thick carpet with their legs folded Indian style.

BOOK TWO: BRAIDY

Rose repeats herself with, "The boys have taken care of the issue at Kenny's warehouse."

Jones, "Thanks Rose. Now I think we need some suggestions about our other problems."

"Do you have something specific in mind, Mr. Jones?" Rose queries.

"As a matter of fact, I do. Specifically, the stuff left over from when Ken was allowing George to reap havoc in the company."

Rose hangs her head in shame. "I'm so very sorry guys."

Jones pulls on her toes and says. "No, no. Not your fault. You are doing all you can to fix the problems George and Ken caused. So, stop feeling guilty my friend."

Rose looks up at him and says. "Do you really think so? I feel like I got us all into this mess because I had my suspicions and said nothing."

Nancy is such a know it all, "Yes, we all think you are doing the best you can, and no, none of us blame you for any of this."

Carmen reaches out and takes Rose's hand, "You're the best Rosy Posy, we all would be lost without you."

Rose gets a giant unexpected lick from Jack who got up so quietly no one noticed.

"Oh Jack, yuck! I don't need another bath from that car washing tongue thank you very much!"

Jack gives her his big toothy grin and licks her again.

22

Don and Joni call Rose, "Would it be possible for us to come see you?"

"Yes of course, that would be delightful, when can you come over?"

"Would right away be too soon?"

"Of course not. You're welcome any time." Rose is smiling.

Don and Joni live close to the headquarters building and are there in twenty minutes. Jones goes down to greet them and after clearing them with security, brings them into the building. After the firing of the last guard at that station, his replacement isn't about to let anyone in without knowing for sure they are security cleared.

Don is not so aloof this time and is much friendlier. Joni is her usual happy self and is glad to see Jones again.

He is taken aback when she steps forward and gives him a little hug as a hello. His cheeks turn pink as he uses his arm to direct them to the elevator. They are whisked to the top floor in no time. Jones leads them past the reception desk and into the office.

Don describes for Joni what he sees, he does it for her because he knows she's interested in knowing everything that is new.

Don and Joni think nothing of the circle of people and dog under the windows even though there are plenty of chairs.

"Come join our happy little group." Rose invites warmly as she pats the carpet with her hand.

Don is a little hesitant until Joni says, "Thank you so much. We'd love to." She takes Don's hand.

Rose offers to make coffee for everyone.

BOOK TWO: BRAIDY

Don remembers and remarks, "I remember the wonderful coffee Ken used to serve." Then realizes that may not be a good memory for these folks, but before he can apologize.

"The coffee is still the same," Rose explains, "Joni do you want to help?"

Joni jumps to her feet with delight and says, "Yes, of course!"

Don doesn't mind sitting on the floor and pets Jack's broad head.

"Don, have you met Carmen?" Nancy asks.

Carmen is still shy about her blindness with strangers, and shyly offers her delicate hand.

Don is not prejudice at all and reaches the extra distance lifting his bottom off the floor to take her hand.

"Carmen, Joni is blind too." Nancy explains.

Carmen looks toward Nancy in surprise.

"Carmen was attacked when Rose was kidnapped. The blow to her head caused her to lose her sight."

Don's expression is full of sadness. "I'm so sorry that happened to you."

Carmen is embarrassed, and it shows.

"Oh, please don't be embarrassed. Everything is all right, it wasn't your fault." Don comforts.

Rose and Joni come back from the kitchen with cups, coffee, creamer, and some fresh baked goodies from the Round the Corner Bakery.

Jack becomes interested in the goodies, but not the coffee and as he stretches his neck to sniff the pastries.

"Hey tubby, you're getting fat again. Leave those sweets alone." Jones commands.

Jack growls ferociously at him.

Joni grins and asks. "Does that dog understand English?"

Jones, "That's the same thing Braidy asks. As far as I know, yes, he does."

Rose refocuses the meeting by asking. "What can I do for you both?"

Don begins, "I have been working for some time now and I believe I have perfected the beaming device."

He looks around at all their faces and sees a lot of anger. He wastes no time in finishing. "And I've built in some extra safety features."

Jones slurping up some tasty coffee. "What do you mean Don?"

"Well, not just anyone can use this new device. It has a retinal scanner, in other words only those that have been approved and their retina pattern has been programmed into the device can use it."

Rose asks with suspicion, "And who are the ones that have been approved?"

"Oh, just me so far."

"Don, do you know if someone can use this device to aim at things using my prosthetic eyes?"

"No, not any longer. I have also developed a new method of aiming."

Rose is cautious, "Just what can you do with this device?"

"Hmmm ok, I can beam small objects anywhere in the world."

Jones nodding at Rose, "ANYWHERE in the world?"

"Yes, with weight up to thirty pounds."

Jones looking skeptical, "So let me understand what you are saying here. You can beam a can of beans say to China?"

"Yes, I can, and even bigger things than that. The danger here is that some explosive material can be beamed the same way."

Rose looking alarmed, "Well I don't like the sound of that. It's been bad enough just sending electricity and sonic beams, but actual bombs?"

"Calm down Rose. That's why there are safeties built in now. And with the new security log, I won't let just anyone use the beam."

Don doesn't see any sign of the concerned and terrified expressions going away. He tries harder.

"I am terrified of Kenny and what he might do."

Jones lifting his free hand, "Hold on. You're afraid of your own cousin?"

Angrily Don says, "Absolutely."

Jones shakes his head to clear his mind. "You mean you want us to protect you from your cousin?"

"Yes, sort of. But Kenny is only part of the problem. You see, there is some guy Kenny calls Marvin."

Rose with a pinched face says. "Oh yeah, we know All about Marvin. He blows up my ships and kills my crews for no reason."

Don playing with Jack's ears. "Oh, there's a reason alright. He wants to control the shipping parts of your company."

BOOK TWO: BRAIDY

Rose touching Carmen's hand, "That's nuts! Why does he want just the shipping part?"

"He's kind of crazy."

"You think?" Rose says sarcastically.

Don holding up his left hand, "Wait, wait, let me finish please. He was around when your grandfather ran the company, and Marvin and your Grandpa were supposedly very close. When Grandpa died and left Marvin absolutely nothing, it kind of made Marvin go off the deep end."

Rose, "Boy what's with all the crazies in this company's past?"

Jones picks up a doughnut crumb before Jack gets it, who has been listening carefully to every word Don has been saying puts in his estimation of the situation.

"It's my belief that at least half the world has gone nutty."

Nancy sitting next to Carmen, "I'll drink to that."

Carmen smirking at her friend, "Silly, you're drinking coffee. You can't toast with that."

"No comment from the peanut gallery, thank you."

Carmen bangs Nancy on the thigh with her small fist and Nancy pretends to howl in pain, "That's the leg that got shot."

Carmen is beside herself with regret, "Oh no, Nancy, I am so sorry."

Nancy pushes Carmen gently on the shoulder playfully and says, "I'll get over it, Honey. It's OK."

Carmen comes back with, "Oh you!"

Jack nudges Nancy and does his best to distract her, wanting to help her not think about the pain.

Nancy pushes Jack away saying, "Get away from me with that car washing tongue, you're a big mutt."

Jack backs off with his head down looking misunderstood.

They all hear Braidy settling onto the landing pad with the helicopter and soon he is there with a stack of pizza boxes in his hands.

"Hi all. I thought I'd drop in at that little Italian pizza joint we all like on my way back from down the coast."

Braidy is beaming he's so proud of his treasure and is welcomed by all. Jack especially is interested and comes over to help.

Braidy carries the food into the kitchen.

Rose turns to her guests with a big smile, "It looks like were having pizza, tonight. Don and Joni, will you join us?"

Don looks at Joni and knowing by now she is always hungry says. "OK, if it's not a bother?"

Rose gets a mischievous little Nome like grin on her face and says, "No bother. You just pick up a piece, chomped down on the pointy end, tear off a bite then just chew. The only thing you have to watch out for is Braidy stealing pieces from your plate."

Joni laughs and says. "We would be happy to stay for pizza, and by the way Braidy," she hollers, "I tend to bite any stray hands that might come near my plate."

"Ho ho! Looks like you've got competition Braidy old boy." Jones informs.

"I'm not shy about food either." Braidy returns.

"Rose, can we talk more about this situation after dinner?"

"Of course; I think there is a lot more to talk about, don't you?"

Don nods as they head to the table where Braidy has placed the now sliced pizzas in the center. They all settle in for some of the best pizza in the world. Jack has taken his place under the table, as close to Braidy as possible. He knows who really cares about his hunger needs.

23

Marvin and Seamus meet in Portland, Oregon for a talk. Marvin is feeling like a big shot and Seamus is feeling like a zoo keeper feeding the animals by buying the gorilla lunch.

Marvin lays out his plan for taking over Rose's company. Leaning forward with his elbows on the table after they are both done eating Seamus listens attentively until Marvin has finished.

Marvin waiting expectantly. "Well, what do you think?"

Seamus sits back in his chair and folds his arms across his chest. He has a patient look on his face,

"The plan has a lot of flaws."

When Seamus points out some of the problems, Marvin grows indignant.

Seamus holding up his hand in a stopping motion. "Hold on laddie, you're putting the cart before the horse so to speak."

Marvin, "What in the hell are you talking about? I didn't say anything about a horse or a cart."

"It's just a metaphor, it doesn't have anything to do with horses!"

Marvin is annoyed, "Just speak plain English, will yeah?"

Seamus looking for a waitress for more coffee. "OK, chill out Laddie. Look at it this way, blowing up ships isn't doing anything but making everyone mad and costing the company money. You're biting off your own nose to spite your face. You got to get to who's in charge of the operations."

Marvin looking confused. "What do you mean? Marvin demands really pissed with Seamus' play on words.

"You're blowing up ships in a company that you want to control. So, you're blowing up your own ships. How is that going to help you once you've got ownership?"

Marvin scratches his head in thought dislodging a plethora of unwanted degree. "I didn't think about it that way, go on."

"First you need to think of this giant company as a living being. If you cut off the head the monster dies." Seamus reveals a world of patience.

Marvin brightens with understanding. "Oh yeah, I get it, you know Kenny tried something like that when he kidnapped that black woman and Rose."

Seamus finally thinking he's making progress with a primate. "I heard something about that. It didn't work because that guy Jones came after Kenny's bad boys."

Marvin revolted by the reminding. "Yes, he did, and Kenny was really shaken up after that one."

"Do you mean Kenny is out of the picture?" Seamus is hopeful.

"Nope, not even close, but you can bet he will be a lot more cautious from now on," Marvin brags, "Kenny can be trained. He might even be house broke for all I know." Marvin laughs at his own joke. Anyway, Kenny is rethinking his plans as well, and will come up with something totally different next time."

Seamus raises his bushy eyebrows curiously. "That will make it interesting, don't you think?"

Marvin pouring more coffee for them both says. "What do you have in mind?"

Seamus nodding his thanks. Now with his elbows on the table has his chin resting on his interlaced fingers

"Oh, it's nothing much, instead of trying to just kidnap one of the big cheeses, we grab them all at the same time."

Marvin getting it, "Oh ho, now I didn't think of that one. You mean grab them all and there's no one to run the company?"

"Exactly, if you got them all then we can move in and start telling folks what to do, and who's left to stop us?"

Marvin looking at Seamus admiringly. "That's brilliant! Seamus, you are a clever bastard."

"I don't mind the clever, but the bastard part you can leave behind."

Marvin is confused yet again, "Say what?"

Seamus with a world of patience, "Never mind."

He knows Marvin isn't too gosh awful bright, "What do you think Kenny is going to do?"

BOOK TWO: BRAIDY

"Kenny is the wild card in all this. Even when he tells you what he is planning he don't stick to it and when he changes his mind, he don't tell you neither." Marvin reveals.

Seamus lays out a plan for capturing all the big cheeses at once.

"It's a simple plan and should work just fine, but some of the success depends on what crazy Kenny does," Seamus admits, "if Kenny stays out of the way, the plan will work." Seamus instructs.

"Got it."

Marvin decides to call this 'The Seamus plan.'

24

Kenny's new place is an old house on a small island. The island is known to nearly everyone, but since it's been deserted for so long, no one pays any attention. There are other buildings around the big house and these structures are mostly empty too. The boat house is good for hiding small boats and provides some protection for the crafts.

Kenny isn't much of a house keeper so the house isn't as clean as the average person would like. However, it's nothing compared to some places he's lived.

Kenny got in touch with his old girlfriend who is from Jamaica and speaks with a lively lilt. She is an interesting woman and does make an effort to keep the house clean. Her best quality is cooking. Fixing meals for Kenny and baking pies, breads, rolls of all kinds and some tarts that are new to Kenny fill the days with pure pleasure. Keeping mostly to herself there is no talk about what happened at the warehouse because it's upsetting to think of that horrible man that killed the five guys. Kenny's hired help were frightening so staying away from them was a priority.

Seamus is kind and has a great sense of humor. Marvin and Seamus come to the island after Kenny collects them from Seattle. Seamus is a little guy and is at least four inches shorter than Kenny's girlfriend, but they weigh about the same. Her name is Barbra and likes to be called Barb.

Her days are spent walking by the beach collecting seashells that are different and interesting and brings her a great deal of enjoyment. She is a kept woman and does not have to do much for Kenny. He has never voiced what he thinks about their relationship, but her natural survival instincts are always ready to make an escape if it becomes

BOOK TWO: BRAIDY

necessary. Growing up around the sea, she knows how to drive a boat. Barb checks on the second boat often. Living by the ocean all of her life, big waves or the incoming tides aren't intimidating. Kenny doesn't think she has much sense, but wisdom has told her to put away a small nest egg just in case Kenny's craziness irrupts again. She doesn't know what Kenny does, because he never talks about it. There is safety in appearing to not know anything about his plans. What she doesn't know isn't a threat because she cannot tell.

Barb likes to fish. When the fishing is good, using recipes shared from other cooks that have come in and gone out of her life she fixes fresh seafood dishes. Kenny and his two visitors gobble down the food. Barb is relieved as she cleans up when they lock themselves into what could generously be called a library.

Marvin always looks like he just came out of the engine room of a ship. Seamus looks like he is going to Sunday Mass. Kenny wears sweat pants and a sweat shirt and usually the same color. Actually, he prefers black, in fact everything he wears is usually black. Kenny can be funny at times and Barb enjoys his humor, but not so much lately. She senses the three men are hatching something very big and very nasty. Her use of English isn't as good as it needs to be to understand everything they say, but she gets most of it. Her English is good enough to determine that there is a large company run by a young woman and the company has millions and millions of dollars just there for the stealing.

Barb trying to appear much more innocent than she really is, "My English not good." Barbra lets Marvin and Seamus know.

With this knowledge, the men feel comfortable and don't mind her listening to their plans. However, she understands much more than they think. Barbra doesn't know what to do with what she is learning, obviously, it's clear they are planning a big crime, and it sounds like there will be murders too. She isn't interested in being involved in any law violations of any kind. Her family is back in Jamaica and they would be sad if she gets into trouble, for now she is discrete and keeps her mouth shut and her head down.

Barb has a runabout Kenny allows her to use for anything she wants. The boat is twenty feet long and has an inboard-outboard engine that lets her zip across the waves nicely. Her father was a fisherman and she learned everything she knows about the sea from him. Barb hasn't many friends where she lives now and it's lonely.

Growing up around family and friends she needs to find people she can be with and talk to.

Kenny isn't very social, he broods and is silent for long periods of time. She knows enough to leave him alone at these times and pleases herself with the things she's interested in. Barb loves the open ocean and boats off for fun when she has caught enough fish for everyone. Barb is very self-sufficient and can take Kenny or not, she's her own woman.

25

Rose's cat is a big kitty weighing in around seventeen pounds. Her name is Miss Kitty, after the saloon owner on the old TV series Gun Smoke. Miss Kitty has all her original equipment including some very nasty claws. Jack tries to be friendly, but the cat wants nothing to do with him. Unfortunately for Jack, Miss Kitty scores a hit every time, scratching his poor nose. Jack just blinks one time but does not yelp. Jones and Braidy witness the act.

"Jack, mind your manners."

Jack looks at Jones and cocks his head with a questioning look, then lowers his chin thinking, *'I didn't do a darn thing to that nasty cat and I'm getting told to mind <u>MY</u> manners?'* Jack lays down and glares at the cat. He uses his paw to rub his injured nose. Miss Kitty isn't at all sorry for her dangerous nose swiping and alternates growls and hisses from the corner.

Jones isn't concerned at all about it; Rose is regretful.

Jones admiring her unique beauty offers, "Rose it's not your fault, dogs and cats have been fighting for ever."

Rose looking at poor old Jack, "Still, I wish they could just get along," she walks over to Jack and kneels down. Very gently she wipes the last drop of blood from his nose with her thumb. "I'm sorry sweet dog."

Jack raises his head off the carpet and Rose kisses the big wet nose as a mother would kiss a child's boo-boo. Jack thumps his tail letting her know he doesn't blame her"

"Well that's true of a lot of other things in life don't you know." Jones adds.

Braidy kneels down, looks at Jack's nose and says, "It's not so bad, not bleeding much now. He pats Jack's head and scratches an ear, you'll live big dog."

Jack plays it for all it's worth. He needs sympathy and of course something to eat wouldn't hurt.

Braidy finds a slightly used piece of pizza and asks, "Hey Jack, would you like this warmed-up, Braidy looks at Rose, "Would you listen to me, now I'm talking to the mutt like he's going to answer me."

Jack decides to have it as is and takes two steps toward the pizza and before Braidy realizes the dog has moved, down it goes.

Rose is trying to conduct a meeting before all the distractions and looks determined. Carmen has taken over coffee duties including grinding of the beans. She has a device that emits beeps when a cup is nearly filled to the top with liquids. She learned about this device from Joni, who uses one herself.

Joni is now working for Rose and holds down the receptionist desk on the main floor. She is attractive and looks professional in her clothes. She dresses eloquently with style. It's quite a change from the casual wear worn on her last job. This position is a public one and employees need to make a positive impression. Joni is a quick study and has learned the locations of all the offices in the building during her first week. She makes it look so easy when directing people where they need to go.

She knows most of the captains by the sound of their voices and usually calls them by their names. Joni is a wonderful addition to the company and Rose is happy to have hired her. Jones and Carmen are busy too, traveling from various divisions of the company. While Carmen talks to the staff and crews, Jones talks to the captain's or bosses. Rose is now completely convinced that goodwill from the top is the way to improve production. She believes happy people are productive people and she is right because it shows in profit and loss statements.

Sometimes Rose can forget most of the past and takes delight in providing employment for so many workers. Her father was a liar and she can never completely remove the painful past, however there are times when the past is nearly gone.

Rose loves people and is so very proud when her people do well. She doesn't think of anyone as a little person. She has discovered that

BOOK TWO: BRAIDY

the size of an individual isn't what counts. She need only look at Carmen to confirm that it's true. Carmen is her best friend and is recovering nicely. Carmen is developing into a real expert in selling more contracts for shipping, lumber, and salvage. She has a rich sense of humor and brings out the best in nearly everyone. Rose has observed Carmen dealing with some of the grouchiest folks in the world and ends up selling them millions of dollars' worth of services or goods.

Carmen works very hard, she takes whatever time is necessary to get things right. She has total control of her computers and smart phones. She stays at work until the day's jobs are complete and final. Rose just loves her friend and delights in her wit and good humor.

26

Carmen and Jones are flying to South Carolina to visit a logging camp. Carmen is looking her usual best wearing jeans and a light weight sweat shirt like Rose does. Jones thinks to himself, *'I wonder if Carmen is wearing one of Rose's outfits? Oh well what the hell, it doesn't matter.'* and decides not to mention it.

Carmen is chatty and talks about the upcoming Thanksgiving dinner she is planning for all.

She is grinning at him looking so pretty, "Jones, what do you think about giving each employee a frozen turkey as a bonus this year?"

Jones smiles at her with lots of teeth, "Do you know how many turkeys that would be? I don't mean people turkeys don't you know?"

Carmen nods to herself, "Of course I do, silly." She gets quiet for a moment.

Jones can see she's counting in her head. "Oh yeah, I guess you're right. I am not certain there are that many turkeys in Seattle and all around."

Jones scanning the instruments checking gauges and direction before answering, "But that's a nice thought. How about just giving everyone, a cash bonus and they can buy their own turkey or whatever they want?"

"That's a better idea. Sure of course! I should have thought about that myself. We have been making money for the company so why not use some of that?" Carmen says and is excited about the holiday once again.

"What do you mean 'we' could use some of that Jonesy?"

Carmen slaps him playfully on his strong arm, "No, not us personally silly, I mean from the general fund."

"Yup, that's where it comes from alright. We can talk to Rose about it if you would like." Jones tugs on her long hair in a pretty braid.

Jones matter-of-factly asks, "Say Carmen do you want to hold the yoke?"

"You mean me fly the plane?" She asks in wonder.

Jones looking at his friend with real affection, "Sure, I'll watch out where we are flying. I mean it will give you the chance to feel what it's like to fly."

Carmen is excited and says, "What do I do?"

"You reach forward with your hands until you find the little half wheel. That's right. Now put one hand on each side. OK you got it?"

"OK I got it I think, now what?"

Jones looking all around the sky, "I am taking my hands off the yoke releasing the plane to you. Now, very gently pull back on the yoke. That's right, just pull it toward you. OK, you got it, do you feel us climbing?"

Carmen smiling bigger than life itself, "Oh yes I do. This is so cool!"

Jones, "Good, now push it slightly forward. Yes, that's got it."

Carmen's face is lit up with excitement.

"Now turn it to the left." Jones pushes on the left rudder peddle and the plane tilts slightly as they turn left.

"Do you feel us turning left?" Jones asks.

"Yes, this is fun, don't you think?"

He grins as he watches the child-like joy on her face.

"Yes, it is. One day there may be a self-flying plane, or car that you can drive or fly on your own."

Carmen thinks, "Wow what a great thought."

Jones, "I had better take the plane back before you fly us somewhere, we don't want to go."

"Hey Jonesy, that was nice, you're the best." Carmen is still smiling big as all outdoors.

Blushing as usual when complimented, "Yes, I know."

By this time in Jones's flying career he can land without any extra bounces. They land at Charleston International Airport. Jones taxi's them to a hardstand where they tie down the plane. Carmen is interested in everything concerning airplanes and hands Jones the wheel chocks to place on both sides of the wheels.

Jones is surprised and asks, "How do you know about wheel chocks?"

Carmen with a self-satisfying smile announces, "I got ears, right? AND I pay attention."

"Of course, you do, and you're apparently good at both." Jones acknowledges her accomplishments.

"Thanks," as she smiles at him, then her expression becomes serious, "I want you to know you can count on me and I can still pull my own weight."

"Thank you Carmen and I do count on you, for many things. You are quickly becoming the company good-will ambassador."

"Oh well I don't know about that, I just want to be useful and never a burden on anyone."

"You are no burden, Carmen, no one can ever accuse you of that."

Jones offers his elbow for human guidance as the pair walk to the rental counter at ground transportation and rent a midsized car. Where they are going isn't difficult to drive too and so comfort prevails. The logging camp is just off a big highway and a four-wheel drive isn't needed.

Jones looks at Carmen wondering, "Are you hungry?"

"Yes, a little, I guess. What are you hungry for?" She is musing.

"Well not fast food that's for sure. That stuff stays with me for days." Jones swallows down some acid.

"I know what you mean, and for sure, no more pizza for a while."

"Yeah, you're right about that too. Braidy just loves his pizza. I think he would live on pizza and fast food alone if he could." Jones speculates.

"Oh, what the hell, I'm needing some salad type food, maybe a big chef salad." Carmen suggests.

"Now that sounds great." Jones agrees. He spots a Perkins restaurant they have visited before. The only danger about Perkins is their killer pies.

As they eat their salads, Carmen asks, "Jones, what do you think we will find at this logging camp?"

Jones wiping his lips, "I think we'll find a good crew and nothing unexpected. It shouldn't be difficult, no one has been complaining."

She sighs and is relieved. They don't need any more problems to deal with. "

Besides, Rose asked us to do a routine check-up and spread goodwill. She told me, that's what we do best. Back in Nebraska they call this job bull droppings.

"What did Rose say to that?"

Jones smiles at the memory, "She said she is impressed with my efforts at cleaning up my usage of the B.S. word."

Jones admires her pretty face, she is trying not to let salad sneak out of her mouth while she is holding back laughter.

"I told Rose it is still possible for me to actually be housebroke, like Jack."

"Oh, you didn't say that?" Carmen is openly laughing now.

"Of course, I did, but she shook her head and looked out at the harbor."

Once they are back in the car Carmen uses the GPS App on her phone and provides Jones with driving directions. Jones thinks, *'What a difference in this interesting woman.'* she has surpassed him in understanding technology and gotten into computers in a big way and keeps on learning more and more. Carmen and Nancy compare notes often and Nancy has created a monster in Carmen's knowledge of technology. She talks about various Apps.

"Did you hear about the new Apps available for estimating board feet of lumber from standing timber?"

"OK, hold on Carmen. You've left me in the dark again. I leave all the computer stuff to you. Just give me the bottom line, thank you."

She laughs at him and says, "You're becoming antiquated in your thinking. You've got to keep up."

"I tried to tell you you're dealing with a dinosaur when it comes to my knowledge of gadgets and the like."

"Oh, you need to take the next exit off the interstate."

Once he takes the exit, she continues to give him directions.

"Drive for five miles and then take a left onto the camp's road."

Jones is still fascinated at her ability to understand the talking phone she uses. He doesn't tell her he already knows where they are going using his own GPS from his prosthetic. His GPS has improved like most everything about his artificial eyes. He doesn't wonder about how or why his eyes work the way they do anymore, he just accepts.

They arrive at the logging camp around noon and the camp looks impressive. There is the usual log structure that looks more or less permanent, the machine shed made from corrugated steel and the scattering of mobile house trailers. The camp is well kept and the weeds have been cut back. More importantly there isn't any junk lying about. They get out of the car and stroll over towards the log building.

Jones is never quite sure what to do in these circumstances. Should he knock or go right on in? "

"Carmen taking his offered arm, where do you think everyone is?" Carmen asks.

"Probably chowing down for lunch it's that time I guess."

"It's a little early for lunch, don't you think?" Carmen offers.

"I guess. So, if they aren't chowing down why are they not out in the woods cutting down trees."

"How do you know they aren't?" Carmen wants to know.

"Because the big trucks are all here."

As he and Carmen mount the steps, she takes his arm with two hands, she holds back some.

Carmen whispers softly, "Jonesy, this doesn't feel quite right to me."

"What do you mean?" Jones looking all around.

"I can't explain it exactly, something's just not right."

Jones has learned to listen to Carmen and others with these little intuitive warnings.

"Let me get you to the car and then I'll come back and check it out."

"Oh no you don't, I don't like being alone even in the car at times like these." She is listening and concentrating on what she doesn't hear as much as what she does.

"Say Jones, let's just stand here for a while until we can find out what's happening."

He looks into her face for a moment before finally saying, "OK, but let's go over to the corner of the building, you know, out of sight."

"OK, good idea. Maybe even around the corner?"

After they move to the end of the building and are just around the corner, they hear a banging door and a bunch of guys come running out of the door they were just standing in front of.

Jones shaking his head at the thought, "It's a good thing we moved. With that crowd, we might have been squashed."

The men go over to a field that has been cleared of everything and begin to play Soccer.

BOOK TWO: BRAIDY

"What are they doing?" Carmen whispers.

"Playing soccer." It looks like.

"They're what?"

"Playing soccer, you know with one of those checkered balls, kicking it with their feet back and forth." Jones thinks, '*well this looks OK*' and he wonders why Carmen felt alarmed.

"Can you explain exactly what you were feeling, Carmen?"

"I don't know for sure," then she tries to make light of it, "it's probably just the blue cheese dressing I had on my chef salad."

"Nope, no way. You felt something and so did I. We shouldn't ignore these feelings."

Carmen agreeing rubbing her tummy, "Yes I agree, and I still feel something funny. Not really dangerous, but still there is something."

Jones moves them back from the corner slightly. They are not visible to any of the loggers, he thinks. He peeks around the corner and watches twenty healthy guys' running back and forth on a field of grass. Carmen moves closer to Jones needing to be reassured by his bulk and strength.

"Say Jonesy, have you looked everywhere else?" she is holding to his arm with both hands.

"What do you mean?"

Carmen listening for all she is worth, "Like behind the building, and up on the roof?"

Jones, "Yup, up for sure, but not behind the building. You stay here, and I'll be right back."

"No way baby, I'm not leaving you for anything. I'm sticking to you like glue."

Jones smiles and takes her hand. "OK, come on, we both go."

When they arrive at the back of the building there's nothing there other than what one would expect to see at a logging camp; trees, grass, a propane tank, an old outhouse, nothing to be concerned over.

Carmen still uncomfortable with something, "Whatever I am feeling is getting stronger back here."

Jones looks at her and wonders what she's talking about. Then they hear it! Something ungodly roars or bellows or makes some kind of loud unusual noise. Jones jumps back in fright and Carmen practically climbs up on his shoulders.

Jones raising his free hand in front of him, "What in the hell was that?"

Carmen starting to understand, her voice shaking anyway, "How should I know, but it sounded like an elephant. Are there elephants in South Carolina?"

Jones starting to think they've gone around the bend, "How would I know, although we both need to calm down and not let our imaginations run away with us."

He starts taking slower breaths to calm down some and get his heart rate back down to something normal.

"Are you sure you want to come with me?"

Carmen grasping his arm tighter, "What do you mean?"

"I have to get closer to see what that is over there."

Carmen with a determined look on her face, "You're not leaving me here. I'm coming with you. I'm just an innocent by stander here, you're the big tough guy."

"Oh yeah, I almost forgot." Jones is looking sheepish.

Carmen has a death grip on Jones arm as they move slowly towards the trees. Finally, Jones sees what made the big sound.

"Hey Carmen, you've got really good ears. There is an elephant standing in the trees munching huge branches of nourishment."

Jones steps back, not wanting to get any closer.

"We need to talk to the loggers about the elephant that shouldn't be here, and not just because elephants don't live in South Carolina."

"Right!" Carmen drags the word out.

27

The two make their way back to the log building and around the front. By this time, the guys have seen the rental car and are looking for them. Jones and Carmen walk over and introduce themselves.

"Hey guys, this is Carmen and I'm Jones, we're from headquarters. We are here to find out how you are doing and if you may need anything?"

The boss guy is about Jones height but weighs less. He is well muscled and is around thirty-five years old. He has bright red hair and warms his surroundings with a giant grin that is slightly mischievous.

"Hey, I'm Pete, how do you do?" He leans a bit to his left as he tries to get a better peek at Jones companion.

With a look of amazement pronounces, "And will you look at that, a real live woman! A little small, but still a real live woman." He teases.

Carmen smiles and holds out her small hand. She greets the guys with a smile and a curtsy. They take to her right away and surround her and Jones.

"Can you tell us more about what's happening at headquarters? We've heard good things about the new woman boss?"

"Rose? Yeah, she's great. She is Ken's daughter and is as good a boss as anyone could ever want." Jones assures.

Pete, "The equipment has been updated, and we didn't have to beg like before. Some of those old chainsaws would throw their chains and could cut a man up."

Jones sympathizes with Pete. He knows all about chainsaws being dangerous.

Jones asks him, "So the new equipment is working out for you guys?"

Pete grinning big as can be, "Yeah, and it's the good stuff, not cheap home owner like equipment, but really heavy-duty chainsaws, some of those German saws," he continues, "and the new Caterpillar D8 dozers with the cable winches are wonderful. They got cabs with roll bars inside too. We got new hardhats that actually fit our heads and will protect us from falling limbs and shit. Oops, excuse me ma'am, I been out in the woods too long I guess!"

Carmen smiles at him, "Oh that's OK, Jones here has provided me with a good education in saying bad words."

Jones nods his head and agrees with her. They have used this gag before as an icebreaker. Carmen is the good guy; the innocent lamb and he's the bad guy barely housebroke.

Pete introduces the rest of the guys all around and Jones wonders at how young they look. Some of these guys aren't even twenty-years old yet. He also sees this is a mixed bunch. There are blacks, Hispanics, and holy cow, a Native American. Jones is relieved that they won't have to deal with prejudices again like they did once in Georgia. He doesn't want to ever go through that crap again. Fortunately, Carmen wasn't involved in that bad stuff.

Carmen continues talking, and tells them, "I will help you with any other equipment you may need, please just ask me."

The men are impressed with her easy manner of talking. She gives the impression that she is everyone's friend and will make things happen for them.

Jones slightly embarrassed, "Say, Pete, I don't mean to snoop, but do you know there's an elephant behind the log building there?"

Pete with a shrug looking all around at the others, "Oh hell that's just Rosie."

Jones looks at him with amusement, "You mean you know all about it of course?"

"Well sure." Pete assures him with a grin.

"What's it doing here?" Jones looks at Carmen.

"We got some other animals scattered around too. You see we all like animals and didn't like what they were going to do with them when the circus went broke."

Jones starting to get a feeling, "Ok, what exactly do you mean? What circus, and how did you guys end up with them?"

Pete responds with energy, "The circus came to the little town near us, so we thought we would go for a visit. When we got there,

BOOK TWO: BRAIDY

there was a legal document on the tent door, and there were the animals and no people. The dirty rats just left those animals to fend for themselves."

Jones still waiting looking at Pete, "Don't that beat all. So, you guys did what?"

"Well, we all grew up on farms you see, and although we don't know about circus animals, we know about animals in general. Elephants like to eat hay for instance and hay is hay."

Jones wondering, "What other animals do you have here?"

Rubbing his unshaved chin in thought, he states, "There's a camel, a giraffe, and a couple of show ponies. We don't know what happened to the lion and the bear that were supposed to be with the circus."

Jones stares at the foreman in disbelief. When he finally gets his head wrapped around Pete's story, "So, you found out what was owed for their keep or something like that and payed it?"

Pete, "Yup, we did, and ah, we needed a little more cash. It was a big bill."

Jones smiles because he knows what's coming next.

"So, you borrowed a bit from your expense account, right?"

Pete, scuffing the dirt with his tow, "We'll pay it back, and soon. It was sort of an emergency."

Jones thinking this gets better and better, "How much did you guys advance yourselves?"

Pete, a little hesitant, "Well you see, um well, it was only um, well it was an emergency."

Jones, "Yeah, I got that part. What I want to know now is how bad of an emergency was it?"

Pete hesitating, "Well, um, I'd rather just not say."

Carmen comes over to Pete and puts her slim arm around his back and says, "You can tell little old me. I won't yell at you like Jones here."

Jones knows her style and tries to look stern, and almost does.

Pete looks down at this remarkable young woman and says, "Ten-thousand dollars is all ma'am."

Carmen just smiles, "Oh well that's hardly worth mentioning at all. Thank you for sharing."

Pete is so relieved, "We been paying it back. We're not crooks you know." His voice is defensive.

Jones snickering to himself, "I think under the circumstances it will be OK, this time," he tries to hide his smile before saying, "do you know that the boss's name is also Rose?"

Pete feeling much safer now, "No shit, is that so? Oops sorry ma'am!"

Carmen swats him on his very hard muscled belly and says, "Shame on you."

Pete see's the slight grin and all the guys laugh at the silliness.

Jones, "I'll have to call it in to Rose, however I'll bet it will be OK this once, but no more circus rescues please."

Pete grinning at all the others, "Oh no more for sure. We got a lot of trees with leaves for the elephant to munch on and we sometimes use her to pull logs around when we have trouble getting the cats in to certain places."

"Well there you go, we can call her a company investment under slightly used equipment."

Pete, "That sounds great. Now what can me and the guys do to say thank you?"

Carmen takes his rough paw in her soft small ones, and says, "We're not here to give you a bad time. Rose feels that a happy crew is a productive crew and so we are here to encourage you all to tell us if you need anything?"

Pete turns slightly red, rubbing his stubbly chin again says, "Yeah know we could really use a couple of new jeeps. The one's we are using are left over from World War II."

Jones is surprised to hear this, "Where are they?"

"They are in the shed over there, and they both are currently broken down."

"Let's take a look at them if you don't mind." Jones suggests.

Pete leads them over to the steel building where they find two open topped jeeps painted red and white of course. The vehicles have five-gallon tanks strapped to the back fenders and both have cracked windshields. The seats are nothing but steel frames and the padding is long gone.

Jones whistles and says, "These belong in a museum not here."

Pete praises his men's mechanical talents, "They had been working alright until about a month ago. Now we can't get any new parts anymore. We been borrowing from Peter to pay Paul."

BOOK TWO: BRAIDY

Carmen touches the edge of the nearest jeep and walks all around it. She doesn't know anything about jeeps but wants to give the impression she does. Pete shows Jones the new D8 Cat with pride. It is still bright yellow for a change and still smells new.

Jones looks all around, "Where is the other one?"

Pete is nervous and says, "We park the other one in the woods where Rosie is grazing. We use a chain to keep her in one place. The dozer is the only big piece of equipment that can hold a five-ton elephant, you know. And it's the only way we can keep her from wandering off and getting into trouble."

Jones marvels, "You mean you are using a one-hundred-fifty-thousand-dollar piece of equipment to keep an elephant from wandering off?"

"Well only when we don't need it you know."

Jones taking Carmen's hand, "Oh what the hell, why not."

28

Braidy has gotten use to the new plane and now allows others to fly it, once in a while. Jones still flies when he can and loves it more and more. Rose has a good handle on managing the different divisions of her company and the need for flying people in an out is becoming less frequent.

Carmen is easier with her disability and doesn't despair about it anymore. Jones looks at her with pride, thinking *'I guess Jack and I really helped for a change'*.

Carmen has gone out on a few dates with guys from around the building.

She shakes her head in disappointment to Jones, "It was nice, and I had a good time." I guess," but offers no other details.

Jones wants to ask her questions about her dates but doesn't, after all it's her business.

Rose and Carmen still are sharing an apartment and are comfortable living together. Braidy and Jones still share Brady's house and Nancy stays over sometimes.

Nancy has been seeing a guy from her church. She sings solo's and directs the choir.

Jones is a little jealous but once again, doesn't say anything.

Braidy is munching on something loud, "So Jonesy, what's up with you and Nance, you know in the dating department."

Jonesy looking out the back door of Brady's house sighs, "Well I don't think I'm the right guy for Nancy.'"

Nancy's new guy is black and is very kind to her, she says at least.

Jones doesn't care what color anyone is. He's a firm believer it's what's inside that counts. He doesn't want to get involved seriously

BOOK TWO: BRAIDY

with anyone because he believes he isn't normal. The scientists put something inside his head he can't seem to control. When he needs super power for breaking down doors or defending his friends it's there, but he's uncomfortable because he knows he still can't control it.

He doesn't feel guilty or bad about doing what he has to do, but he wonders if it will always be used for good. What if this madness inside his head gets out of control and he start knocking people down for the fun of it? These thoughts make him shutter. He hopes that never happens and he is OK as long as no one tries to hurt people. It's then that he just loses control and <u>boom</u> they're dead.

Jones is sad to hear his old friend in Nebraska has passed away in his sleep of heart failure. Elwood was 89 years old and lived a good life. What's strange about Elwood's passing is that Molly died just three weeks later. They both gave a great deal to others in their lifetimes, and their sons Gary and Galen will continue farming the same good way carrying on traditions and providing lots of food.

Jones, isn't entirely sad however because he believes as long as people can live a good life without suffering then it's probably alright, they pass. After all we got to make room for the little guys, children and grandchildren. Jones doesn't ever want children. He may never know if this madness that he shows when there is danger may be passed on to the next generation. He decided to never get married to anyone and realized that's stupid. Of course, he can marry, he just can't have children.

The memories of his old life on the dairy farm don't make him feel so bad anymore. After all, he has a new life here with Rose and everyone else. They are like family to him now, and he will do whatever he can to help them.

They are not out of danger by a long shot and he knows Kenny and Marvin and who knows who else wants to destroy Rose and her company.

Carmen and Jones continue going on good-will trips, and Carmen is effective in talking to mostly the men. She doesn't mind roughing it sometimes and is a wonderful partner and does more than her share. Jones sometimes just sits back and lets Carmen do all the work. She is organized and communicates well.

Even when there are catcalls, she just smiles and says, "Down boys, after all, we are all gentleman."

They laugh and say, "You isn't no gentlemen that's for sure."

She comes right back at them by saying, "Well I thought you'd never notice," and does a little curtsy.

She is easy to be with and the guys just love her wit and humor. No one notices she is blind and it's not mentioned. She treats everyone equally and is warm and friendly without being slutty.

Jones and sometimes Jack, just hang out on the sidelines watching her due her job and work well with guys too.

Rose is delighted too and tells Jones, "You've been so very wonderful at bringing this damaged fledgling woman out of the closet so well."

Jones just can't take a compliment and is embarrassed.

Braidy notices and complains, "How come Jones gets all the easy jobs?"

Rose goes over to him and hugs him around his slim waste, saying, "You're still my favorite uncle and always will be."

Braidy turning red grinning big time at her, "Yes, you're right, I am wonderful."

Getting back to work, Rose talks about the newest part of the business, and that is container shipping.

She shoves her hair off her face and nods at everyone, "This initial investment is very big at first, but eventually it will pay off, I think. I am phasing out some of the bulk carriers and buying a few new container ships.

These ships are bigger and faster and they can carry nearly every kind of cargo there is, including non-conventional materials. The shipping business is changing, and we have to keep up with those changes."

Braidy from out of the blue for who knows why, "Speaking of keeping up with new things," as he traces an invisible figure eight on the table with his index finger, "We could really use another King Air."

Jones backs Braidy up by adding, "You know Boss Lady, we do have a lot more flying time between us and another King would really help out."

Rose looks from Braidy to Jones and back to Braidy again.

She crosses her arms tapping her left foot, says, "Braidy, if it was just you asking I would bet dollars to donuts it would be because you simply want another new toy to play with."

"Awe Rosie, you hurt my feelings," you know if I had any, as he puts his chin on his chest pretending to be hurt.

Rose walks around the table and pats him on top of his head and chuckles, "Oh, poor baby. Life's just tough all over for you?"

"Jones, do you think we need another King Air? I think I'd better keep my mouth shut so I don't end up putting my foot in it." He's embarrassed looking everywhere accept at Rose.

Rose raises her eyebrows, "Seriously, do you really think we need another King?"

Jones and Braidy silently agree, "Absolutely we do. Braidy and I are spending lots of our time in the air these days and having another King-Air that's faster than the rental would sure help cut my flying time down. Plus, if I can get to assignments quicker the more I can get done."

Rose with her fist under her chin, "I'll think about it, I guess we can work out getting a second King."

Rose makes a note on her pad.

Looking at both guys, "Just so you both know I'm not completely convinced that we need a new airplane," she adds reluctantly, "You are like little boys wanting another toy to play with I guess you two are no different." She chuckles.

Jones getting a bright idea, "Well this time Rose, you will be the first to fly with me in your new plane."

Rose knowing she's ben had, "That's better! When do we pick it up?"

Jones and Braidy laugh at her, "Not for a month or so. It still has to be painted the company colors like the one we have already."

Rose gives them a stern look., "Ah, you two were so sure you'd get your way you've already ordered it and are having it painted? I should have known." Her voice light-hearted.

Braidy and Jones look across the table at each other and grin like two little boys who just got caught with their hands in the cookie jar.

"I have to admit I really do like those colors, and so does most everyone else. What do you think about the idea of painting some of the new ships in the new colors?" Rose wants to know.

Braidy hesitates some, "saying, "I'll have to check on that, I don't know how those colors will stand up in harsh sea conditions. Red can look OK even if it's faded some."

"What other colors do you think would be best for my new ships? She really needs the answer to be blue."

"I'll look into that for you." and Braidy writes himself a note. He carries a small note book in his shirt pocket and brings it out for reminders of what he needs to do.

Carmen and Jack are talking under the windows, they are sitting on the floor. Carmen is talking, and Jack is listening with both ears up. She and Jack meet this way often and communicate comfortably. Jones looks at his dog and is wondering what he is thinking about. Could it be what Carmen is telling him? Jones hesitates to believe Jack can understand English, still, there are times when Jack makes him wonder

There are so many questions about Jack's abilities and his own as well. He doesn't feel guilty after taking out some scumbag bad guys. Jones knows how to kill, he learned that in the military. So, this killing is so confusing to him. The army teaches soldiers to kill and rewards guys when they do. However, when anyone kills someone in civilian life the law calls it murder. What is the difference, killing is killing!

Jack is more resourceful and intelligent too, Jones wonders if he feels any remorse or guilt after killing? Jones and Jack are different that's for sure. Still he just cannot let the bad guys kill someone that Jones is responsible for keeping safe. Jack probably thinks that as well.

Jones decides to live with it, after all if he hadn't killed those bad guys, someone he loves would be dead instead.

Jones and probably Jack too often has these dark feelings that cause and Jack too to become very depressed. These friends help, they are like family and Jones has never had so many people care for him and about him.

Jones has to admit to himself that even on that peaceful farm he got melancholy from time to time. Even though Nancy and that Gray-haired dude whatever his name was oh yeah Harold, came to take him away it turned out to be a relief. Jones has discovered that he is a social being and likes people. This shipping business is rough and tumble and everyone here needs to always do their best just to keep heads above water.

Jones is brought back to the present by Rose calling his name.

"Oh well what the hell."

29

On the island the three men are meeting in the library. Marvin doesn't understand what Seamus is trying to explain.

Seamus tells them for a second time, "We need to think outside the box here."

Kenny doesn't get it either he is ready to kill this little jerk, "What in the hell are you talking about?"

Finally, Seamus finds a large rolled up tube of paper and spreads it out on the oak table. He holds down the corners with empty coffee cups, the paper wants to roll back up into a tube.

He sighs with exasperation and tries again, "OK, let's start from the beginning, right?"

He draws a pretty accurate outline of the headquarters building in the middle.

Marvin admires the drawing and says, "Say Seamus you should have been an artist."

"I am an artist. I told you that already."

Kenny ignoring the slight, "OK that's good, now what?"

Annoyed at the distraction, Seamus draws lines coming out from the picture of the headquarters building.

Continuing, saying, "These lines indicate the various directions this huge company extends to. At the ends of these lines near the edge of the paper are businesses like; logging."

He draws a logging camp, complete with log main building, housing for loggers and a steel machine shed.

"These lines are for shipping," and he draws an exact simulation of one of Rose's bulk carriers.

Marvin is fascinated and gets excited like a kid at Christmas, he has never seen anyone draw so well and with such ease.

Seamus continues he has their interest now, "These lines are for salvage and oil platforms the tugs move about. These lines indicate storage facilities in the United States and all around the world. The other figures show the increasing transporting of containers.

"These containers are wonderful inventions. You can ship them on the ocean and when they get to a port, the containers are transferred onto trains or trucks. That company of Rose's keeps on growing all the time. With good management, it can't help growing."

Kenny absently scratching his chest, "So this Rose is a good manager?"

Seamus laying down his marker nods, "Absolutely! She is either very good or someone in the company is, because companies don't grow like this unless someone at the top knows what they are doing. The growth isn't rapid; but it is steady."

Seamus pulls out a legal pad with pages of numbers in columns. They indicate the changes in the profits ever since Rose's father passed.

Kenny points out with a finger with a manicured nail "Before Rose took over the company, there was a steady loss all be it slight, hardly noticeable but still a loss. And now there's a profit?"

"Yes, it's not earthshaking, but the numbers don't lie, they are getting better." Seamus admits.

Marvin notices with disappointment that most of the profits are not in shipping, he asks Seamus, "What about the shipping part of the profits?"

"Shipping takes a bit longer to turn around and the company is converting to container ships instead of so many bulk carriers. The real money in shipping is in the new cargo boxes," Seamus admires, he continues to explain, "The containers are placed on vessels in their countries of origin and shipped to their destinations. When they get to, say the U.S., these containers can be shipped by rail, truck, or even smaller ships. They are very universal and can be used over and over again. Anything and everything can be shipped in containers and the cargo is protected and usually kept very safe."

Barb comes down the hall singing one of her lovely island songs and the men look up with delight. She brings coffee, fresh baked goodies; doughnuts, cinnamon rolls, tarts, and Marvin's favorites, long johns on a large silver tray. The coffee is dark and rich, Kenny gets it from Guatemala in large cloth bags.

BOOK TWO: BRAIDY

Barb grinds beans each time she serves coffee and from somewhere she provides fresh cream.

Kenny plays with a spoon full of rich cream, "Where did you get the cream?"

Barb smiles her warm island smile, "The tiny dairy on other side island."

Kenny licking off his spoon, "No shit, I had no idea. How long has that dairy been there?"

"Always there, if you get out of house, you'd know about other side of island yeah-man."

Kenny looks stupid at that.

Seamus admiring Barb, "I knew about the dairy, and there's a small fishing village too."

Kenny defends himself with, "I haven't gotten around much because I've been concentrating on hatching this new plan."

Seamus shakes his head at him and says, "You need to get out more."

Marvin knows enough to keep quiet and slides a big long john into his watering mouth. The pastry is filled with sweet cream that squirts part way down his throat exciting his waiting taste buds with pure pleasure. A big bite of long john then a slurp of dark rich coffee. *'It just doesn't get any better than this'* he thinks.

Barb is always cheery and bounces all around waiting on everyone at once. Not a second goes by without her topping off cups, passing goodies and filling the room with sunshine.

Kenny marvels at her delightful cheer and is glad she is here to provide goodies and entertainment. He doesn't really care if there is a bit of dust in the other rooms, especially the ones they don't use. The magic Barb does in the kitchen is well worth it. He knows she fishes and goes out in the little boat each day if the weather is good. He does wonder what the secret is that allows her to catch so many fish. The preparation of each seafood meal is right next door to perfect. He thinks these folks from the islands are truly people of the sea.

Barb does like her Rum, however, and doesn't mind telling Kenny she likes it. She insists it be Jamaican Rum and no other. He thinks of himself as generous for allowing her to have opportunities he supposes. Kenny admires her spirit and her optimism for life. Hearing her laugh and sing brings what little joy he allows himself.

Barb enjoys good living and cooking for these lazy guys isn't so bad. Still she has hopes for a better life. She knows the sea and fishing. She can cook as well as anyone she knows. Also, she is honest and those who know her well find that out right away.

30

When Jones and Carmen get back to the office they meet with Rose. Carmen can hardly keep from busting out with laughter.

Rose sees her friend smiling and asks, "What's going on?"

"You won't' believe it, no, nope, not at all. I barely believe it myself and I was there." Carmen breaks out into side-splitting laughter so hard she can't talk.

Jones is left holding the bag.

Rose smiles because Carmen's laugh is contagious.

She is trying to look stern and almost does, "Well, I'm waiting!"

Jones doing his best not to join in Carmen's laughter, says, "You see it's like this, the guys have a sort of a pet out in the South Carolina woods and they have named it after you."

Carmen is now holding her sides and has tears streaming down her cheeks.

"That's nice," Rose returns, still not understanding the humor, "do you mean like a dog or a cat, or something larger?"

Jones is hesitant.

"So, what kind of pet is it?" Rose pushes a little more. She looks from Jones to Carmen and back to Jones. You don't mean they have something like Babe the Blue Ox, do you?" Rose's voice now has a hint of suspicion to it.

Carmen roars harder with laughter and Rose is getting annoyed.

"Alright you two, what kind of pet is it?" She demands.

Jones looks to Carmen for some help, who turns away with her hands over her face trying to play dumb.

Jack knows there's something up and comes over to share in the fun and he is ready to play.

Rose looks stern and says again, "What kind of pet is this that is apparently my name sake?"

Jones with one last look at Carmen for help, "Well it's all innocent, and the guys felt sorry for the critters."

Rose brushing the top of her blond curls asks, "What <u>exactly</u> do you mean by critters?"

"There's more than one, but only one is named Rosie."

Rose looking determined, "You're not helping here, and you can be replaced you know."

Jones isn't worried, "I guess I could get a job taking care of Rosie the elephant."

"Say what? Did you say an elephant?"

It's a good thing there was already a chair behind Rose or Jones would be picking her up off the floor.

Carmen heard the wheels on the chair rolling across the mat and the sound of Rose plopping into it.

"It was like this, there was a circus that was going out of business." Carmen begins to explain.

Jones chimes in with, "And the animals were to be destroyed if the bills weren't paid."

Carmen bull dozers right in there, "The guys sort of borrowed some money from the general fund, you know from the logging camp's expense account…"

Jones once again, "And they paid the bills and took possession of the animals."

Rose getting a sinking feeling, "You mean they own an elephant?"

"Yup and a camel and a giraffe, two show ponies."

Rose is nearly in shock, "If this isn't the damnedest thing I've ever heard in the whole of my life."

"In their defense, Boss, they have already begun to pay the money back."

"Exactly how much money do they still need to repay?"

Jones starts to raise his hands and shoulders at the same time while almost whispering, "Nine-thousand-eight-hundred dollars."

Rose simply stares at him without saying a word.

Jones finally breaks the silence by informing her, "They are still using the old Jeeps that are red and white that were used during World War II and are no longer working."

BOOK TWO: BRAIDY

Rose throwing out her hands in defeat exclaims, "Why do they need Jeeps when they have elephants and horses? And what about that worthless camel? Isn't he good for transportation at least?"

Jones backing up a step holding up his hands in defense, "According to their resume's they aren't trained in logging, however they are great for keeping the guys company." Jones pauses. "I think their best work has been in the entertainment field."

Rose shaking her head replies in exasperation, "The things I have to put up with because of you guys."

Carmen with a tiny little grin getting bigger, "We should put in for a Metal of Honor for you ma'am!" Her uncontrollable laughter tamed only some.

"No comments from the peanut gallery, thank you very much."

And that set Carmen back into belly rolls of laughter as she reminds Rose, "Elephants like peanuts too."

Rose shakes her head and gives in, "Well I guess we're in the circus business now. Why not." She looks to Jack for an explanation, Jack lets out a nasty puff of gas and looks completely innocent.

31

Back on Kenny's island', as Marvin calls it, Barb gets friendlier with some of the women who live in the village. She finds they are from everywhere and are diverse. They are impressed with her ability to handle a boat. After fishing, she shares her catch with them. Spending time in the village enjoying coffee and chatting about nothing makes her feel less lonely for her family. She doesn't mention to Kenny of her visits and is careful not to mention him to the villagers.

Barb believes if no one knows anything about Kenny it's better for her. They talk about baking and the women share recipes. They are a gay group, enjoying a nip of Rum. Barb is teaching them all about Jamaican Rum and brings over some interesting samples for them to try

The village people are a simple people and live as close to the land and sea as they can. There are many in the village who are educated however they want to live a simple life avoiding modern chaos.

Barb fits right in, she's no dummy after all. She hasn't got a formal education, although she has enough experience to earn some sort of degree. If there was a degree in fishing, handling a boat, cooking, or many other skills she can't think of at the moment, she would probably be a PHD at least.

Barb wants to have a place to land if that crazy Kenny and company pull off this big heist. She wants no part of anything like that. She used to enjoy Kenny and believed him to be funny and nice. Since he started hanging around with George, his values have gone away, far away. These new guys especially Marvin scare her to death.

BOOK TWO: BRAIDY

She knows Seamus likes her, she can see it in his eyes when he looks at her. He is at least intelligent enough to carry on a conversation. She can't say that about Kenny or Marvin. They used to play table games and although Barb had difficulty understanding Spades or Hearts or whatever those card games were, it was fun.

Barb writes to her family often and is always glad to hear back from them. She thinks she should just go back home to Jamaica where she belongs. She knows she would be welcome there but enjoys the challenge of living on her own. Her family are nice although somewhat overbearing.

Barb does what she usually does and decides not to worry about it. After all, not worrying is always easiest.

32

They go to watch the first of Rose's new ships being launched. Carmen, Jones, Rose, and Jack are all there. Rose smiles with pride at the huge container ship. It cost millions and she is nervous about what could happen to this beautiful vessel. The ship is soft sky blue over deep royal blue. They are the same colors as the new plane and the slightly older one. The engineers have convinced her that the paints are much better and will stand up as good as any. The color doesn't really matter much in the long run.

The ship is over one thousand feet long and has very comfortable quarters for the crew and visitors. Rose and company will sail with the ship on her maiden voyage for a short trip to a second facility where the completion of the rigging will take place. She takes the tour of the bridge and admires that it is equipped with all the latest in electronic technology. There is even a voice command navigation system.

"Isn't she beautiful?" Rose asks the others, "You just tell the ship what you want, and it responds. It does still need a backup-system too and some crew and a captain."

Rose has chosen a young captain. He has only fifteen years of experience on the sea of which five are as captain. He is confident and knows what he is doing. He has shown good judgment in past difficulties and she feels comfortable with him.

She looks into his shining face and reassures him, "You will get all the support from headquarters that you want or need."

She strives to find him the best crew.

The captain is married and has two kids and a lovely wife, and they all live in Seattle. He beams with pride with his chest out, shoulders back and looks like he could take on the world with ease.

BOOK TWO: BRAIDY

The ship has a name that Rose isn't completely satisfied with, but she can learn to live with it. The ship is called the Kenneth Martin after her Father.

Jones knows very little about container ships but looks her over. He can't help but wonder what's coming next.

This ship is bigger than some people's farms, at least it looks that way. If you count the other decks, then it is very large indeed.

This ship can carry thousands of containers and it moves through the ocean faster than any of the bulk carriers. The crew is smaller too and more and more of these ships are automated.

He begins to think, *'one day these ships will be fully automated and no one will need to be aboard.'* Jones sighs and wonders *'what if the ship loses control and goes on its own way or when the ship gets to shore it keeps on going over docks, warehouses, and anything else in its way?'*

It's probably better not to think about that kind of possible disaster. There have been enough problems without adding more.

Rose turns to him and says, "Well my friend, what do you think of her?"

Jonesy smiling big as the sea looks back at her, "I'm happy for you Rose, I really am. We'll be alright. You are making the right decisions."

Rose smiling into his eyes admires her employee and friend and says, "Well I hope you're right Mr. Jones. I have made a very large investment and who knows what will happen in the future."

Rose thinks about the board of directors that sometimes gives her a bad time concerning some of the choices she has made. She wishes the company didn't have to have a board of directors at all. She believes they just get in the way. The board knows nothing about shipping, logging, or salvage, but there they are. She spends most board meetings explaining details of the business they should all know but don't and she has to work hard to keep her calm demeanor, when she sees their eyes glazing over. There are times she has the urge to just shout, *'If you're so bored listening to the details of this company then why don't you all resign and let me run my own company?'*

Jones is always beside her at meetings now and when he sees the frustration in her face or hears it in her voice he takes her pinky finger with his thumb and fore-finger. It isn't anything except a way he uses to tell her he is there for her and everything is alright. She is reassured by this tiny gesture and winks at him.

"Well, if you know what's in the future, you won't have to worry about what your ships are doing. You can plan with knowledge instead of just human experience." He tries to give her encouragement.

Rose smiling at his warm reassurances tells him, "I'm not sure what you just said, but I will defend forever your right to express yourself."

Jones snickering at Rosie's offer, "Just give me one of your big hugs and we can call it good."

She smiles comfortably at him, "OK, it's yours my dear friend. I believe in you Jonesy."

"And I in you Rosie."

Carmen has been traveling all over the new ship with Jack. She and Jack work well together, she has a short leash that she attaches to his collar and simply tells him what she wants. Jack loves this delightful young woman and often knows ahead of time what she needs. They move about the huge ship into open and hidden places alike. She lingers in the engine rooms with the giant Caterpillar engines. She helped design this ship at least as much as she and others in the company could.

Jack walks beside her close enough to touch. He without thinking about it travels over and around objects in their way. He watches out for what's ahead of her so there's never a time when she crashes into something painful.

The crew that are on the ship for this limited voyage at first are startled by Jack's size. However, since Jack is so friendly, they are soon put at ease. Carmen is a where of their discomfort at first, so she smiles big and beautiful when she knows people are near.

Carmen and Braidy or Jones will most likely visit this ship on a good will tour, so laying the ground work ahead of time is only good.

Carmen likes to know about every part and each piece of machinery on these vessels. She knows much more about engines, pumps, winches, cranes, capacities of the holds and more. Her job At Big Lift is to sell shipping and knowing how much a ship can carry is important. She understands these vessels because she has investigated the actual sizes for herself. She tours the accommodation block, for the crew quarters and the visitor's quarters too. She has a reasonable idea of how the navigation systems work and a little bit about each crew member. The most important member of any crew is the captain of course. Although there are those who would say that the cook is more important. Carmen has interviewed many of the crew before hiring them in the first place. Those she didn't interview she researches and makes a point to introduce herself to them. Even though this company is huge, she and Rose both believe that the personal touch is what makes the difference.

The good will visits are probably not entirely necessary, however the profit and loss statements show that after these visits the profits increase. Not always a great deal but some, and that's always good. A little increase is better than a loss. Carmen is comfortable wandering around this mostly empty ship and organizes the information she and Jack have obtained into file like memories in her head.

She is blind that's for sure, she is reminded every time she bumps into a half open door or some other obstacle in her way. She has bruises on her shins and has learned to ignore the pain that these encounters cause. Jack and Carmen are a good team and she knows that Jack is much more than any ordinary mutt. He stops for her when there's something in their way. She has to open up her folding cane at times and explore the problem before moving on. Sometimes the problem can be avoided and other times she can simply close an open drawer or close a door.

Carmen is a wonderful addition to Rose's company and she is beginning to almost be happy in her very changed life. She knows if it weren't for good old Jack, she wouldn't do as well.

33

Braidy has the day off and decides to fly his float plane.

He sneaks up on Jones and asks, "Hey Jonesy, you want to go flying with me today?"

Jones jumps only a little wanting to hide his surprise, "Sorry, I'd love to, but I promised I'd help Rose with whatever this stuff is."

Braidy moves on to his next victim, "Nancy, you want to hit the wild blue yonder?"

"Nancy not looking sorry at all says, "Sorry Braidy, but I've got something planned with my friend."

Finally, he asks, "Carmen, what about you. I know you're not going to turn down a chance to go flying with me, are you?"

She turns toward him followed by her long beautiful hair and sadly tells him, "I'm so sorry Braidy, but I'm working on something that just can't wait. It's time sensitive."

At last he asks Jack, "Well Jack, you got something more important to do than keep me company flying?"

Jack is up and bouncing around Braidy like he is on fire. Then he lays down at Braidy's feet and looks up at him as if saying by raising his ears and slightly tilting his head, *'So what's in it for me?'*

Braidy looking hopeful admits, "Atta boy. And since you're so enthusiastic about keeping me company, we can stop for lunch somewhere really nice. My treat."

That does it, Jack is definitely in.

Braidy believes Jack hasn't any idea what he is talking about but enjoys the conversation anyway.

The two drive-out to the hanger where the mechanics are working on the planes.

BOOK TWO: BRAIDY

Braidy sneaks up on Jim and bangs his big fist on a wing, "What are you guys wrecking now?"

Jim dropping his box end wrench on the cement with a clang grins at Braidy saying, "You see Mr. Braidy sir, we are trying to keep these planes that you guys keep on ruining all together. We are changing the oil and maintaining the engines like the book says."

Braidy picking up Jim's wrench for him, "The planes are built well so there's not much you guys can destroy."

Jim looking all around the hanger, "So what do you want to fly off with today?"

He looks down at Jack smiling up at him, finishes with, "You and that great worthless hound?"

Jack just grins bigger and takes Jim's coverall pant leg in his teeth and tugs rather soundly.

"Hey stop that you menace to society." Jim is dancing on one foot.

Jack just tugs harder pulling Jim practically off his feet.

Braidy laughing at that crazy Jack commands, "Down boy, we might need Jim here, although I don't know for what exactly." As he smiles.

Jack lets go of the pant leg and sits back on his butt grinning up at Jim showing most of his large bright white teeth.

"Good grief, I wouldn't ever want him to really go after me with those huge choppers."

Braidy rubbing Jacks ears warns, "Then you'd better stay on his good side." Braidy advises.

Jim smiles, and pets Jack on his broad head, saying, "What a nutty mutt you are, but I like you."

Jack lets out a big loud, long bit of gas, and the air turns blue. Fast food that Braidy prefers doesn't agree with Jack and there are consequences for these intakes of what one could say are very explosive foods.

Jim hiding his nose with his hands, "Oh shit that stinks." Than waving his hand in front of his face, "What have you been feeding that dog?" He grabs a square piece of left-over cardboard and begins fanning in front of his nose as fast as he can. "That's worse than limburger cheese on a hot engine."

Braidy places his palm under his chin considering, "Let me see, I had four big Mac's and Jack had, um, well only 5."

Jim slowing down slightly with the cardboard wonders, "He has a tummy ache because of all that garbage you feed him. I get a belly ache just hearing about his lunch! Are you trying to give this great hunk a heart attack? That kind of junk food will clog his arteries."

Braidy smiles down at Jack, "He loves big Mac's. Hey, any chance I can convince you guys to help me get my float plane out of the hanger?"

Jim at first thinks about saying no just to be ornery, "Oh, now you want a favor?" Jim joshes. "You mean you want to actually fly that antique?"

"Why not, isn't it airworthy?" Braidy enquires.

"Yes, I guess it might be, but you haven't flown it for what, two years?" Jim looking amused.

"Something like that, I guess. I'll take it for a test flight and make sure it's OK."

"That's a good idea and if you fly out over the ocean when you wreck this one too, we won't have to clean up the mess." Jim is grinning big time.

"Thanks a lot, you bum. Besides," Braidy looks down at his co-pilot, "Don't worry, Jack fly's good."

Jim looking doubtful, says, "Say what? You don't mean you have been forcing the mutt to fly?"

Braidy can't help chuckling at his own joke, "Oh sure, everyone learns to fly if they want to, even Jack, and he's not a mutt. He's and all-American dog." Braidy brags as he puffs up his chest and stands very straight.

Jack sees his pal and sits up on his butt with his chin pointing straight towards the American flag flying near the weather sock.

"Now I've seen everything." Jim laughs. A dog with a patriotic heart. I still don't trust his flying."

Jack just looks away and thinks, *Some people think they are the only ones who can learn to fly these crazy things. If Jones can do it, why do they think I can't?*' Jack blows air out his nose as if in a huff.

Jim calls to the others and they push Brady's float plane out of the hanger.

Braidy notices the dust and says, "You guys haven't even kept the dust off my plane."

Jim shrugs and waves it off, "Oh hell Braidy, that's just a little angel dust, you know to help you get this crate off the ground."

BOOK TWO: BRAIDY

Braidy looks lovingly at his own plane and thinks, *'I should get it painted.'* The plane is mostly white with dark red stripes on the fuselage. *'It isn't as bad as Jim is saying.'* The guys have maintained his plane well over the years. They take pride in their work and it always shows. Braidy opens the door and turns the key. The batteries have been charged and the lighting up of the instruments excites him a bit. His plane still has some life in her and he touches the seats, the yoke and other surfaces too this old plane and he go back a long way. This old girl was his first plane that he owned by himself and he is still proud of the fact. He knows the characteristics of this old jewel and loves her for what she represents in his past as much as anything else. He has missed taking her up. He makes his usual inspection, walking around and looking at every inch of her. The floats are in good shape and Braidy walks all around touching surfaces and getting a feel for the plane again.

He shouts to Jim, "You guys turned the engines over lately?"

Jim shaking his head with pity, "No, we just wave to her as we walk by."

There's a mixed tone of joking and annoyance in his voice, "Yes, we start both engines about once a month letting them run for a while to keep the battery's up and check out the gages."

Braidy looks at the tires and moves the rudder back and forth. He watches the yoke move slightly and is satisfied that the cables are tight enough. Braidy is happy with the plane and the way the Jim and his crew have taken care of it.

"You guys have done a good job and I'm very grateful, thank you!"

Jim recognizes the sentiment in Brady's voice and knows how special this plane is to him, "You're welcome." He can't resist to yank just one more time on Brady's chain, "You gonna fly today or just admire her?"

Braidy gives him a sideways glance, "Yup, for a little while. I miss flying this old plane. It doesn't have any of those modern gadgets on it of course, it's just basic flying."

Jim looks up into Brady's warm eyes saying, "Yup, although sometimes that's the best."

"Pure flying perfection." Braidy brags. "Hey Jim, you got time to fly with me today?"

Jim looks around at the work that needs doing, "Well not really."

The other guys have been listening, and say to their boss, "Oh hell Jim, you got time, we can handle this tiny bit of work."

"I don't know, if you guys screw things up, I'll be here all day and all night for a week."

"Oh, hell Jim, you know better than that, we're better than you anyway."

Jim sighs, "Yeah you're right, I'm getting too old for this much excitement watching you guys place all these nice planes in so much danger by working on them."

"OK Mr. Braidy, let's go flying, but do we gotta take the stinky mutt along?"

Braidy looks at Jack and wonders if he would rather stay here with the guys.

"Say Jack do you want to stay here or come flying with Jim and me?"

Jack puts his head down and walks away from the float plane to sit by the guys and looks back at Braidy

Jim laugh's at Braidy and says, "It looks like Jack has decided to stay on the ground. Maybe he doesn't trust your flying after all."

Jack barks once and turns his head looking toward the trees behind the hanger, to show his dismissiveness for flying. Braidy isn't miffed at Jack, he knows the big dog doesn't always enjoy flying. Braidy believes the changing altitude may hurt Jacks ears. Jack always looks forward to being with Braidy outside the office. However, flying is sometimes very uncomfortable for Jack.

Braidy goes over to pet him on his big block head, saying, "OK Jack, you can stay here and help the guys over hall the Cessna's engine if you like. I promise I'll take you with me another time."

Jack licks his friend's hand and smiles up at Braidy, *After all, he's just human.*

The two men climb in the float plane and strap themselves in. Braidy looks around touching the faces of the gages getting the feel for his plane. Jim, is a curious man and watches his friend, enjoying the moment.

"Say Braidy you gonna just fondle the poor thing or are we actually flying today?"

Braidy smiles and nods, "Yeah sure, we'll go," Braidy starts the engines, "Hmm, that's a reassuring sound of well-kept machinery."

Jim says, "You OK with your plane?"

"I'm happy with the work you guys put into her and I'm grateful. Jim, you have your ticket, don't you?"

Jim looks at him wondering what the heck he's talking about.

Then it dawns on him, "Oh yeah, I can fly, I haven't kept up with the physicals lately."

"How come?"

"Just lazy I guess."

"Well I won't tell, if you'd like to fly her."

"Are you sure?"

Braidy nods.

Jim takes the controls. The plane isn't as powerful as the King Airs and trundles down the strip taking forever to build up enough speed for rotation. When they finally reach seventy-five knots the wheels leave the ground and they are flying.

Jim is smiling like a little boy with a new toy. Braidy thinks this day is already good just watching his friend flying with so much pleasure. Braidy believes that mechanics need to be able to fly to truly understand the characteristics of an airplane.

Jim happy as a bird on an updraft says, "So old man, where should we fly to, which direction?"

"Let's just head out to sea, anywhere."

Jim climbs to two-thousand feet and heads west. With the clear water below and barely a cloud in the sky, the day couldn't be finer, for once there's no rain. Jim is a bit rusty but soon settles into a relaxed, but alert posture.

Braidy relaxing, "The engines sound good and the cables are OK too. You guys have kept her in good shape."

Jim looking proud, "Well if I knew you were going to force me to fly this antique, I would have fixed everything that was wrong."

Braidy knows he is kidding, and says, "I'll ignore the funny rattles coming from the floats and rudder then."

Jim feeling happy and full of fun, "Oh well, what the hell. We'll probably be alright."

Braidy hears Jones's favorite statement in his head for times like this and asks, "How's everything else for you Jim?"

In a reserved tone Jim says, "You know my younger brother died, right?"

34

Braidy looks shocked, "No I didn't know, I'm sorry man. When did he die?"

"It's been over three months now. He had some problems with drinking, and I guess the booze finally got to him," Jim pauses, "He was only fifty-eight years old. He was a wild one and never took care of himself. He always said that guys like him played hard and worked hard too. He lived his life fast and furious not worrying about tomorrow."

Braidy sighs, "Jim there are a lot of folks like that, and unfortunately all that fast living catches up with everyone eventually."

Jim nodding at his friend, "My brother had been married at least eight times and as far as I know divorced only once."

Braidy with a surprised face says, "Wow, that isn't so good, is it?"

"Like I said, he was a wild one and paid in the end."

"So, how many of these alleged wives knew they weren't the only ones married to your brother?"

"I don't know for sure. I believe some of those women weren't even American citizens. I know of one girl from Peru and another was from Brazil." Jim is embarrassed and it shows.

Braidy exclaims, "Holy Cow, he did get around."

"Yup, he was a pipe fitter, and he was apparently very good at it. For sure good enough to keep getting more work to do."

Braidy asks, "What is a pipe fitter again?"

"Pipe fitters weld steam pipes together that are used for a lot of high pressure. I'm not totally sure what the difference between a pipe fitter and a steam fitter is. I think they both do some sort of welding that has to be X-rayed."

BOOK TWO: BRAIDY

Braidy is interested watching over Jim's flying, "Hey Jim let's go north toward that island over there." As he points his finger.

Jim turns them to the right and they fly over a small island that has a little village and a dairy farm. There are black and white cows contentedly munching on some forage. Braidy thinks of Jones and will remember to tell him about this island. Jones likes looking at cows and will enjoy this small herd.

Jim, "Say Braidy, do you see that big house at the other end of this island? Jim continues, "It would be nice to own a big house like that on a mostly private island."

He begins to make a second pass.

"Would you look at that!" Jim points out the woman in the runabout apparently fishing. "Now that looks relaxing. Maybe we should go fishing some time."

Braidy shaking his head, "Nope not me, who wants to just sit there doing nothing waiting for something to hook itself. That's not my idea of getting a meal. You have to work too hard for it."

Jim holding up one hand, "You're not doing nothing, you're fishing."

Braidy asks, "So what do you do until the fish actually bites?"

"You contemplate the worlds affairs."

"Now why do I need to sit in a little boat in the hot sun to try and figure the rest of the world out? I can do that from my favorite recliner."

Jim, "Oh hell, you'll never make a good fisherman that's for sure."

The woman looks up and they see that she is lovely and, isn't dressed for fashion, but her natural beauty is clear.

Jim is wondering, "Why do you suppose this lone woman is fishing by herself and having such good luck according to the catch we can see."

Braidy looking oh so wise, "You know Jim, I'll bet that she grew up fishing and it's in her blood."

"You're probably right, she sure is working at it. I'll bet she's catching supper for someone. Jim states.

"You know Jim, some fresh fish would be just right for me."

Braidy remembers he hasn't fed for three hours and is suddenly hungry.

He tries to be humble, "You want to find us some lunch?"

Jim is disappointed, "Do you mean out here? Do I just land the plane beside her boat and invite ourselves for lunch?"

"That's not such a bad idea, why not?"

"Nope, you gotta take us to a restaurant or somewhere like that."

"Is that what you want me to do?" Jim wonders.

Braidy rubbing his belly, "Well I wouldn't mind, I'm not on a diet you know."

Jim sighs and turns the float plane toward land, even though he was hoping to get the chance to land the plane on water just for fun.

Jim sounding resigned, says, "So after we find something to eat, it will probably be late, and we will need to get back to work?"

Braidy laying his big paw on Jim's arm, "No man, we got the rest of the day to play, and just relax."

Jim is anxious, "Well I don't know, I don't need trouble."

Braidy like a big brother who knows it all reveals, "Jim since Ken is gone, everything is better for us. Rose is trusting and if I tell her it's OK then it is."

Jim isn't used to having any slack and looks at his friend with a troubled expression.

Braidy reassures Jim, "It's alright, for sure man you're good, don't worry about it."

Jim shrugs and fly's them back to the airstrip. Jim comes in so smoothly like an old pro and when they taxi back to the hanger, Braidy realizes he didn't fly the plane at all.

"Say Jim you did all the flying."

Jim grins like the cat that eat the canary, "Yup your big dummy, I suckered you into letting me have all the fun."

Braidy isn't really disappointed though. After all he flies every day, not only fixed wing but the helicopter too.

The two continue chatting while Braidy drives them to a nearby eatery.

35

On Kenny's island Barbra notices the plane flying low and slow looking her over, she doesn't mind. Barb wants to fly in a little plane like that, one that can land on water or land. She wonders how difficult it might be to learn to fly. She looks over her catch and is satisfied. She will cook the fish with a special recipe from home. The dish does contain a touch of Rum, hardly noticeable though. Rum is quite useful in cooking and adds secret flavors not there with other spices. Barb knows all about cooking tastier dishes like fish and can present a fish dish that doesn't even taste like fish. She likes the oven in the big house, someone some time was really into cooking and using a commercial oven is a good start. She drives her boat into the boathouse and ties it up. She calls this her boat, mostly because she's the only one who uses it. Kenny prefers the 40-foot boat, it's more of a cabin cruiser than a runabout. She can drive any boat, but this smaller one is easier to fish from. She looks over her catch again admiring the size and the firmness of her fish. She cleans and guts them near the boathouse letting the birds clean up the unusable parts. She doesn't like to litter and allowing the Gulls and others to eat the offal is ok. She has five fairly big fish, it will be more than enough for everyone to eat as much as they like. She will give the extras to the village people; fish doesn't keep very well uncooked and not much better after it has been.

Barb sings some while she is preparing supper. She has some nice potatoes, corn, and salad fixings. The dinner will be very nice, and there is some fruit from the village ladies too. She whips up a topping from fresh cream that she bought in the morning from the dairy.

Kenny is talking again with his two strange friends. The door to the library is shut tight, that can only mean they talk of something that must remain secretive. Barb doesn't care if those guys want their privacy, that's not the problem, she is concerned about what they will do to others. She will not allow them to kill people who are innocent. She has her father's big revolver and knows how to use it.

Kenny doesn't know anything about that gun and she likes it that way. She likes Kenny ok but not always what he does, he has a nasty plan and that plan scares her. Barb never shows her discomfort however, she smiles and laugh's and sings often; she is like a ray of sunshine.

Kenny and Marvin are listening to Seamus telling them about a wild plan that they don't completely understand. Seamus is light years ahead of them in the smarts department. He puts up with them because he needs the mussel. Seamus has no problem eliminating them when the job is done. They are like a used car or other piece of equipment. He is a small man and doesn't have the strength of Marvin or even Kenny. Seamus really admires Barbra and wonders if she might learn to like him if Kenny is out of the picture. She is so bright and cheery and my, what a cook. He doesn't usually like women, they are sometimes nasty to him because of his size. However, this Barbra isn't that way, she is considerate of everyone, even him, she smiles at him and laughs at his corny jokes. He likes the way she looks, clean and fresh even though she goes out fishing nearly every day.

She has long curly dark brown hair that reaches nearly to her hips, and everything about her is feminine without being snobbish. He doesn't care that she is 4 inches taller than he, it's what's inside that counts, right!

Barb has laid out the fish and covers them with her special mixture of bread crumbs, spices, and herbs, and some of that delightful Jamaican Rum. She is singing and the sound is so joyful filling the house with a wonderful sense of wellbeing. Seamus has come out of the library to get some coffee he says, but really wants to say hello to Barbra. She looks up in surprise at him and wishes him a cheery good afternoon. She is saying that dinner will be ready in about a half hour if that's alright. Seamus looks at what she is preparing and smiles at her, he tells her she is wonderful and so efficient. She thanks him and continues preparing dinner. He notices the Rum bottle and asks her if that is part of the recipe?

"Oh, yeah man of course, I cannot make fish properly without using a touch of Rum." Yeah man!

BOOK TWO: BRAIDY

Seamus shuffling his tiny feet with doubt, "Oh I see, so that's the way of it?"

"Yes, sir it's an old family recipe from home don't you know." She smiles over at him.

Seamus fills a cup of that very special coffee that Kenny buys and includes some fresh cream from Barbra's bowl of whipped topping.

Barb pretending to be stern, "Say now, my good sir that cream is for our dessert." She is pretending to be firm but isn't really, she finds him interesting and fun. Seamus looks horrified and jumps back in fright. She shakes her finger at him.

"Ah no man, you can have all you want, I'm just having some fun with you." Yeah man!

Seamus looking relieved and grinning back at her, "Well ok, I don't ever want to be on my favorite cook's bad side."

Barb looking so innocent winking at him, "No man you're good, at least you communicate, unlike your pals in the library there."

Seamus lifting his eyebrows, "Well if you are looking for intelligence those guys lost out in the beginning, they're not the brightest fellows around."

She shakes her head and goes back to fixing dinner. She has prepared the potatoes in wedges that will cook up crispy, and the corn will be flavored just so, bringing out all of the flavor there can be. She knows about fixing all foods and adds this and that as Seamus watches. He is taken by this very talented woman and thinks that maybe he can be her favorite man.

Barbra doesn't think about it one way or the other, she knows who she is and believes in herself. She will survive and be ok with whatever happens. She goes back to humming softly then sings right out. Seamus takes his coffee and returns to the library.

36

Rose and Jones are talking about what Jones and Carmen have been doing. They have been visiting lumber camps and ships that are near enough to fly to. Braidy has been teaching Jones to fly the helicopter; he is better at the helicopter than flying fixed wing aircraft. He is a natural at flying the helicopter and Braidy tells him he is doing very well. Jones can understand the how-to's of flying helicopters easier than flying fixed-winged aircraft. He catches on right away, something about his prosthetics he believes. Whatever the reasons he learns quickly and Braidy is only the observer on most flights.

Braidy and Carmen and sometimes Jack fly out to ships and talk to the crew. They are always glad to see Carmen. By this time, she has become somewhat famous.

She looks so interesting in the clothes she wears and is so humorous and can get the guys laughing right away. She is a clown and knows she has a good effect on the crews. There aren't many women on ships, once in a while one is part of the crew. These women are rough tough women who can defend themselves against anyone and are stronger than many men. They are dedicated to doing a good job and are dependable.

Rose doesn't hesitate to hire any woman, unlike Ken, who was obviously prejudice against women. Rose tells Jones and Carmen to just treat everyone equally and that's all. Carmen has no problem dealing with men or women and Jones is the same way.

Carmen tries to dress accordingly depending where they are going. If she is going on a ship that has nice accommodations, she where's a pretty dress and if she is going out into the back woods than she wears something more appropriate. In any case, she is warm and

BOOK TWO: BRAIDY

responsive and provides information in a precise manner that leaves no doubt but is entertaining.

She has a real gift for speaking to bunches of men and sometimes women concerning subjects that are not always easy for her to talk about. Carmen has found a niche for herself and is an asset to Rose's company.

Carmen has more money than she can spend comfortably, she lives in the headquarters building with Rose, paying no rent, and Rose provides her a clothing allowance and so Carmen doesn't need much of what she is paid. Rose tells her that she is worth every penny and loves having her near, the two women have traveled to other places and Carmen has no problem using alternative techniques to do what she needs to do. She is becoming so natural at what she does that no one seems to notice any blindness issues. Jones is proud of Carmen and tells her so. Carmen just smiles at him and if she is near, she takes his hand for a quick squeeze.

Jones thinks she is getting more beautiful all the time, sometimes women get better looking with age and that's the way it is with Carmen he thinks.

Various divisions within the company are doing mostly well, Rose provides incentives and rewards good work. She wants everyone to be happy with their employment.

Joni helps too, she provides everyone with a warm welcome right from the start. She is at the main desk on the first floor of the headquarters building and makes a lasting impression. By the time the problems get to Rose on the top floor office the grouches are in a better mood. Rose has selected a young man from shipping that is shipping of small parts to work at the desk outside of her office. She is recalling to Jones how Joe came to work outside the upper office. She is explaining to him where she found him and a little about why she decided on Joe. Rose and Jones discuss the many various aspects of this giant company and Rose is happy for Jones objectiveness.

He is about 25 years old and has blond hair. His smile is bright and inviting. His eyes are blue, he seems to like everyone. Carmen comes and goes now, more out of the office than in, and so doesn't notice the young guy for a few days. His name is Joe, and he is appreciative of Carmen. She is so bouncy and happy he says to her that she is the sunshine of all their lives. In Seattle sunshine isn't nearly often enough for some folks and so telling her that she is sunshine is a real compliment. Carmen always has a smile for Joe and tells him he is cute. Joe is embarrassed and turns red when she tells him that. Joe wants to ask her out for a date but hasn't gotten up the nerve as yet. He likes her and wants to say so but not yet. Carmen likes Joe and can't say so either.

There are more than five hundred employees who work at Headquarters Building. The upper management of Big Lift like to welcome everyone, however since there are so many employees it's not always possible to include everyone. Rose travels around the building greeting people and getting to know as many as she can. She is on the fifth floor looking for a missing package that she ordered for Carmen.

Rose looking all around says, "Hello, are you new?"

The bright young man smiles big as all outdoors at his pretty boss. He hasn't met her before however of course he knows who she is and what she's like.

Joe smiling right into her eyes, "Hello, I'm Joe, I am happy to meet you at last. I have seen you around the building but haven't met you yet."

Rose likes the way this young man looks her directly in the eye. She puts out her small hand and they shake.

Rose taking back her hand, "Of course, it's nice to meet you as well. So, do you know anything about a missing package? We have been looking all over for it, I did ask down here in the mail room but no one knows."

Joe holds up a big hand, "Oh ho, I might be able to help, you see over here is a room we use for packages that don't have a home. These packages are missing names or departments and we don't know where to deliver them. We are still developing the idea and need to make things happen however it's a start."

Rose approving says, "Oh good, anything is an improvement, I think. Show me what you got please."

Joe opens the door to a small room and shows her the shelves of packages that don't apparently have anywhere to go. The packages are various sizes and have mostly missing labels. The parcels do have dates on them stuck on with red tape with white cards containing as much information as available. By using the dates, they were delivered there is sort of a system.

BOOK TWO: BRAIDY

Rose looking at everything, "Say Joe this looks organized, and maybe you can find out where these packages need to go by sharing their dates of delivery and maybe the contents too."

Joe explains, "I am not sure about the legality of opening someone else's packages. If there is something very personal than I could be in trouble."

Rose, shaking her curly head, "Nope no way, I'm the boss and I say its ok to open packages when there's no way to identify them."

Rose wants to know more about this very caring man and invites him to the upper office for an interview. She needs someone to work at the front desk at the upper office.

Rose asking, "Say Joe, do you know anything about computers?"

Joe smiling right into her eyes, "Yes I do, I built my first computer when I was twelve, I still have it. I can type ninety words a minute without mistakes and I know every program Microsoft sells or has. I am getting a little bored working here, I'm not complaining but I want to advance myself if possible."

Rose nodding, "Oh good, I like your attitude, of course that's what I want for my employees, so show up at the main office tomorrow and we'll talk some more. In the meanwhile, I think this is the package in question. Thanks to your system of dating arrivals, and the general shape and size, this is the one I believe."

Rose opens the package and sure enough, it's the surprise she ordered for Carmen. The device is a sonic resonator that a blind person can use to locate objects and shapes in a room. The device is still experimental and maybe Carmen will hate it, but still it's worth a try.

Joe is curious and wants to know more, "Hey Mam, what is that you have there, it looks interesting. Does it emit some sort of echo maybe?"

Rose is surprised, "You can tell that from one look?"

Joe turning red, "Oh I'm sorry Mam, I didn't mean to intrude."

Rose shaking her head no, making her curls bounce, "Oh no its ok, you can be curious its good. This is an experiment for Carmen, do you know Carmen?"

Joe not sure, "Maybe only in passing, isn't she that pretty Hispanic girl that hangs around with that big black dog?"

Rose, is impressed with his delicacy says, "Yup she's the one."

37

Jones and Rose are flying to a conference that Rose needs to attend. They are flying the Jet Ranger and lift off the roof of the headquarters building. Rose still marvels at Jones's ability to fly so quickly and apparently according to Braidy so well. He is jovial and light-hearted and greets her with a big warm smile. Usually Carmen flies with the guys and Rose isn't used to just flying off. She is nervous and tells Jones that she hasn't flown much lately. Jones reassures her that she is perfectly safe. Rose knows she is and says she is probably acting silly. Jones tells her that she isn't silly at all, that even though he is the pilot these flying machines make him nervous too.

Rose looks at him with lifted eye brows and says, "No way!"

He admits to her, "Yup one can never know for sure if everything will work like it is supposed to."

They fly out over the harbor and Rose looks down at her ships and dock facilities with pride. Some of the ships have been repainted in the new blue over blue colors and she thinks compared to the original red and white colors the ships look fresh. The red and white is old now and faded, the blues look nicer to her eye.

Jones is relaxed and flies them off towards the south. They will fly down the coast for about one hundred miles and land at an airport than rent a car for the rest of the journey. Jones flies out to sea off the coast, he likes to watch the ocean. Sometimes there are dolphins playing and are fun to watch. Rose too likes watching dolphins and is excited at the possibilities. They are flying along at around one-hundred-twenty-five knots, and the water is clear below, they can see the bottom a little.

BOOK TWO: BRAIDY

Jones flies so smoothly that Rose begins to relax. She knows that how she feels is only because she hasn't flown much at least in the helicopter. She has to remind herself that this aircraft belongs to her since her Father died. She thinks they should paint this aircraft the new colors and asks Jones what he thinks.

He smiles with his big bright white teeth with a wise grin, "Well, I am not so sure it would be worth the expense, this is an old helicopter now."

Rose looks around her and notices that the interior does look shabby. The seats are nearly warren through in places and the colors have faded to the point that the original colors aren't apparent. She asks him if he believes that they are safe.

Jones replies with that confident grin again, "Yes of course, the aircraft is perfectly safe, it's more cosmetic than mechanical."

She believes him and looks down at the sea for something interesting. Jones flies them along the coast and whistles through his teeth some little ditty she doesn't know.

Rose with a wrinkled brow, "Say Jonesy what's that tune you're whistling?"

"Oh well it's nothing, it's just a tune I use to whistle to my cows back on the farm to help them relax before milking." He glances at her.

Rose looks at him in horror, "Do you mean I have replaced your cows?"

Jones looks at her in surprise, "I never had a cow that looked half as good as you do."

Rose looks relieved to hear that, she says, "She wouldn't want to be a milk cow thank you very much!"

Jones shakes his head and says, "Sorry about that, I wasn't thinking about you."

Rose smiles back at him, "Oh well, I'm just being silly don't you know." She is being goofy.

Jones feels the helicopter vibrating somewhere in the tale section, its slight than growing stronger. Rose doesn't notice at first and goes on talking about the changing colors of the water below them. Jones keeps quiet and is trying to understand the problem. He doesn't think there's anything wrong with the maintenance, Jim and the mechanics take good care of all the aircraft. The problem gets worse and finally Rose looks over in alarm.

Jones cannot reassure her, he has no idea what the problem might be. He turns them towards shore thinking they can land on the beach. They have flown further out than when they started and the beech isn't in sight. Rose is becoming terrified and holds on to the edge of her seat with desperation. She hasn't completely recovered from some of the horrible events from the past. Jones is confused and isn't sure where the beech is. He is feeling dizzy and disoriented. Rose doesn't seem to be affected by whatever is getting to Jones. He knows he has to keep on flying for both their sakes and concentrates intensely.

The helicopter is becoming impossible to fly and they settle down toward the water. Jones tells Rose that they will crash-land on the water and to pull out a flotation device from under her seat. Rose is so terrified she cannot move, Jones is fading fast and the helicopter isn't flying, rather it's just falling.

Just before they hit the water Jones pulls back on the collective and brings the nose up. They smack the water with enough force to collapse the skids and they roll to the right. The helicopter is laying on its right side and Rose and Jones are hanging by their seatbelts. Rose is conscious and understands the danger they are in. She can push the door open that is now above her. She forgets she is strapped in for a moment and can't get loose. When she releases the seatbelt, she falls against Jones. Jones isn't moving, she can tell that he is unconscious. She has to get them out of the sinking helicopter and right now! She remembers that there is a life raft on board and finds it behind the pilot's seat. She pulls it out and pushes it through the door she has opened. The helicopter is settling in the water and will be under soon. She finds the tab on the raft and gives it a tug, nothing happens at first and she panics. Brady's words come back to her than and she calms down. She remembers that there's a safety lock, no one wants a raft to inflate inside the aircraft. The raft is an 8-person raft and is the best that money can buy.

They have never had to use one of the rafts that are aboard all company aircraft but everyone knows how to inflate them. Braidy made sure that anyone who may fly knows how to save themselves in the event of a water landing.

She ties the painter to the door handle and goes back in the sinking aircraft to try and help Jones. He blinks his eyes asking what happened. Rose tells him that they crash-landed in the ocean and could he please get the hell out of here?

Jones grins goofy like at her and says, "Oh well, what the hell, why not!"

She makes him focus on the present and he helps her help him climb up and then out of the helicopter. By the time, she gets Jones out of the inside of the cabin the helicopter is only a few inches above the surface of the ocean. She un-ties the raft from the door handle and ties the rope around Jones's chest. She doesn't understand what's wrong with Jones and that scares her. Jones has always been so strong and dependable. She wonders if they have become too dependent on this very wonderful man. She notices that Jones is becoming more alert and is relieved. Jones looks around in surprise asking what are they doing in the water. Rose tells him that they have crash-landed in the ocean and she wants him to help her get him into the raft. Jones looks at the raft and understands what's needed of him. He slides over the side and into the inflated raft. The raft has a canopy and can protect people from the elements in most any weather and any seas. Rose is feeling better as Jones comes to life.

Jones says to Rose, "There must have been something in the helicopter that was knocking me out."

Rose looking like a wet hen with ruffled feathers, "I don't know why but I don't feel anything but terror. Just like a wet hen and a real mess. Would you look at my hair?"

Jones finds the ores and rows them away from the sinking chopper. He tells Rose that he is ok, whatever it was is passing out of his system. Rose, shudders to think what could have happened if Jones was completely out. She isn't stupid and realizes that someone is attacking them yet again. When will this ever end, and what do they want of her now?

Rose hates her father and Uncle George for starting all this trouble. She believes that they both were mad. She can only hope that nothing like that ever happens to her. She is glad for once that she was adopted and so genetics won't have any effect on any children if she ever gets around to having any.

She looks at Jones rowing them away from the crash site and is glad he is with her. She thinks she is in love with this old duffer and doesn't care any more about the differences in their ages. She wants to ask him how old he is but has to laugh at herself. Why on earth would she care how old someone is at this time? Jones looks around at her with a questioning gaze. Rose smiles back at him, he is so perceptive.

She has a funny thought and asks, "Oh well, Mr. Jones, can I ask you something?"

He tells her to go ahead and ask, what the difference is now.

She bites the bullet and says right out, "How old are you?"

Jones with a shrug, says, "You know that's the same thing Nancy always wants to know."

Rose, tells him that it really doesn't matter, it's not important. Jones, reminds her that all she has to do is look at his personal file he filled out when signing on with her father.

Rose looking embarrassed says, "That would be dishonest of me and she wouldn't do that."

Jones sighs and says, "He is 51 years old."

Rose does the math quicker than she realizes and says that's not so old. Jones knows she is 34 now and he too realizes that they are 17 years' different in their ages. Jones looks at Rose with a different point of view, he has noticed how perfectly beautiful she is, at least he thinks so and tells her she is pretty. Rose looks down at her wet clothes and stringy hair and tells him she doesn't feel pretty. Jones reminds her that he's not exactly a basket of fruit himself. In spite of their predicament they chuckle at their thoughts. Rose asks if there is a responder on the helicopter, does anyone know we have crash-landed?

Jones looking over his left shoulder at her, "I don't know, I was sort of out of it when we came down. I am afraid the helicopter is done for and will probably sink to the bottom."

She asks, "How far down is the bottom?"

Jones tells her it's much too far to retrieve the Jet Ranger. She is sad over that, she used to play around the helicopter when she was still a kid. She thinks oh well, *'at least they won't have to worry about painting it the new colors.'* Jones uses his prosthetics GPS to show him where they are.

Jones groans," Oh hell, we're further out from shore than I thought we would be."

Rose pushing her wet hair off of her face asks, "How far?"

Jones tells her they are 40 miles from the nearest beech. The shore is rocky along this part of the coast and they may have a difficult

BOOK TWO: BRAIDY

time landing. Rose isn't as upset as she thinks she should be, she believes in Jones's abilities and as long as he is awake, she is safe.

Jones hasn't any doubts, the helicopter was definitely sabotaged, and him too. Someone planned this crash and wanted them both dead. He doesn't know why they are still alive, he guesses it's just his stubbornness that kept him from passing out completely.

It's than that Jones notices that the compass has been removed from the raft. The water bottles are gone and the food supplies too are missing. Jones is surprised that the paddles don't break when, one does break right in two. Jones doesn't even swear he just looks around for another way of getting to shore. Rose notices his looking and asks him what's the matter? He tells her that there's no water bottles, food, compass, and now the paddle brakes.

Rose is alarmed, saying, "You mean the raft has been sabotaged too?"

"Yup it has, whoever or is it whomever wants us dead has been efficient at removing everything."

Rose swallows at that and looks all around. Jones tells her that there's nothing around that will hurt them. Rose is glad for that, she is wondering if they were visible on radar? Jones doesn't think so, they didn't really have a flight plan, but, Braidy will search for us. He will rent another helicopter or look for us in his float plane. Rose, has forgotten about Brady's float plane, remembering that it can land on water or land.

She asks Jones, "How long until he becomes concerned?"

Jones tells her he believes right away, Braidy is a worrier. Rose, thinks that's good for a change, he will find us she just knows.

38

Marvin and Kenny have been monitoring the helicopter because of a tracking device that one of the new mechanics placed on board while the chopper was being serviced. He has been paid a large sum of cash from Kenny's ill-gotten money left over from George's estate. The money is enough for Kenny and company to do the nasty deeds they have planned but not enough, it's never enough for Kenny and Marvin.

Seamus is a genius at planning everything, he says he thinks outside the box whatever that means, the two guys aren't certain. They are waiting a mile or so off the raft's location, they have a tracking device in Rose's purse as well. She doesn't always examine the contents of her very large handbag. She has managed to snag it on the way out of the sinking helicopter. The two bad guys have a plan for capturing Rose and Jones that Seamus has invented. They will show up seemingly accidentally to rescue the downed people. They have worked on this plan that Shamus has invented for them. The two are so impressed with their difference in appearance that they barely recognize themselves. Kenny looks like a very old man hardly able to move, and Marvin looks more like his real self, crazy and very stupid. He has been practicing drooling and mumbling nonsense words. He is dirty and his shirt isn't buttoned properly. They are using the 40-foot cabin cruiser from the island. Kenny thought of making Barbra drive the boat but he doesn't want her to hear about any greedy schemes. She doesn't ask where they are going with the other boat, she keeps her head down and her mouth shut.

Kenny drives the boat towards the raft not directly but from the side. He intends to make the finding appear like they weren't looking for Jones and Rose when they sight the raft. Kenny turns the boat

BOOK TWO: BRAIDY

suddenly, and it does seem that the folks in the boat saw the raft accidentally. Kenny slows the boat and backs up toward the raft. This isn't at all accidental, he wants to come at the raft with the back of his craft. He wants to tow the raft instead of transferring passengers to his boat. Kenny knows how dangerous Jones can be and wants to keep some distance from him. Jones doesn't wonder at this maneuver, he is just glad to get rescued. He does however wonder at this very old man and his innocent looking son. Kenny introduces himself as Ward and this is his son Ward junior. He says they can call his son Junior and he is just plain Ward.

Jones tosses over the painter from the front of the raft and Junior ties it to a cleat at the back of the bigger boat. Ward, asks if they are ready? Jones answers ok, take it easy please. Ward goes slow heading at first toward shore but gradually turning to the south. Jones wonders at the change in direction but keeps still, he doesn't know these waters as well as Ward does.

Rose is shivering even though the weather isn't cold, she is wearing a lightweight dress that's more for showing off her figure than keeping her warm. Jones finds one of those space age blankets and offers it to her. She finds that it is surprisingly warm and soon is more comfortable.

Jones is reviewing the GPS numbers in his prosthetics and says to Rose, "I don't know where this old guy is taking us?"

She looks at him in alarm, and says, "You mean they aren't going toward shore?"

Jones tells her no, "We're going south and slightly out to sea."

Rose shrugs, and tells him, "That she doesn't know these waters either, she should, after living around here all of her life."

Jones pulls her closer, and she is warmed by his concern. She has come to trust this very special man and feels better. Jones doesn't feel better however, there's something about this rescue that stinks. The boat is moving slowly enough that the raft doesn't swamp and the Diesel fumes are getting to him. The boat is about 40 feet long with a marine Diesel, apparently and isn't very well kept. The paint is peeling off the wheelhouse and the brass looks dull. The engine hasn't been serviced for quite some time he thinks. Jones is alert and ready for anything he hopes.

Rose is warmer after wrapping the space blanket around herself. She is asking, "Jones what's happening here?"

Jones tells her he doesn't know, maybe nothing, I suppose were going to a port that we can use to get back home. Rose comments that she will miss her conference, she wonders if they will get along without her. She is kidding, no one keeps track of who's there or not it doesn't matter. Jones is watching the man at the helm of the boat ahead of them.

"Say Rose, do you think that old man driving that boat moves rather well for seeming to be so old?" Jones looking out of the corners of his eyes.

Rose, "Well let me look at him for a second, yes he does move quite smartly for an old guy, do you think there's something amiss?"

Jones trying not to stare directly at Ward Jr, asks, "How about Junior there?"

Rose also trying not to be obvious replies, "He isn't as dumb as he would like us to believe that's for sure."

Jones sighs and tells her, that he doesn't think the helicopter had a mechanical problem caused by lack of maintenance, the mechanics are the best we can find anywhere. Rose, says to Jones, that there's a new guy, she hired him about 6 months ago, he had good credentials and an amazing resume.

Jones touching Rose's hand lightly, "All those reports can be faked these days, I'm not doubting you Rose, I'd never do that of course! I have been fooled many times myself, it can happen to anyone."

Rose feels bad that she may be the one to cause more trouble and looks to Jones with sadness. Jones sees her discomfort and takes her hand and holds it tight against his chest.

With a warm smile just for her softly says, "Rose its ok, you're doing just fine, think about all the individual parts to this giant company of yours. There are countries with smaller budgets than there is in this company. You have to look at the positives rather than the negatives." Jones thinks he sounds ridiculous saying statements like that.

He smiles with a silly grin," Sorry Rose, I didn't mean for that to come out sounding so goofy."

Rose doesn't even notice and snuggles in close to Jones and is comforted by his strength and bulk.

Jonesy, she asks, "Do you think we can be alright?"

BOOK TWO: BRAIDY

Jones knows what she means, but asks anyway, "Rosie, what do you mean?"

Rose is shy and looks away, then says in a rush, "Could you love someone like me?"

Jones, wants to say yes, but tells her that he doesn't want to ever have children with any woman. She is surprised at that, she hasn't ever thought of children. Rose tells him that she was adopted remember, and if she wants children that would be the way she would have kids. Jones thinks *'well now that's probably OK, maybe yes that might be good.'*

Jones, thinks about Rose and smiles down at her, saying, "Yes Rose I do love you and have for a long time now."

Rose, "What about Nancy?"

Jones, "Well I confess, I thought that because she is of a different color that she would never want to marry me for any reason. I don't know if that's so, maybe she was getting some sort of unspoken message who can know."

Rose, "So you don't have a problem loving me, even though I'm saddled down with this albatross of a company?" She shyly smiles into his loving eyes.

Jones, "Rose don't worry about your big assed company, we can handle anything it has to throw at us."

Rose is reassured by Jones's words and presents, she will be ok with Jones's help. She tells him that she depends on him for sanity from time to time and needs him to be there for her.

Jones hugging her, "Well Rose, when we were helping Carmen some of my past came back to haunt me. I remember all too well how it was for me in those early days of blindness. Carmen is doing just fine and has become a valuable part of this company; the employees just love her and she has become quite the comedian too.

"You're so right my friend, she keeps people informed and entertained at the same time. She has a good future with us and we will take good care of her whatever happens."

Jones asks her about Joni, too.

"Joni, is also doing well, she is polite and does her job well, however she isn't the comedian that Carmen is."

Jones tells her that "Joni is slightly older actually about 20 years older."

Rose, "Well old man does that really make a difference?"

Jones moves to kiss her soft sweet lips and hesitates, "Nope not as far as I'm concerned, the older the goofball the goofier the jokes become."

Rose doesn't wait, and just lifts her face up and kisses him with a really good smack right where it counts.

39

Braidy comes walking into the office hungry as usual. Carmen is petting Jack and they are communicating in that special way they have. Ever since Carmen was injured, she has depended on good old Jack for a personal friend.

Braidy is asking with a look of concern, "Carmen where is Jones and Rose?"

Carmen with tears welling in her pretty dark eyes, "Oh Mr. Braidy, I don't know, I call on the phone but no answer."

When Carmen is anxious, she reverts back to her Spanish accented English. Braidy enjoys hearing it usually but not now, he hears the concern in her voice and goes over to her.

Braidy kneeling down beside her and Jack, "So, Carmen when did you hear from them last?"

Carmen wiping tears from her face with the palms of both hands, "Oh, it's been at least an hour or more, that's not like Rose, she is always dependable at answering the phone. When she knows, it's me calling her always answers right away."

Braidy laying his big paw on her soft hair trying to calm her, "Did they leave from here with the helicopter?"

Carmen melting into his touch, "Oh yes Mr. Braidy they flew off the roof more than an hour now and I'm worried."

Braidy is also worried but doesn't say anything yet, he knows that problems can develop and wants to know more before getting too worried. Carmen hugs Jack closer and is very upset, people in this company are her family now and she shutters to think of losing any of them. Braidy isn't good at comforting people and says to her that he will figure out what's the matter. Carmen isn't convinced and cries into Jacks fur. Jack turns to her and licks a big tongue full of dog slobber onto her face.

Carmen stops crying long enough to snicker at Jack and says, "Oh Jack yuck!"

Jack doesn't understand what the problem is, it's clean dog slobber, not too bad.

Braidy checks with Jim at the hanger and is told that the helicopter isn't there. Jim informs Braidy that Jones and Rose flew off in the helicopter almost 2 hours ago, Braidy wants to know if Jones indicated where they were flying? Jim tells Braidy that Rose had to attend a conference somewhere in California Jim doesn't know what place only that there wasn't an airport big enough for the King Air.

Braidy with a sigh of exasperation, "Ok thanks Jim, is the Cessna ready to fly?"

Jim tasks at Braidy and groans, "Of course the plane is gassed up and ready for his terrible flying."

Braidy suggest to Jim maybe he can give him flying lessons designed for an old man!"

Jim complains, "Yeah, yeah, I'll old man you buster."

Braidy says to Carmen that he wants to fly down the coast for a bit and see what he can see. Carmen asks him what should she do in the meantime. Braidy looks at Carmen and sees her concern and tells her that she can come along if she wants to. Carmen lights up at that, she wants to be included and is excited that he is asking her to help. She cannot see what's below them but can be there for anything else. She has become more confident in her abilities and will do whatever it takes to help her friends.

Braidy and Carmen take the elevator down the lower level where the company vehicles are kept. Braidy takes one of the newly painted trucks and calls Joni on the way out, he says they will stay in touch. Joni is worried, she really likes these people and wants to be useful. Braidy drives quickly out to the Hanger not even stopping for food on the way. Neither one of them are hungry just worried. Jim is waiting there with the others and is worried too.

Jim wiping his hands on a paper towel looking a mess, "Say Braidy I can fly too and help you guys look for Rose."

Braidy with a warm smile for his old friend, "Thanks Jim, I don't even know where were going except south. We can fly to the little

BOOK TWO: BRAIDY

town where Rose was supposed to be but we've already asked, they didn't show up there."

Jim looking up at the clouds, "Ok, let us know, we will do whatever you need us to do."

Braidy, says they will take the Cessna since its newly overhaled, maybe it will stay in the air long enough to find Rose and Jones. Jim tells Braidy that he is nuts, that plane is like new.

Braidy smiles at his old friend and says, "I don't doubt it one little bit, I believe in you Jim."

Jim has to look away, he isn't used to such nice compliments from Braidy.

The guys help Braidy push the Cessna out of the hanger and Jim helps Carmen get into the passenger side of the aircraft. She is very anxious and isn't as skillful at moving about as her usual self. She is on the verge of tears and doesn't want to lose it again. Jim is reassuring and kind to her, he tells her directions rather than just pushing her around. He is really a very kind man in spite of what Braidy says about him. Braidy helps her with the seatbelt and she is ok, she tells him that once Jones let her hold the controls in the King Air. Braidy looks at her and can see that she isn't kidding, and says to her,

"Well that's ok, maybe you will need to bring us home."

Carmen smacks his arm with her small hand and says he is as goofy as Jones.

Braidy with a grin, "Well ah shucks mam, thank you very much."

Braidy goes through the check list and starts the engine. Jim is right, the plane starts right up and runs smoothly. Jim really does it up right when it comes to maintaining airplanes, Braidy thinks he is the best. He has bet his life on Jim's abilities for many years now and hasn't any problem with continuing. Jim and the guys are there waving them good luck and they roar off down the runway heading into the sky.

Braidy likes these little planes, they are easier to fly then the turbo props that the King Airs use. The cabins are smaller of course but turning and maneuvering smaller aircraft is more like the flying he learned long ago.

40

Kenny, alias Ward, notices the two in the raft staring at him and looks away toward the front of his boat. Marvin is smart enough to stay out of sight, he doesn't like acting like a dummy. He finds something to do below decks and peaks out once in a while. Marvin has been told what to do when they arrive at the small island, they are taking these two captives to and reminds himself of what he needs to do. Seamus has written out the directions with precise timing of every part of the job. Marvin doesn't trust this little squirt and will probably just have to crush him like an empty beer can. He thinks about how it will feel to crunch the little bastard into pulp, what a thrill. Marvin doesn't like the sound of the engine, he knows engines and this one is bad bad. He has asked Kenny about working on the engine but Kenny says no why bother. Marvin doesn't know what that might mean, he lets it go.

Kenny spots the island just ahead and drives the boat directly for it. Rose says to Jones that she sees a small island ahead and wonders if that's where they are going? Jones doesn't like this one little bit and says so.

Rose, "what do you mean, what will happen to us do you think?" She shivers.

Jones "well I don't know, but whatever it is I don't like it."

Rose, "you said that already, don't you remember?" she has that little Nome like grin on her pretty face.

Jones, "I thought I heard that before from somewhere."

Rose just kisses him again, and says, "You're my man now no matter what happens."

Jones tells her that he will do his best for her whatever comes. He tells her that these are dangerous characters, he isn't invincible,

BOOK TWO: BRAIDY

like she might think, just be ready for anything. Rose gulps and nods her head, ok.

Kenny drives his boat into a lagoon, over to the beach, and stops in shallower water. Marvin comes up from below and un-ties the raft from the back of the cabin cruiser. He wades through the water to the beach and ties the painter to a piece of dock that is still there. He tows the raft into shore and pulls it partly onto the sand. Jones and Rose climb out and walk up the beech towards some trees, and then stand together on the sand looking around. Marvin goes back to the cabin cruiser and Kenny drives the boat out to see. Jones has to wonder at that.

"And says to Rose, "What do you think about that?"

Rose isn't there she has vanished in an instant. Rose is gone, and Jones stands on the sand looking and feeling stupid. He thinks of calling her name.

And says quietly, "Rose, where are you?"

Rose answers from below, she has dropped down through a hole under the sand. Jones looks around and finds the opening where she has gone.

"Rose, are you down there?"

"Jones, I'm down here, I'm not sure what's happening."

Jones tries to stop himself but slides down the hole like Rose has. He meets up with her in a heap, and some sand falls around them. Rose, is terrified and giggles too.

She asks snickering a little, "Now what? Do you feel like Alice in Wonderland?"

Jones, "I feel like a complete idiot." Standing up.

Rose looks around and says, "This looks manmade to me."

Jones, says, "Yes, it is, it's a cement structure like a pre-cast culvert maybe."

Rose has no idea what he is talking about and says that.

"Well, it's something they use to put under roads and highways to allow water to flow through. They dig up the roadway and then insert something like this piece of cement than cover over the road and very soon traffic can drive over the culvert not even knowing there's an opening below the road. The difference here of course is that the culvert is vertical instead of horizontal."

Rose brushing sand off her legs, "Do you mean someone has planned this structure to be placed here?"

Jones looking around agrees, "Yup, just for us, I cannot brake out of this cement I don't think, and the sides are smooth and we can't pull ourselves out of here. It's like a pit they use to capture wild animals in Africa, you know like elephants."

Rose in spite of the seriousness of it all says, "I hope you don't think I'm an elephant?"

"No silly, maybe a tiger or something better looking than an elephant." He smiles into her warm brown eyes.

Rose grinning back at him, "You're gonna get yours, you bum you."

Jones, is looking all around, he is seeking a way out. The top of the structure is at least 10 feet tall, way over their heads, and he wonders why they didn't get injured. He notices that the bottom has lots of soft sand, in fact their feet have sunk in about a foot or so. Jones tells Rose that the sand has cushioned their fall. Rose has bare legs because she is wearing a dress and agrees with him. She looks up too and asks Jones if he can think of a way of getting them out of this place? Jones doesn't think he can, the top is too far above them. Even if Rose stands on his shoulders, he doubts she can reach the top. He wanders around the bottom and is looking for sand that may be firmer. Near one edge it is a little more firm and close to an outside wall.

He looks at the spot and says, "Say rose, maybe you can stand on my shoulders over by this wall and reach the top."

Rose looking more than willing, "Ok I'll try if you like, I'm not as athletic as Nancy of course, but why not, I'll give it a try."

Jones kneels down and she steps up on his shoulders, with bare feet, he rises up and she uses her hands on the wall to keep her balance. She rises up the wall like she is on an elevator marveling at Jones's strength. She can touch the top of the cement container with her extended finger tips and says she can almost pull herself up. Jones pushes her up by her ankles, she can reach. She isn't strong and it takes everything she has and then some to pull herself out of the pit. She doesn't worry about what she must look like from below, she loves this man and doesn't care. Everything she has Jones can have and if she can bring them happiness she will. Jones doesn't look up under Rose's dress, he isn't a creep. He knows that she will show him everything sometime later if there ever out of this dilemma.

Jones has wondered at all the crap they have to go through just to survive in the world. Rose looks all around from above and calls

BOOK TWO: BRAIDY

down to him. She looks at everything and all around and there is nothing but this small island. The boat is gone, and he thinks what a surprise with that one. Rose says she will look around for some way of getting Jones out of the hole he's in. Jones has to smile at that one, man oh man what a hoe he's in. Rose comes back dragging a long limb from a downed tree. It is long enough but will it be strong enough to hold his weight? She tells him that she will drop the end into the hole. Jones looks up and see's the man behind Rose holding a gun to Rose's head. She screams and fright and her eyes are as big as saucers. The man is a little guy and says with some sort of Irish accent.

"Now lassie just stay still and you'll be just fine."

Rose looks down at Jones with fear and regret and starts to cry. Jones knows now what the plan was, they want to separate Rose and him, in such a way that he cannot protect her. Jones begins to see red and gathers himself, not knowing what he will do but knowing something is coming. With a single leap, he is up through the hole and smashing this little turd into paste. Rose has never seen this kind of violence from Jones and is shocked. She is also glad to be out of danger. Jones isn't even breathing hard. He smiles at her, and asks if she is alright? Rose has heard of his powers but has not witnessed it like Nancy has. She just hugs Jones close to her chest and sighs with relief. She says to him,

"I'm glad you're on my side!"

Jones assures her that it's ok, he isn't dangerous to her or anyone else he loves. Rose looks down at what was a man and wonders who he was and where did he come from? Jones looks around at an empty island and wonders how they will get back home from here. Rose asks if the raft is still over on the water. Jones doesn't know and says they will find out.

They move away from Seamus's dead body and walk to the edge of the water. Yes, the raft is still there tied to the piece of broken dock. Rose asks if they may be able to find something to move the raft with since the paddles are ruined. Jones, isn't worried about the paddles as much as the other two bad guys. He thinks he might know at least one of them. Jones, asks Rose,

"Do you think the bigger guy on the boat looked a little familiar?"

Rose, asks him, "What do you mean?"

Jones tells her that he thinks that guy looks like Marvin's size, although the face was very different. Rose, says the guy is Marvin's size that's for sure, but he was mostly out of sight.

Jones "Well we will find out if they are still around." He gazes everywhere.

Rose looks at her man and wonders what else he is capable of. Jones doesn't know either, only now he can feel his temper is boiling. He has just about had enough of this Bull Shit. He tells Rose that he will get to the bottom of this mess, and he is sorry if that upsets her. Rose agrees reluctantly, she doesn't like violence but also has had enough loss of life and destroyed equipment and ships. Rose, asks Jones if he can find the others? Jones tells her that he will try and keep on trying until their all found out. She believes him and decides that maybe his way is the only way for them to find peace and happiness.

41

Braidy and Carmen are flying the Cessna along the coast not really with a plan just feeling their way, hoping for something to show. Braidy doesn't say much, he is concentrating on thinking like Jones might. He cannot feel anything that Jones feels and is just wasting time and fuel.

He turns to Carmen and asks her, "Do you have any ideas or feelings?"

She answers with a shaky small voice, "Oh no Mr. Braidy, I'm just worried and scared."

Braidy touches her hand and tells her that, "They will find their people."

Carmen tries not to cry so much but cannot help herself. Braidy turns back toward home and is still looking around, see's nothing, just open sea on the left and sand on the right. When they get closer to home, he tells her about the little island where he and Jim saw the woman fishing. When they come to the island, he tells her about the big house too. The dairy farm on the other end of the island. Carmen knows nothing about cows or dairy farms but is interested in the house. Braidy describes it to her from 1000 feet. He tells her that the house is 2 stories tall and has a large space under the roof. He thinks that there could be a big room on the top above the second floor. The house has to have at least five bedrooms and the rooms must be quite large. There are smaller buildings all around the property and closer to the shore is a boathouse. He tells her that there is a woman fishing out on the ocean in a boat. She is dressed in some sort of swimming suit and wears a man's shirt over the top. She looks up at their plane and Braidy tells her how pretty she looks. Carmen is interested in what he is saying and wonders. Braidy flies them toward home and they land on the company strip. He taxi's over to the hanger and Jim helps him put away the plane. Jim can see they have had no luck, they didn't expect any but still hopeful. Jim tells Braidy that there's nothing from the office either.

Braidy isn't happy and says so, "When will this crap ever end?"

Jim is frustrated too, "Hey man I don't know, but please let him know if he can do anything?"

Braidy placing his big hand on Jim's shoulder says, "Oh hey thanks Jim, I will."

42

Kenny and Marvin are terrified when they find Seamus's remains, they know that Jones is capable enough to smash Seamus into paste, but how did Jones get out of the pit. The pit has slick walls and is deep enough that he shouldn't have been able to get out. Kenny and Marvin just leave Seamus's body where it lies and head back to their home island. They will have to tell Barbra some lie about Seamus, why he decided to skip out on them or something like that. Kenny wants to get back to the zapper that Dr. Don Hamilton invented, for one thing, you don't have to be near Jones to zap him. Being near Jones is very dangerous and in fact as it turns out deadly. Man, oh man what kind of man is Jones, how does he do what he does? Kenny is really very frightened. Marvin isn't so cocky any more, he has seen the results of Jones's strength and is reluctant to get near him.

The two men discuss Jones and what they can do about him.

Kenny looking around for his cigars says, "It's too bad they don't have any superman killer stuff, what was it called kryptonite or what the hell was it."

Marvin looking lost and kind of stupid replies, "Well I don't know what you are talking about, but some of the zapper stuff would do wonders on Jones I think."

Kenny lighting a big Havana, "How do we find the creep, and where do we look for him?"

Marvin for once gets an inspiration lighting up like a light bulb announces, "Say doesn't that girl friend of Don's work for Rose's Company?"

"Yup, so what, what do you mean?"

Kenny blows a smoke ring.

Marvin drags out a well for ever almost and reveals, "We grab the broad and then the jerk will follow."

Kenny thinks that's almost poetic. Marvin hasn't a clue what Kenny is saying, he knows nothing about poetry. He knows Diesel engines and maintaining other heavy equipment but nothing about culture of any kind.

The food services on the island has certainly gone downhill since Barbra disappeared. Kenny wonders what's up with that. After all the only job she had to do was to feed them once in a while. He let her play around with that other boat and if she caught some fish, she manages to cook than that's only good.

Kenny flips his cigar into a plant and growls, "What a worthless bitch, after all I did for that broad. If I ever get my hands on her that will be the end of that worthless foreigner."

Kenny isn't really positive where Barbra came from, he thinks it could be somewhere south but not for sure. Marvin knows exactly where Barbra came from and lords it over Kenny.

Kenny snarls at Marvin, "So how is where the woman came from any of your business? After all she is my woman not yours. You had better be watching your manners here or you will end up as dead as good old Seamus."

Marvin holds up his dirty paw and fights back, "Now hold on there, I got no desire to have anything to do with that woman except for her cooking. After all a man has to eat, right? Do you expect me to cook for myself, oh no, not me that's for damn sure?"

Kenny lights another cigar and offers one to Marvin. Marvin has been looking at those very fine Cubin cigars with only a little drool falling from his bottom lip. Marvin smells like a Diesel engine and the odor is plugging Kenny's nose.

Kenny lighting his cigar again complains, "You know Marvin, you stink like a dirty engine, why don't you take a bath or something?"

Marvin looking really pissed off, "You watch your mouth asshole, after all, I can squash you like a bug whenever I want. Keep your big bad mouth shut or I will shut it for you."

Kenny pulls out a double-barreled derringer from nowhere. Marvin recognizes it for what it is and what even that little toy can do.

BOOK TWO: BRAIDY

"Hey man, I didn't mean nothin', just put that little toy gun away."

Kenny grins, "So you can be taught to respond, maybe you need some better training. Just remember, don't forget, I'm the boss, you're the worker."

Marvin lights up one of Kenny's cigars and disappears into his own world of not knowing or caring.

Marvin is watching Kenny get madder and madder, he is turning red and then purple. Marvin hopes that good old Kenny will simply blow up like an overheated engine.

43

Jones and Rose find the raft and decide to wait until morning now before trying to navigate their way home. Jones tells Rose that they are 47 miles from the mainland, and if the tide is incoming, they may be able to drift partway to shore in the morning. Jones searches the raft looking for anything they can use for shelter. There is nothing much, the raft has been stripped. Jones does find some fishing line and hooks.

"I wonder how they missed this stuff."

Rose looks at eh fishing line and hooks and asks, "What do they do with that?"

Jones, smiles back at her, and tells her "That they can catch some fish maybe!"

Rose is curious and asks, "Will they be cooked?"

Jones looks back at her and see's that she is smiling back at him, and tells her, "That she is silly."

She says, "But she is his silly."

He agrees," Yup you are that."

Jones finds a rubber worm too and says this is their lucky day, theirs line hooks and some fake fish food.

Rose looks at the worm and asks him, "Does a fish really think that's real?"

Jones allows that he doesn't think fish are very bright, they bite at almost anything. Rose finds a stick they can use for a fishing pole to fish with and Jones ties the line to the end of the stick. Jones finds a long limb like the one Rose brought him to try and escape with. The limb has some branches on it and Jones strips off the extras from the limb, he uses it for a pole to move the raft over the little lagoon toward the open ocean and Rose begins to fish. The fish are willing and soon she has caught four nice fish. Rose is proud of herself, she tells Jones that this is the first time she ever fished. Jones tells her she is pulling his leg, and she says no, scouts honor. Jones has to wonder at that, how can someone live this close to the ocean that happens to be full of water and never fish before?

Jones poles them back to shore and has another search for some matches.

"Nope there isn't any matches, not a one." He throws up his hands.

Rose pulls out a Bick lighter from her giant purse and offers it to Jones.

He asks her, "If she has been secretly smoking all this time?"

Rose tells him with a wink, "That she doesn't smoke but likes to be prepared."

He asks her, "What else she has in that giant bag of hers?"

She dumps it out on the sand and shows him a woodsmen's knife.

Jones also notices a GPS transmitter, and exclaims, "Oh shit, no wonder they knew where we were, that's a tracker."

Rose looks horrified covering her mouth with her not so clean hand, "You mean that I was the one that they were following?
"

"Yup, don't worry about it now, we'll be ok Rose." He reassures her.

Jones smiles at her and just has to tell her what a woman she is, how cool that is.

"She says she has never used that knife for anything but opening beer bottles." She looks so wise.

Jones finds there is a; scaling blade, carving blade, plyers, screw driver, corkscrew, scissors and more.

"Holy cow woman where did you get this killer knife?" holding up.

Rose looking a tiny bit superior proudly announces, "My father gave it to me, he said this was the present for a girl that has everything."

Jones tells her that he was right, it would be a present for the girl that has everything.

"Well I'm glad you're the girl that has everything, it means we'll eat fresh caught fish tonight."

Rose, asks "If this is their first date?"

Jones fanning smoke away from his face replies, "Why not, we're on a private island, and it's not too cold, we got a fire started and fish to fry. We can share that space blanket you got there, and I think there's another one in the raft."

Say Jones, "Why did they take out the water compass and other stuff but left these blankets?"

Jones tells her that they probably just didn't think we would be able to use anything after we were killed in the helicopter crash or maybe they were just plane lazy.

Rose, asks him, "What about the helicopter?"

Jones tells her that the helicopter is probably done for, once an aircraft is submerged all the electronics are ruined. The helicopter is at least twenty years old and would need to be replaced soon anyway."

Rose moves a little closer to him," You're probably right about that, Braidy has mentioned that to me before."

Jones wishes he could call Braidy somehow, and asks Rose, "Does she have a satellite phone in that giant suitcase she calls a purse?"

She shakes her head no but does produce a couple of wrapped up cupcakes.

Jones looks at her in admiration and says, "Things are looking up, not only fresh fish but dessert too."

44

The two lovers enjoy a rough night, they are happy to be together but the accommodation isn't the best. Jones has cooked the fish using a stick to hold them over the fire, trying to keep it from catching fire. Rose found salt and sugar packets in her giant handbag.

"Boy oh boy, how much does that suitcase like bag hold?"

Rose is worried about what's out in the dark, but Jones can see well enough and tells her there's nothing. Rose finally settles down and gets some sleep leaning against Jones. They save the cupcakes for breakfast and Jones says he wishes for some coffee.

Rose smiles at his wishes an offers with a knowing look, "You can have all the coffee you want later."

The island isn't very big less than a half mile long and less than that wide. It's just a little bump on the ocean, no one cares about these little islands, most are too small to be noticed. There's nothing worthwhile and people visit them just to explore for fun. In the morning, Jones and Rose look around and decide they will have to use the raft to get back to shore.

Rose asks Jones, "Hey Jones, what's that engine sound?"

Jones has heard it too and wants to find out who is coming nearer to this island. Jones tells Rose that the smoke probably gave them away, boaters on the open ocean can see smoke on an island for miles on a clear day. They hide behind some bushes near the lagoon where the raft is tied. On board an open boat is a pretty woman driving it. She comes right over to the raft and looks it over. She is looking all around, she is trying to find something or someone. Jones sees that she is alone and decides to come right out and talk to her.

Jones, steps out from behind the bushes they are hiding behind. He is surprised when the woman pulls out an old six shooter. He thinks it's a 45 revolver, he can see the shining brass cartridges in the ends of the cylinder. Jones hasn't seen one of those forever. He stands still just waiting for the woman to make the next move. She speaks with a lilting accent that is musical to hear.

Barb holding her pistol steady as a rock enquires, "Are you alone on this island?"

Jones wanting to be evasive offers, "Why do you want to know?"

She is surprised at that, she thinks that her big pistol speaks loud enough but maybe not. She decides that this man isn't any danger, he is unarmed. She lowers her gun and asks him if he has seen a very small man? Jones knows who she is looking for, it's the man he has killed. He doesn't want any more trouble, he tells the woman that the man she is looking for was killed.

She shakes her head, and sighs, "I knew they were up to no good. I should never have denied my inner thoughts."

Jones is not certain what she is saying, he knows about inner voices, and wonders if hers are like his?

Jones, asks her if she can give them a ride to the mainland? Barb tells him, "Oh sure, and who are you?"

Just than Rose decides to come out from hiding and Barb is impressed with Rose's beauty. Rose looks like she has spent the night in her clothes, but still manages to look bright and delicate.

Barbra after lowering her big gun, "I'm Barbra, and live on the island over there pointing towards the island where she lives with Kenny."

Jones tells her that Rose and he survived a helicopter crash and a couple of strangers brought them to this little island.

Barbra's curiosity is peaked she wants to know, "What did the guys look like?"

After Rose tells her, Barbra is confused, the men she describes aren't Marvin or Kenny. Jones goes on telling her about the boat and then Barbra gets it and shakes her head. She thinks to herself, *'so Kenny and Marvin have disguised themselves'*

She asks Jones, "Do you work for that big shipping company in Seattle?"

Jones looks at Rose, and reluctantly nods yes.

Rose wants to know and simply asks, "Why do you need to know that?"

BOOK TWO: BRAIDY

Barbra with lots of resistance reveals, "Oh well never mind, it's nothing, I know a little bit about your company."

Jones, doesn't like this, he wants to find out more from Barbra but decides a ride to shore will be enough for now. Barbra invites them over to her boat and asks about the raft?

Rose has to think about that for a second, "Oh you can have it if you want it."

Barbra says she will think about that later and takes them out through the lagoon toward open ocean. Jones is suspicious and watching Barbra closely, he doesn't want any more tricks. He notices that she is taking them directly toward shore, not so much to the closest shore but shore where they can get transportation home. Jones decides that this woman isn't a bad person, she has an honest face and does what she says she will do.

When they get to shore, Rose thanks Barbra gratefully and hands her one of her business cards. Barbra looks at Rose's card closely and again shakes her head. Rose wonders what that head shaking is all about, she doesn't know this woman but Rose feels that the woman knows her. Jones offers Barbra his hand to shake, and she looks him right in the eye.

"I'm glad to know you both, and please be careful."

Barbra drives her boat out to sea and towards the island, they came from. Barbra needs to find Seamus's body and give him a proper burial, she hardly knew him but still he was nice to her. Barbra will do what's right, and she will feel better in that. She finds the island and the hole in the beech, she has no idea what happen to her friend, she decides to place Seamus in the bottom of the cement pit and fill it up with sand. She is responsible and wants no one to fall in this weird cement hole in the ground.

Rose says to Jones, "What do you make of that last statement?"

Jones rubs his whiskery chin making a rasping sound, "Well I don't know what she met but it sure sounded like a warning to me."

Rose agrees with him and says she will have to think about that woman some more.

Jones and Rose call the office from a pay phone in a drug store. Jones thinks there can't be very many of those phones left. Joni answers the phone with the name of Rose's Company and is excited to hear from them. She sends the call up to the main office and Carmen nearly jumps out of her skin with excitement. She is so excited she reverts to Spanish and Braidy doesn't understand her. Joe does however and translates for Braidy. Braidy runs out of the office and forgets Carmen, she yells at him to stop! Braidy looks around in surprise wondering what that bellow was. When he sees that it is Carmen, he goes back for her and takes her hand dragging her along. He is a man on a mission and can't wait for anything. Carmen is much shorter than Braidy and her feet barely touch the floor while she is towed along by him. Braidy demands that the elevator move faster, when he discovers that he has forgotten to push the button. Carmen realizes the problem and reaches around Braidy and pushes the button for him. She laughs at him in spite of the circumstances and he says oops.

    Carmen doesn't let his hand go even on the elevator, she doesn't want to lose him in his mad dash for a vehicle. Carmen tells Braidy to calm down, everything is ok now.

    Braidy looks down at his friend and says, "You know you're right, sorry Carmen, I'm alright, I won't leave you."

    Carmen still holds his hand as tight as she can and says she will just make sure of that if he doesn't mind.

    Braidy is calmer and finds a truck with a back seat, this one will do, for collecting Rose and Jones.

    Braidy and Carmen arrive in the little village where Jones and Rose are waiting and suddenly Braidy is starving. Rose hugs her favorite Uncle as she calls him and he is smiling. Rose and Jones are hungry too, and Rose tells them that she isn't dressed for anywhere fancy and thinks they should find a fast food place. Braidy looks all around but there isn't one in this small town. He sighs and tells them that they will have to wait until he drives them to a bigger town. Carmen has her phone out and finds them a nearby fast-food place in the next town and gives Braidy directions. Jones admires Carmen and her abilities on that smart phone she has. He can't hardly make a call on one of those silly things and she finds fast food places for them.

    Rose is really hungry and doesn't even care if it's a junk food place as she calls them. She will power down anything that resembles food and oh yes coffee too.

45

Back on Kenny's island, Marvin and Kenny are licking their wounds, they are frightened of what happened to Seamus. Kenny is looking around for Barbra and doesn't find her. Marvin isn't concerned with where Barbra is, he is shaking with fear.

Marvin says to Kenny, "Did you see Seamus, he was smashed like a melon or something.

Kenny tells Marvin that is what Jones can do, it looks like Seamus wasn't so grate after all, he is no more. Marvin thinks they need to be more careful even more than they were with Seamus's help. They need to find Don Hamilton and make him do what they want. That zapper thing that Hamilton has will take care of Jones. They can zap that bastard Jones from miles away and not take any chances. They have forgotten some of the reasons they need to get rid of Rose. They are focused on getting Jones out of the way and not so much on Rose's money. They aren't the brightest guys around and will stick to the basics from now on.

Kenny tells Marvin that the way to get to Don Hamilton is to grab the broad Joni. Marvin tells Kenny they have talked about that before and Kenny says he knows but it's the only way. Marvin also is wondering where Barbra is, he is getting hungry he misses her delicious cooking.

Kenny finds them something to eat and does an adequate job of warming it up. He has found some left overs and almost doesn't burn the food on the big stove. He doesn't do cooking and tells Marvin he doesn't. Marvin doesn't care, he just powers it all down anyway, its food and that's all he cares.

Barbra has returned to the island after taking Jones and Rose to the mainland. She is distressed by what has happened to Seamus. She hasn't felt good about Kenny for a while, he has been too devious for her liking. She lands her boat at the village dock on the other side of the island. She asks if she can stay with the village people for the night, they are glad to have her. She doesn't know what she will do next, she needs some time to think.

Barbra likes these folks and could just stay for the near future. She feels guilty about Kenny and Marvin's nastiness, and believes she should have given the people from the shipping company more information about the two guys. She really hasn't much more to say, mostly it's a bad feeling. She knows that Kenny is capable of criminal behavior but she has no real proof. Marvin is a different story, he has been involved with killing some of the local cats. She thinks killing is killing and has seen Marvin picking up cats, petting them, then throwing them down an abandon well. The well is deep enough that the cats cannot ever get out and eventually starve to death if they aren't killed in the first drop. She knows that Marvin is deliberately vicious and she is afraid of him, more than she is of Kenny. At least Kenny can pretend to be polite, although she doesn't trust him anymore either.

She will definitely have to find another place to live and she will need to find work too. She has been living off of Kenny's money and has to admit to herself she has been lazy. She likes living easy, after working all of her life not having to go to work every day is nicer

Barbra doesn't worry much about her future, she can take care of herself. Kenny and Marvin need to be watched at least from a distance. They are cooking up something bad and Barb believes that shipping company is right in the middle of their evil schemes. Barb wants to warn them of what she almost knows but doesn't know exactly how. Her command of English isn't the best and she is embarrassed when she tries to express herself. The language she uses for everyday talk is ok, however, when she has to talk about difficult subjects, she gets tongue tied. She will think about the problem some more and maybe one day she will find the right words.

Barbra needs to find work for herself and soon. She knows cooking, fishing, and not much else. She is a survivor and will do what she has to do to be ok.

Barb thinks about the mostly white sea plane that flew over when she was fishing. Wouldn't it be fun to learn to fly a plane like that? She could fly guys anywhere and show them how to catch fish. She

BOOK TWO: BRAIDY

likes the sea and hopes to find work on the ocean. Her family are fishermen and she is too. She will be alright.

46

Rose's new ship is a beauty, it is huge, and can carry thousands of containers. She travels at 25 knots and has comfortable crew's quarters. There is also visitor's accommodation that rival the best hotels. The ship is blue over darker blue just like Rose wanted it to be. She and Jones travel on board just for the novelty. They walk amongst the cargo and are impressed by the thousands of containers on board.

Rose wearing a wind breaker with company logo on front and back for all to see, "Well Mr. Jones, I bet you never saw anything like this ship in Nebraska?"

Jones wearing a matching jacket, "Well of course we don't have much of an ocean in Omaha, just the mighty Mo don't you know."

Rose holds his hand and doesn't care who knows she loves this gentle-man. Jones wonders too at his good fortune. He checks the chains that hold piles of containers in place, he can't help himself, it's just a habit. He checks everything that is mechanical, making sure that equipment looks right, and even tugging on a nearby chain.

Rose looks at her man with so much love, asking gently, "Does it feel ok?"

Jones looks up in surprise and asks her, "Is it that obvious?"

Rose kisses him saying, "It is but its ok, we gotta be safe don't you know."

He knows that she is kidding him but doesn't mind. They wander the ship from the back to the front, or excuse me, the stern to the bow. The crew are here and there doing their jobs efficiently and wave or smile or just say hi to them. Jones and Rose haven't gotten married, and maybe they won't, they are their own bosses. Rose has to wonder at how the company has grown since Jones came along. Probably it

BOOK TWO: BRAIDY

would have grown anyway however she thinks because of his efforts. She believes that sending Carmen and Jones out to visit logging camps, ships, and other facilities has helped to make the company grow bigger. Maybe it's just because her Father isn't steeling from his own company that's also helping it's difficult to know.

They will get off this ship in Los Angeles and fly back to Seattle. Jones hasn't flown commercial very often, he usually flies himself in one of the company planes. Rose and Jones talk about getting a replacement helicopter sometime soon. Braidy will be involved of course, and he has investigated what's available. Braidy favors the Bell Jet Ranger model 505 X, it is Bells replacement for the model 206 Jet Ranger. The company has been manufacturing Jet Rangers for around 45 years. Jones believes the new helicopter is ok, its cost is just over one million dollars. Braidy and Jones both agree that they should equip the new helicopter with floats. They want to be able to land on water if necessary since they are in the shipping business. Although every ship has a helicopter pad on the decks of Rose's ships it might be a good thing to be able to land on the water too. In the end however they decide no floats are really necessary. Rose has little or no idea what they are talking about, she trusts her guys, and will follow their leads. Both Jones and Braidy are considerate of Rose's wishes and explain to her as many times as necessary about the new chopper. Rose and Jones have been talking also about the mechanic that Rose hired around six months ago, they don't have proof, but they know that someone bugged the old helicopter and sabotaged it forcing it to crash land on the water. They are watching this new guy and have told Jim of their suspicions. Jim will keep an eye on that guy and does it so that it looks like he is just watching because he is new. The biggest reason for suspecting the new mechanic is because Jack is wary, he stays close whenever he visits the hanger. Jack is a dog who is not fooled and Jones has come to rely on the dog's cautions.

Jim is turning sixty-seven years old his next birthday and is talking about retiring soon. Rose has known him since she was a young girl and would miss him. She is sentimental about old employees and will provide Jim with a comfortable retirement. She hopes he will stay a little longer, at least until the new helicopter arrives. Jim tells her that he will.

When Rose and Jones arrive back in Seattle Braidy and Carmen meet them at the airport. Carmen is anxious again, she tells them that they haven't seen Joni for days. They call her apartment and even have gone over there but no Joni.

Rose and Jones grown and say, "Oh hell, not again!"

Carmen clings to Jacks collar and Jack leans into her trying to help in his doggy way. Braidy has looked in her old places that she has told them she goes too and theirs nothing.

Jones rubbing his weary face wonders, "Has anyone seen Don Hamilton?"

Braidy tells him no, he's gone too. He says that he can rent a helicopter and look around from the air although he doesn't know how much good that may do.

Jones touching his friends' arm, looking thankful says, "No that's ok Braidy, if Kenny or that Marvin have them their out of sight, out of sight out of mind."

Rose has asked Joe to take over Joni's desk on the main floor. Joe is willing and helpful and goes down willing of course. He is considerate and doesn't ask what's the matter, although his face shows his concern. Rose likes this young man and she thinks Carmen does too.

47

Kenny and Marvin have the two alright, and they are smart enough to move to another secret location. They have taken Don and Joni to a small town nearby. They rented a house near the Sound and keep the cabin cruiser close tied up at a nearby marina. This little town is out of the way and is mostly quiet. The two captives are locked in a basement, the basement is damp since the water table is so high. The two are always cold and damp and soon Joni develops a nasty cough. She says to Don that she never gets sick, but this damp basement is killing her.

Every day the bad guys try to get information out of Dr. Don Hamilton but he says nothing. He tells them that he would rather die than allow them to use his creation to kill more people. Don is weakening however when he hears what they are doing to Joni. Joni is trying to be brave but these brutes are experts at torturing innocent people. Joni bites down on her lower lip so hard she bleeds and finally cries out loud enough for Don to hear. Don finally gives in and tells them alright, they can have the new zapper.

Kenny is a real bastard and enjoys making Joni cry out in pain and doesn't stop until Marvin grabs his arm. Kenny looks at Marvin like he is from a different planet. Kenny has been burning Joni with a lighted cigarette just like he did to Nancy. The difference is Jones isn't there to stop him. Marvin isn't a nice guy either but he realizes that a dead Joni will be no use to them.

Don shows them the new device and Kenny is impressed. The new unit is much smaller and the viewer is now part of the zapper. Don tells Kenny that he just aligns the crosshairs over a target, by moving the mouse, then push the button and zap! Kenny gets excited and wants to try it. He pushes Don out of the way and aims the device at a boat out on the water. He doesn't care whose boat it is or who's aboard he just wants to see this thing work. When he gets the crosshairs aligned on his chosen target, he pushes the button, and nothing happens. Don has gotten the final laugh, he hasn't told Kenny of the Retinal scan that only works with Don's eye. Before he knows it, Kenny pulls out his gun and kills Don.

Joni screams and tries to get loose from her restraints. She is screaming and sobbing trying to get at this slimy bastard who killed her man but cannot. Marvin looks at Kenny and shakes his head, he just walks away. Kenny kicks the device and goes over to Joni and slaps her until she is silent. He doesn't care if he kills the bitch, she needs to shut up. Joni, isn't dead nor is she badly hurt, she is pretending to pass out, her intelligence has control over her pain. She knows that she will kill this bastard if it's the last thing she ever does. Kenny goes outside and walks around trying to cool down. He didn't mean to kill the golden goose, it's just that Don made him really mad. Kenny knows that there's no way for him to activate the new zapper. Dam dam dam, what bad luck. After a good long walk in strange neighborhoods he wonders to himself? He decides to try and cut out Don's eyes and hold the eyeball up to the retinal scanner and make the zapper work anyway. He needs to get rid of that Joni, and he means permanently. He thinks he will tell Marvin to have his way first then just dump her body in deep water with a lot of weights attached. Marvin isn't there when he returns, he has left with the zapper and Kenny sees that Don's eyes have already been removed. Kenny gets mad all over again and looks for something to kick or hit or do something too. Surprisingly he passes Joni over, she is laying in a heap not moving, he wonders if Marvin has killed her. Joni isn't dead, she is playing a desperate game of possum, she is hardly breathing. Kenny goes out and notices that Marvin's old truck is gone, but his van is right there where he parked it before removing Joni from it. Kenny drives off, not knowing exactly where just away.

Joni stays still for a long while not moving afraid that Kenny or Marvin will come back. She doesn't know what she will do without Don's love, it will be nearly impossible. She gives in and cries and cries, her tears flow freely and soaks down the front of her. The more she cries the more slippery her wrist become. She notices that the ties are getting easier to move and with an effort she doesn't think she has she is free. The zip ties weren't tight in the first place and she made her wrists stretch when they were tying her up. She doesn't know why she did that, maybe from watching to many crime-shows on TV, whatever the reason she is loose. She goes over to Don's body and makes sure that he is really dead. She feels for a pulse but there is none, he is growing cold already. She will miss him more than she can say. She wonders where she is, what town is this they have taken her to. She remembers that she heard a boat and also, the creeps were talking about one too. She believes that when they were done with Don and her, they were going to take their dead bodies out onto the ocean and down they would go. Joni remembers hearing that in some places the ocean was very deep and no one would ever know what happened to Don or Her.

48

After driving around aimlessly Kenny comes back to himself, he killed his cousin, that doesn't matter. What he is really mad about is Marvin. He has grabbed the zapper and Don's eyeballs, and Marvin can take the entire prize. Kenny doesn't know what to do, not yet, he will have to think for a while. Thinking isn't Kenny's first priority, he usually acts than thinks. He finds a small café and settles into a back booth. He orders coffee, it isn't very good, and a piece of blue berry pie that is delicious. The pie isn't quite as good as Barbra's but this piece is close. After eating the pie and drinking the coffee he decides he is still hungry. Kenny calls the waitress over and asks her what's good. She tells him that everything is good, what is he hungry for? Kenny, doesn't know, and finally decides on a hamburger steak. She asks him how does he want it cooked? He tells her medium rare, and lots of catchup too please. She says he sounds like her son, wanting lots of catchup. Kenny couldn't care less about this witch's kid, he just wants to be left alone. She fills his cup and moves off to take care of other customers.

Kenny looks into his coffee cup like it could tell him what to do. The cup doesn't say a thing, and finally he decides to just let it ride. He hardly tastes the food, even with lots of catchup, he is really upset about killing his cousin Don. After eating and having another piece of pie, this time Pecan with ice-cream he thinks he will need to get the boat back to his island. How does he get the boat back and his van with him being the only driver?

Joni doesn't waste time worrying about something she cannot do anything about, she is terrified that one of the bad guys will come back for her. She doesn't have a cane and finds a broom in a cleaning closet. It's not what she is used too, but she makes it work for her.

BOOK TWO: BRAIDY

She figures that anywhere is better than waiting here for Kenny or that other guy. She finds her way out the front door and down the driveway to the street. She can't find anything that looks like it might be another house, and so she walks down the street. She knows which way the water is, she hears boats, she walks toward what she hopes is town. She has a bloody shirt, and a bloody face too. She supposes she looks like a mess, but what can she do, it's not her fault. Joni, can't stop crying over Don, she will get those bastards no matter what it takes.

A small dog comes over and sniffs her all over. She likes dogs but all dogs aren't always friendly especially to strangers. At the end of the block an old man calls for his dog, the dog that is sniffing Joni trots off to his owner. The old man talks to the dog like it was a real person, and the dog wines back. The old gentleman looks down the street from where the dog has come and sees Joni.

He is concerned and exclaims, "Hey miss, are you hurt?"

Joni, wants to say, "No not really I always dress like this," she says instead, "I am Joni and I have been kidnapped."

The old man comes over to her and clucks his tongue. He tells her that she is a mess, and can he help her?

Joni, tells him, "Yes please, you see I am blind too, and I don't know where I am."

The old guy says, "No, oh no that can't be. How bad can some people bee, why would anyone want to beat up a blind woman?"

Joni, takes charge, and tells him, please don't worry, I'll be alright. He asks her if he can call anyone for her? Joni can't think of anyone except the company where she works. She follows her rescuer into a small house that smells like old medicine. He says his name is Frank and this is his wife Flossy.

She exclaims sucking a quick breath saying, "Oh Dear God, what happened to you?"

Joni isn't religious and says she'll be ok, it's not as bad as it looks.

Flossy shaking her head no says, "It's bad enough, I've seen hamburger that looks better than you."

Joni smiles at that in spite of what's happened to her and says, "May I use your phone please?"

Flossy says where the phone is, and Joni finds her way over to the kitchen without knocking all of Flossie's plants on to the floor. Joni tells her new friend that the call will cost a little but she can pay her back. Flossy tells her that's ok, don't worry about a few cents. Joni calls the company and Joe answers.

"Big lift Shipping and lumber, how may I direct your call?"

Joni, tells Joe she wants to talk to Rose please."

Joe recognizes Joni's voice and says, "Hey Joni we been looking for you, are you alright?"

Joni, says to Joe, "Oh really, who has been looking for me?"

Joe, "Everyone, Jones, Braidy Carmen Nancy, probably even Jack."

Joni swallows and says, "Well I'm ok, can someone come and get me?"

Joe tells her that he will find someone for her right away."

Joe is true to his word, and there is Jones, asking her, "Are you alright?"

Joni, just can't tell him about Don yet, and says to him, "Could you come and get me, I'm not sure where I am exactly but I'm with some people who can tell you if that's ok?"

Jones, hears the pain in her voice, and tells her that he will come right away, don't worry, just let him talk to who's there with her. Joni is glad to hand the phone off, to this very kind old gentleman because she is ready to start with tears all over again. Jones gets the directions and calls Jack, Jack is ready, he knows something is up, he is ready to offer nice dog stuff or kill the bad guy. Jones tells Rose about Joni, and that he will go get her. Rose wants to know how far? Jones tells her about two hours, and he will stay in touch. He informs her that Jack is coming along incase Jones needs some backup. Rose believes that Jack is a good backup and feels better because Jones is taking Jack along.

On the way, down from the top floor, Jones runs into Nancy, and asks her if she can come along. Nancy says she can, just let her tell her people she will be gone. Nancy never goes anywhere unarmed, she carries an automatic on her hip like an old western gunslinger. Her slim body looks unnatural with the gun sticking out like that. She has vowed never to be taken by surprise ever again. She and Jones use to be lovers in a limited way and she is professional in their relations currently. Her new guys name is Melvin, he is Deakin in the church where Nancy directs the quire and sings often. She doesn't dislike Jones, she is just uncomfortable. Jones understands how she feels and thinks of her like an old friend. Nancy wants to know details

BOOK TWO: BRAIDY

and of course Jones doesn't have many. He tells her that Joni has been kidnapped and got away. She is in a little town, and when he tells her Nancy says she knows exactly where the town is.

She and Jones take one of the old trucks, it is still red and white. It doesn't matter to Jones, as long as it works and can get them there. Jones remembers that Nancy likes to drive and offers her the job. Nancy likes the idea, and chirps the tires taking off, just for sport. They drive for two hours until they find the little town, and then the address Joni's new friend has provided.

49

When Kenny gets back to the house where Joni was being held, he is surprised to find that she is gone. More than that, Don's body is gone too. He looks around and finds not much, no evidence to indicate that anything went on. Everything has been removed and rubbed out, the only thing to indicate that any of them were there is a big oil stain on the cement driveway from Marvin's old truck. Marvin's old truck always leaks oil and nearly everything else, and he has to top off the oil with at least a quart a day. Kenny shakes his head and sighs and decides to go over to the marina to check on the boat.

When he gets there, the boat is gone also. He talks to the dock boy.

The boy trying not to look like he's lying smirks, "What boat, there ain't no boat like that here, and hasn't been either!"

Little does Kenny know that Barbra paid this dock boy to lie about the cabin cruiser ever being there, she wants to mess with his mind. Kenny is beginning to think this must be a bad nightmare, he doesn't know what to think. He finally drives off back toward Seattle. Kenny is so confused that he doesn't know which way is up. He doesn't know that there have been forces at work that he can't know of. Marvin has taken Don's body away and will plant it in the ocean way down deep. He also doesn't know that Barbra has driven her boat all the way over from the island. She has tied the smaller boat to the back of the cabin cruiser and towed it back to the island. She is out on the open ocean out of sight of anyone driving on the highway. Marvin and Barbra had no idea they were working together to drive Kenny mad, it's just coincidence nothing more.

Barbra came looking for Kenny and Marvin with her Father's big revolver, she would have killed both those dogs, but no one was there.

BOOK TWO: BRAIDY

She had no idea of the rental house and Joni and Don. She just knew about the bigger boat and the marina. Barb doesn't know what she will do with two boats but figures anything goes, she will work it out later.

Kenny has no way of returning to the island and stays in a Motel 6 he knows of. He gets a room next to a very busy one, there are guys coming and going all night long. He knows that there are women who make their living servicing men but man oh man this room takes the big prize. He thinks about 1 an hour even into the early morning. He never does get a good look at the woman or women who are working so hard all-night long. How can the management not know what's happening here? Oh well it's not his business accept he hasn't gotten much sleep.

He finds a café like all the others, greasy spoon places that probably should be shut down but are not. He needs to get in touch with Marvin at least long enough to kill the slime ball, he had no right steeling what Kenny stole. Kenny has another hide out of course, he always has a backup plan or in this case place. He wonders for a moment where is Barbra but then forgets it and refocuses on killing that Marvin. Kenny dumps the van he is driving and grabs an old Ford Crown Vick. These old cars use to belong to the cops, some sort of pigs, and have big engines and other extras.

Kenny has his gun tucked into his pants and feels it whenever he sits. He tries to be discrete when settling back onto a booth bench. He doesn't really care who knows he's armed, it's just that he doesn't want any cops knowing where he is. Kenny has a very checkered past, and for sure he can't remember every single tiny little murder he committed. After all there were so many and in so many different places. Kenny has been lucky for so long staying away from cops that he takes his freedom for granted. He recognizes that killing might be wrong but when he thinks of the slimy bastards he has killed he finds that what he calls his conscience is absolutely clear.

Kenny misses the Island girl because she was so cheery. He wonders to himself, how can anyone be cheery when there's so much trouble all around. What right does this Rose have keeping him away from all that fortune that he rightfully deserves. He can't explain how he deserves it, it's just a strong feeling. Kenny responds to impulses more than thoughts. He has always had problems thinking things through. He is very impulsive and doesn't really care if he is or not.

Kenny does whatever he wants when he wants and if people don't like that than to hell with them.

50

Jones and Nancy bring Joni back to the headquarters building and Rose and Carmen comfort her, they are cleaning up her injuries. When they ask her about Don she sobs and can't get the news out. They all know that Don has been killed before she can say the words. Jack snuggles into her, making his presents known to her buy being close. He doesn't lick her instead wines some and is there for petting and hugging. Carmen stays close too and is telling Joni little comforting words that are meaningless but are reassuring. Joni, finally stops crying long enough to tell them the details as far as she knows them.

Jones laying his big warm hand gently on her shoulder softly says, "Hey Joni, your safe now, we will take care of you, just believe that please."

Joni, wipes her eyes and says, "Thanks Mr. Jones, I will tell you more in a minute, can I have something to drink?"

Rose brings her a cold soda and Joni gulps down a big swallow. She hasn't realized how thirsty she has become. Those bad guys never did give her much to eat or drink for that matter. She isn't hungry but feels empty inside.

Rose says she will heat up some soup for Joni. They are all in Rose's apartment with a couple of Nancy's security folks guarding the surrounding hallways. They are armed of course thanks to Nancy's insistence. They are armed and look tough, they have body armor and those little hat cameras. Their guns are large and very visible ready for action. Jones thinks those guys scare him sometimes, they are nuts who work out often, their muscles are well developed and he knows most know the martial arts too.

Nancy and Rose both know what it's like to be kidnapped and sympathizes with Joni. Nancy is gentle with her asking questions that will provide information but hopefully won't cause Joni anymore stress.

Nancy working hard to sound less tough pries, "Hey Joni, can you tell us how this all began?"

Joni takes in a big breath and begins, "Don and I were coming back from lunch, you know at that little Italian restaurant at the end of the street down the stairs."

" Yes, we know what you are talking about, its berry nice." Carmen wanting to reassure Joni.

"Well, we got to the top of the stairs and were heading for home when this big guy grabbed Don holding a gun to his head. Another guy pushed me in the alley too, he had something pushing into my back, he said it was a gun. They shoved us into a van and tied our hands behind our backs, they were very fast and strong. Don wasn't a strong man." And at this, she starts to cry all over again.

She asks for a minute, Jack puts his head on her hands in her lap and wines. Joni pets Jacks big head and ruffles his ears. Jack sounds like a cat purring, it's sort of a growl low in his throat but non-threatening. Joni recovers some and continues.

Joni sips some more soda before continuing, "They had bags that they slid over our heads, I cannot see anyway, but I guess they didn't know or forgot. Anyway, they drove us out of town for around two hours, some of the time they took us along the interstate, I think. They didn't say anything after they captured us, we were piled on the floor in the back of a van, there weren't any back seats only the two in front. Before we left the alley, someone covered us over with a plastic tarp, it smelled like new plastic. When we got to that little town where they killed my Don, they drove into a garage attached to a house. They closed the big door and dragged us both out of the van and into that house. They pushed us down some steps into a basement. The basement was damp and smelled musty. They put us on an air matrass that was mostly deflated and left us there. The next day they came after Don and took him upstairs. They wanted him to show them how to use some peace of electronic equipment. Don kept saying he would not tell them anything and I could hear them slapping him and hitting him with their fists.

BOOK TWO: BRAIDY

One voice kept saying, "Take it easy you dumb shit, you're gonna kill the bastard."

Joni sniffles some but doesn't cry, she is a brave woman Carmen thinks and moves closer. Carmen is comforting for Joni, she knows what Joni is feeling some. Nancy does too, and touches Joni's back rubbing in a circle motion. Joni continues in a minute.

"After two days Don was getting weaker and finally said he would show them what they wanted, but first they had to let me go. He told them that I knew nothing about the zapper and if they let me go, he would show them all the things the device could do. They didn't ever let me go, they just kept hitting Don, until he couldn't take any more, but by then he couldn't talk. Then one of the creeps I think it was the bigger guy came down and dragged me up the stairs. They tied me in a chair and said to Don that they were going to burn me with a lighted cigarette if he didn't cooperate. Don agreed to tell them and they untied his hands and they both held their guns on him. Don said that he loved me and Joni starts crying all over again. The rescue party consisting of Jack, Carmen and Nancy with Rose nearby moved in. Joni, waves her hand and says she's ok, thanks, she continues.

"I don't know what the device was, I don't think it was very large, maybe like a laptop computer? Anyway, when he turned it on, one guy, maybe his name was Kenny, got excited and couldn't wait for Don to finish. Don told him how to use the device and the creep pushed Don onto the floor. Don didn't say much then; the creeps were doing all the talking. They aimed the thing at a boat out on the water, and when Don protested, they kicked him knocking the breath out of him. I could hear him gasping for air, I was so mad I could only think how I would kill those guys. After the one guy pushed the button and nothing happened, he got mad all over again at Don. It happened so fast, in only a few seconds, Kenny shot Don. One moment Don was alive laying there on the floor and then he was dead. After that I'm not sure what happened I guess I passed out some. Anyway, when I came back to consciousness, I was all alone. I worked my way out of those plastic tie things and when over to Don, but it was much too late, he was getting cold. I found a broomstick in a closet to use for a cane and found my way outside and that's when the little dog found me. The rest you already know."

Everyone is quiet, not knowing what to say after all that. Nancy lays her hand on Joni's shoulder and tells her she is a brave Woman.

Rose kneels before Joni, and is crying too, "I am so sorry Joni, you should have never been involved with my troubles. My father was a crook and had some violence in the past before he died and unfortunately that past is catching up with us," she continues, "those two creeps want to take over the company and will do anything to get what they want. We have been fighting these bad guys for more than a year now and haven't been able to catch them yet. Jones and I were in a helicopter crash out over the water, and the bad guys picked us up and took us to a small island. They had a trap there for us and Jones here got us out. We were rescued by a nice woman who just showed up in the morning and took us to land. We don't know where she came from or where she is now, she did tell us to be careful. She seems to know more than she was willing to say, and I think we need to find her and ask more questions."

Rose, brings a big cup of soup for Joni, and Joni is grateful. She didn't think she was hungry and probably would never be again, but after the first spoon full her appetite took over. Rose tells Joni that there is plenty and asks if she needs anything more? Joni answers no, no thanks, this is wonderful, just right.

Jones's phone buzzes then, and he answers, its Braidy flying in and landing on the roof. Jones tells his friend that they are in Rose's apartment and to come down. Soon Braidy comes to the door, and reluctantly the security folks let him in. He is surprised at the increased security and wonders what's up with that. When he comes in, he sees Joni surrounded by the other women and guesses the rest. He did hear about Joni being gone somewhere but didn't know she was kidnapped. Braidy and Jones exchange looks and an unspoken agreement goes between the two men. They are determined to rid Rose of these bad guys and think they should go on a man hunt. They are tired of just waiting for the next shoe to fall. They believe that they should do some ass kicking. Jones has been teaching Braidy about guns, they have been practicing out at the company airstrip, banging away behind the hanger. Jim and the others laughed at them at first but soon they could see the determined looks on Braidy and Joneses faces they laughed no more. The men get better and better at hitting what they shoot at, and Jim just keeps still.

51

There are six mechanics who work on Rose's airplanes and helicopter, they are all qualified in everything concerning aircraft maintenance. Jim mostly supervises and doesn't do much heavy lifting. He is easy to work for and knows what he is doing. The guys know all about Jim's experience and most respect him for what he knows. The new guy is called newbie, although his name is actually Johnathan. He prefers Johnathan rather than John, and the guys find the extra ending is too cumbersome and just call him Newbie. Newbie is quiet keeping mostly to himself, his work skills are adequate not exceptional but ok. Jim has been watching closely and Newbie is getting suspicious. It is impossible for him to sabotage any other aircraft, he was able however to place a tracking device on the Jet Ranger that sank. He also covered the pilot's controls with a substance created to cause the pilot to become unconscious after handling the poison. He placed a weight on the tale that gradually shifted as the flight continued. The aircraft would fly just fine at first, but as the flight continued the sabotaged component shifted, and the entire aircraft became unbalanced. The aircraft would begin to shake uncontrollably and in a very short while down they go.

Johnathan doesn't have anything against Jones or Rose, he hardly knows either one, he just wants the money. He likes working on airplanes it's fun for him, but he likes having lots of money more.

That guy Kenny paid him five thousand dollars for just that one little job. He thinks a life of crime can be profitable and getting caught never occurs to him, he will never get caught he thinks. Jim is a problem now however, he is watching Johnathan like a hawk, and that big black dog gives him the evil-eye. He doesn't know what's up with the mutt, but the dog makes him nervous. It's like that dog knows

Johnathan is up to no good. When he is watching for an opportunity to bug another plane that dog is there staring at him. Johnathan tells the mutt to go away but the dog sits down and stairs harder, he doesn't go away. Jack doesn't like this guy, he doesn't know what Johnathan has done but he does know there's something suspicious about him.

The other five mechanics have been with Rose's Company for many years and have proven themselves as being very loyal. They go the extra distance to make sure planes are safe and ready. Some of them have learned to fly from Braidy and have their own planes. Some of the guys buy small planes together and fly just for fun. Jim is convinced that a mechanic who is a pilot makes a better mechanic. Someone who flies himself can understand about cable tension for instance and how it feels when control surfaces aren't quite right.

Jim likes all the guys except he doesn't really know Johnathan, he keeps to himself. Keeping to one's self isn't a problem for Jim, everyone needs their privacy but he does want guys to talk about what they have been working on, everyone needs to know about each aircrafts condition.

Jim remembers the days when Ken was the boss and the working conditions were ok for the most part. This Rose is so considerate of people's needs that it's like the difference between night and day. Jim has worked for Big Lift for as long as Braidy and thinks he has had a good life. His career is nearly over and he reflects on all the changes that have occurred in the past thirty-five years. Jim gets tired easier than he used to and that concerns him. He knows that everyone gets old but so soon? Jim enjoys working but his arthritis gets him down. If only it wasn't so damp around here it would be better.

Jim has a younger brother who lives in Arizona and invites him to come there to retire. Jim thinks that would be nice, the problem is of course all their friends live around Seattle. Jim watches Newby out of the corner of his eye and feels like theirs something wrong with that guys attitude. Newby is an ok mechanic; however, he keeps looking around all the time. The guy should be concentrating on what he is working on not on what others are doing. Jack that big assed dog doesn't like Newby that's for sure. Jim has to laugh at what that big mutt does from time to time. The dog definitely has something extra under the hood

BOOK TWO: BRAIDY

Jim thinks to himself, *"Maybe I need to get me a big silly dog like that one, having a pal like that around could make days more interesting."*

52

Kenny remembers that he has Marvin's phone number and calls. Marvin answers, that surprises Kenny.

Marvin is smug, and is surly, "So what the hell do you want you bastard?"

Kenny is mad, it shows, he growls, "Marvin you are an asshole!"

Marvin doesn't deny it, "So what do you want, you but wipe!"

Kenny not restraining himself in the least growls right back, "I want to kill you like Don, and where is my zapper?"

Marvin with a silly grin knowingly says, "Well I don't think the zapper will do us any good, I tried holding Don's eyeball up to the little screen on the zapper but nothing."

Kenny nods to himself he knew that wouldn't work, calms down some, after all he did leave the house without telling Marvin anything. He supposes he would do the same thing in Marvin's place. Marvin suggests that they bury the hatchet, after all they need each other's help, and Kenny agrees although he has his fingers crossed. He remembers that from when he was a kid, if you crossed your fingers you could lie without a worry. Marven has fingers, feet and arms all crossed, these guys are both lyres. They help each other because it can benefit them both, but when the music stops, out comes the guns. Kenny is more devious then Marvin but Marvin is more calculating, as a matter of fact, they both help each other without knowing or admitting anything.

Kenny agrees to meet at another café for some lunch and planning. Neither one has been to this little café before, to them their all alike. Sort of dirty and smelling of old grease, and the waitresses are all the same, complaining of sore feet and looking well used. They are older around 50 to 90 and needing to be overhauled desperately.

BOOK TWO: BRAIDY

The two guys find a booth in the back and order up burgers and fries. The burgers are at least hot and not too bad, and the fries are salty and hot. Kenny uses tons of catchup and Marvin prefers his without. They are like wolfs, tearing into their food without restraint. It looks like they have been starving for weeks when in fact they are very well fed

Kenny with a mouth full of burger asks if Marvin knows anything about Barbra?

Marvin chewing with his big mouth open wide blubbers out, "No not a thing."

Kenny tells Marvin that the boat was gone from the marina, and does he know anything about that?

Marvin looks up in surprise, "No way man, do you mean it's gone?"

"Yup not there, and when I ask the dock-boy he knew not a thing and was evasive."

Marvin wiping his mouth with his sleeve replies," They need to get back to the little island and see if the boat is there."

Kenny, thinks that Barbra is capable of doing something like that, she has some friends on the other side of the island, people who live in that little village.

Marvin loudly slurping up coffee, "Well ok that's what we'll do first, and maybe Ms. Barbra knows more than she has been telling us.

Kenny uses a napkin to remove excess catsup from his mug, "For sure I know one thing, she is one hell of a good cook!"

Marvin drives them to a marina by the docks in Seattle. They rent a speed boat and drive over to their island. The boat house is empty, neither boat is there. When they look in the house, they find that all of Barbra's belongings are gone, not a sign of her. Marvin touches his gun and says that he thinks they should visit the village people. Kenny says ok that's a good idea.

Marvin curiously asks, "Say Kenny, how did Jones and that broad get out of the hole and how did they get off the little island?"

"Right, it looks more and more like Lady Barbra may have had a hand in this."

Kenny drives them around the island to the village. There is no boat tied up at the makeshift dock they use. They get out and go ashore and find that people are just minding their own business. Kenny asks an old lady if she knows Barbra, and the sweet old lady tells him no, and who does he mean? Kenny moves on to a small boy playing in the dirt.

"Say kid do you know Barbra?" Kenny looks disgusted.

The little boy looks up from his play and answers in a language Kenny doesn't know, Kenny moves on. Marvin has been asking too, and he gets the same result, no one knows anything about someone named Barbra.

The two men Marvin and Kenny take their boat back to the boathouse and walk up to the big house. They are both hungry but neither one wants to try and fix something. Kenny is getting mad all over again at Barbra and kicks a chair out of his way. Marvin looks at Kenny with amusement, he thinks Kenny acts like a clown. Kenny is glaring at Marvin like he wants to just pull out his gun and shoot him too, like Don. Marvin finally gives in and begins to search the refrigerator and cupboards. He finds some left-over soup and sniffs it. Well, it doesn't smell spoiled and there isn't green stuff, must be ok. Marvin finds a big sauce pan and remembers to spray the bottom of the pan, he believes that spray stuff is supposed to keep the food from burning or sticking. He thinks, *'maybe I spray the pan because my mother did.'* Marvin has no idea how hot to cook left over soup and so he turns it up all the way. Kenny isn't paying any attention to what Marvin is doing. Finally, Kenny looks up after the kitchen fills with smoke.

Marvin comes running into the kitchen and yells at Kenny, "Why in the hell didn't you turn it off?"

Kenny doesn't even get mad, he has forgotten all about the stove. He finds a note that Barbra left for him to find later.

She writes, "Kenny, you are a bad man, I heard what you three were planning to do to that nice girl Rose. You and your friends are criminals and need to be arrested and locked up forever. You are a killer and vicious too."

There is more, but Kenny doesn't want to read on. He looks out the door toward the sea. Marvin turns off the stove and the smoke dissipates with the breeze. Marvin decides the food is still ok, just a little burnt not bad. Kenny is staring out the door for some stupid reason, Marvin doesn't even bother trying to figure this guy out. Kenny finally stops with the thousand-yard stair and turns to Marvin. He asks Marvin if something is wrong. Marvin looks at the pan and back at Kenny and sighs.

BOOK TWO: BRAIDY

"Hey no man, nothing wrong."

Kenny doesn't get the nasty reflection in Marvin's voice. Marvin dishes up the stew, it's not bad, even with the slightly burnt flavor. Kenny doesn't say a thing, it tastes good to him.

The two men heat up some coffee and retire to the library. There are overstuffed chairs that can be pulled up to the fireplace when it's chilly enough. The guys don't need any fire now and Kenny wishes for a cigar. Marvin offers him one from a cigar box. Kenny tells Marvin, you must be reading my mind?

"Well I don't know anything about reading your mind, I just felt like a cigar." Kenny settles back in the soft chair.

Kenny accepts a light and puffs away. These cigars are hand rolled and the tobacco is very fine indeed. Each cigar is wrapped in its own cellophane and tastes fresh. Marvin has traveled all around the world on various ships, and so he knows more of the world than Kenny. Marvin isn't at all cultural but he has been around.

Kenny and Marvin sip coffee and smoke cigars and try not to think of their mistakes. Marvin doesn't like torturing people, but he does like blowing up big ships. He likes to watch when they burn, and when the ship goes down, the water makes a lot of steam putting out the fire. Kenny likes hearing people scream in pain, it's up close and personal. He especially liked burning the black woman from the shipping company. Kenny's secret person who works for Rose's Company tells him the black woman in security looks really tough. She tells Kenny that all of the security folks are well armed and there are more. This woman Kenny hired to spy for him works in shipping. She has to deliver packages and other mail all around the building and so can go anywhere. She hasn't been with the company long, about a year, and so doesn't really know anyone at the top. She pushes a four-wheeled cart to offices, work rooms, printing, and even to the lower levels to mechanics that service the company vehicles. This woman has nothing against Rose or her company, she has no loyalty, she does what she does for the money Kenny pays her. Kenny offers the woman three thousand dollars just for listening and reporting to him. The woman is around fifty-five years old and has nothing remarkable about her. She where's loose fitting clothes and her hair hangs down and is wild and free. She doesn't wash it often and it's not to pleasant to sniff. Unfortunately, she also smokes, quite a lot. Rose doesn't approve of smoking but has to allow it in certain places. She has provided a place in the alley behind the building. There's a couple of parking places that were used long ago, but now can be used for the smokers. There are umbrellas and tables, also she has provided five-gallon buckets filled half way with sand for still burning Coles. The area has a five-foot fence around mostly to keep out homeless folks and others.

Rose doesn't like to see homeless folks around her building but can't always prevent them. She offers people on the street some work at least for the day. Some do work around the building and are cheerful and agreeable. The next day when they should be back, never being. Many of the workers are drunks and blow all their hard-earned money on booze. Rose keeps track of these guys and reminds the person of how they acted the last time. They don't like to be reminded of past failings and beg for another chance. Rose gives them two more chances, saying three strikes you're out like that and snaps her fingers. The snap sometimes makes the guys jump back. Rose can snap her fingers incredibly loud and even Jones is startled. Rose is fair, she wants to sort out these people herself, she does admire her father for one thing. She remembers how her father would help guys who were down on their luck. He helped them to help themselves and supported them until they were able to make choices. If after the guy, he helped still wanted to work for him, then he offered them a job. Rose reflects on her father, she tries to forgive him but cannot, he allowed all those men and women to be killed. He could have stopped that killing anytime, why protect someone who is a criminal. Even though George was his brother, Ken should have protected his people. Rose has a deep compassion for others and tries to keep all situations on a level playing field. She thinks about her friend Carmen, she and Carmen used to share an apartment, but since Jones and Rose have gotten together Carmen has moved. Rose offers Carmen a smaller apartment in the headquarters building and Carmen is delighted with her new home. She has never had her own place before, she always needed a roommate to share with the expenses.

Joni decides to try and get past her loss. She tells Rose that she is willing to go back to work if that's ok. Rose worries about Joni, she feels responsible for Joni's losses. If only and so on she says over and over again. Rose is a very considerate woman and Joni's problems become her problems. Rose is not herself, she talks about appointing someone else to be the boss. Jones, holds her close, telling her that he can help, and that she is the very best. He tells her that she knows the company better than anyone can, she grew up in shipping. She loves this very special man so much, she trusts him completely and tells him all the company secrets. Jones isn't surprised and doesn't say much, he knows that Rose has had a hard life too. Jones offers to take her flying.

Rose with a little chuckle says, "Mr. Jones the last time I went flying with you, I went for a swim too. Are swimming lessons included in all his flights?"

Jones picks her up and bounces her on their bed. Rose can't help herself, and howls with laughter. They are good together and are considerate of each other's feelings. Rose has forgotten about Jones's surprising strengths and decides for better or worse he is her man forever. Jones tickles her and enjoys hearing her giggles. They aren't very quiet in their love making, and soon there is a banging on the door.

Rose gasping for air still laughing, "Oops, I'm sorry Mr. Jones, I guess I must enjoy that too much"

Jones doubts that their love making aroused anyone outside their apartment. The knock turns into a banging. Rose pulls on a robe and starts for the front door. Jones jumps up and pulls on a pair of pants from the floor. He isn't armed except for his hands but decides to check it out anyway. Jones is right, there are a couple of big bad guys standing there. At first, he doesn't recognize them, but then realizes that these guys are part of Nancy's security gang. One guy, maybe Lloyd, tells them that the building needs to be cleared, we've had a bomb threat. Jones really gets mad but does nothing about it yet.

Rose looking very alarmed holding on to Jones hand demands, "How long do we have?"

The security guys tell her right away mam, the bomb is apparently ticking. Jones and Rose throw on some more clothes and go with the security men and drive off in a company truck. Rose is asking Nancy if everyone is out of the building. Nancy tells her yes everyone is on their way to hotels around the town. Rose, wants to know if they know where the bomb is? Nancy reveals to them that the bomb was left in a mail cart. Nancy knows and informs Rose that the woman who usually pushes the cart around delivering packages and mail is gone. Rose remembers the woman, she was not homeless, but something else concerned Rose at the time. Rose mentioned that to

Jones and he just shrugs. He isn't trying to ignore her, he is trying to sense all around the building. He doesn't know why he does that, it just comes to him. He only wants to get Rose and others away from the danger and have a look for himself. Rose doesn't like what he is saying about going into the building. She tells him they can always build another building but there is only one Jonesy. Jones tells her that he will be ok, he has a good idea what this is all about. He finds a hotel for Rose and checks her in, she wants to go with him but he insists, please stay here where it's safe.

53

Jones and Nancy meet up at the front of the headquarters building and talk about what's going on. Jones asks her how does she know where the bomb is. Nancy tells Jones that Jack found the bomb.

She asks Jones, "Does Jack have any training in finding bombs?"

Jones doesn't know, he got Jack pretty young, but still there could be something else. When Jones was away getting blinded Jack was with some others. He could have been trained in finding bombs.

Nancy being careful and polite wants to know, "So where was this place where Jack was when you were gone?"

Jones not really wanting to talk about it, "Somewhere in Omaha, it was for about a year."

Nancy knowingly responds with, "You know that a year can be a long time, lots of training can be accomplished in that time."

Jones reluctantly admits, "I wouldn't be surprised, after all they did lots of nasty things to me."

Nancy thinks about the violence that Jones is capable of and looks at him with meaning.

Jones has feelings for Nancy and looks at her softly wondering, what she is thinking about?

Nancy looks at her former lover with gentleness saying, "I am thinking about the way that you smashed the bad guy's heads together when she was shot on the beach. She also remembers the twin brothers that were dispatched at Brady's house and of course the five guys Jones used for bowling pins."

Jones tells her that she is right, he doesn't know either, and maybe those scientists did something to Jack's head too."

Nancy isn't so sure about that one, what if Jack is capable of causing death so quickly like Jones. He tries to reassure her and says that he thinks he is safe, I gotta get really mad to brake heads. Nancy shivers and hopes he is right, she doesn't like things she cannot control.

Jones wanting to get off the subject of his head wonders, "Nancy, what do we do now?"

Nancy isn't sure, asking "What would you do if this was a military operation of some kind?"

Jones, tells her that he wasn't much of a soldier, but he supposes that someone has to go in and look at the stupid bomb.

Nancy thinks he sounds like a kid who doesn't want to do his homework.

Jones says to her, "You can stay here if you like."

Nancy does want to stay there, but says "I will go along, after all it's really my job as security."

Jones holds up his hand and stops her and asks, "What about the police, aren't they supposed to do this job?"

Nancy tells him that she hasn't contacted the police yet. Rose asks me to try and figure out what's going on first.

Jones shakes his head and sighs, "Good oh Rose."

54

Jones and Nancy go back into the building. Nancy tells Jones that the bomb was last reported to be on the fifth floor. Jones is asking where Jack is. Just than Jack comes strolling around the corner pretty as you please. He sashays up to Jones and licks his hand. Jones wonders what the hell are you doing you silly mutt? Nancy has to wonder too, and asks Jones what's up with the dog? Jones doesn't know of course.

He suggests to Jack and Nancy, "Let's find out what's not happening here ok?"

Jack turns and heads to the center of the building where the elevators are and waits for someone to push the button. Nancy pushes the button for the fifth floor and when the car arrives, they all step aboard. Soon they are at the fifth floor and everything is quiet. There's no one around of course and the seen takes on a spooky Aire. Nancy pulls out her gun, like that might help with a bomb, but there's nothing else to do. When Jack leads them to the cart he stops, barks, once and then sits on his but looking back at them. Jones is confused, and he wants to ask Jack what's up, but remembers that's not going to help. Jack isn't bothered and sits calmly not showing any alerts. Nancy finally goes over to the cart and there it is, something that looks like a bomb alright. She doesn't know anything about bombs except they go boom. Jones watches his dog, he hasn't seen Jack act like this before. Nancy looks at the bomb.

She is more curious than afraid, "I wonder where the timer is or the whatever triggers a bomb like this might be?"

Jack is just sitting there not moving not showing any concern.

Nancy making a decision explains, "They need to get the cops, they need the bomb squad for this one."

Jones agrees and wants to call them, but stops, what if the bomb is set to go off with a phone call. He doesn't know what he is talking about and doesn't mind saying so. Nancy admits that she doesn't either. They all leave the building and move about a block away. Jones calls the police and after a lot of switching finally is talking to the very same cop he has talked to before. This cop knows there's something going on with this company but can't say what. Jones explains to the police all about the bomb scare and the cop is at least listening. He agrees to send over the bomb squad and says he will wait on the corner next block over. When the bomb squad arrives, everyone surrounding the building has been evacuated also. The shop owners did manage to lock their doors and so looting shouldn't be a problem. Jones lets the cops into the building and tells them where the bomb is located. After a short while they come down with a bomb in a specially designed cart. The bomb container is on a self-propelled cart that can be remotely guided from a safe distance. They have several small cameras on the cart and can see where it is going. The bomb container has an arm, that can lift up the bomb and place it inside the box. The technicians simply drive the cart with the bomb aboard down to street level and into a special van. Jones wants to ask them how did that little mechanical beasty push the elevator buttons? They just grin a little and tell him that is their secret, you gotta be a cop to know. Jones lets it go, who really cares how they do their jobs as long as they do them right.

Jones and Nancy have organized a search party with the security people and look all through the building. There's nothing else to worry over, the building is clear. A long time has passed since the bomb threat was new and everyone who lives in the building just decides to stay where they are in hotels.

Rose sneaks Jack up in the elevator, it's not easy with Jacks bulk. Jack tries to look innocent and does it simply because no one else uses the elevator when they do. Rose is waiting, she knows that the bomb didn't explode and is feeling calmer. She is reading under a lamp and looks adorable to Jones. She looks up when Jack licks her bare knee.

She puts down her red book and exclaims, "Oh you're a big goof ball, I don't need another bath from you."

Jack sits back on his tail and grins at her. She just has to grin back and rubs his ears. Jack accepts the compliment with good grace and doesn't cut one of his nasty gaseous products. Jones tells Rose all

BOOK TWO: BRAIDY

about the bomb squad and how they removed the bomb, he continues to tell her that the police will take it to a place where they can check it out further. He says they have this neat little robot to do the actual removal. The technician steers the device watching a small screen and can manipulate the bomb grabber from a safe distance.

Rose is impressed and smiling at him says, "That's nice!"

She is so relieved that they are all safe she doesn't even think what could have happened to her home.

Jones and Rose enjoy a nice dinner from room service and decide that this isn't so bad, they could just move into a set of rooms like these and be ok. Next morning Jones calls the captain at the police station and the copper tells him that there was indeed a bomb that could have taken out at least the fifth floor, probably not the entire building. He tells Jones that the bomb was intended to kill people more than destroy property. The bomb was loaded up with led pellets that would fly out in all directions and would no doubt kill anyone in the way. Rose shudders when she hears that, she doesn't want any more deaths because of the creeps. Jones asks the cop how come it didn't go off. He tells Jones that the technicians say that someone removed the timer.

Jones not understanding looks around for Jack, "Say what, removed the timer?"

The cop allows, "Yes, someone just pulled it right out of the explosives."

"Why didn't it blow up when the timer was removed?" Jones looks around at Jack.

Jack knows nothing about anything. He is licking off their breakfast plates enjoying the remains of pancakes eggs, and sausages. Jack is after all still a dog and dogs can't help themselves, they just gotta eat. Jones tells the cop thanks and what's next? The cop says that's sort of up to Jones, we don't have anything except the bomb, and that tells them not much. Jones is really getting tired of cops who are corrupt and apparently lazy too. He thanks the nice officer anyway and tells him to let them know if they find anything else from the bomb evidence.

55

Marvin is disappointed to hear nothing concerning the building where Jones and Rose live, he was expecting a very large fireball. He wanted to see that witches building go up in a giant bonfire. Oh well, he hasn't even told Kenny of his latest try, and so he won't have to deal with Kenny's temper. If he had succeeded Kenny would think he was a genius but nothing gained nothing ventured or something like that. Marvin likes exploding things and has a dependable supplier of C4 explosives. Marvin is convinced that anyone can get anything from the internet. There are Guns, bullets and all kinds of nasty devices for killing people off and destroying property. Marvin maintains a private mail box and goes there after most everyone else is sleeping. He doesn't know exactly who owns the mail boxes they are private in a building not used for U.S. Mail. Kenny doesn't know of Marvin's secret mail box, he plays with his gun more and more, and Marvin stays out of the line of fire.

They haven't heard anything from Barbra, she has disappeared along with both boats. Marvin and Kenny had to purchase a small fifteen-footer with an outboard engine. The boat is fast enough but doesn't keep them dry, the water splashes on them when they travel at a reasonable speed. The only way they can stay dry is to travel slowly and that takes forever. They both get wet, and even when they use rain slickers, they still get wet.

Kenny and Marvin have made compromises and can get along. They have purchased a microwave oven and got lots of frozen dinners. The dinners aren't as good as Barbra's cooking, how could they be, but they get by. Kenny is researching Rose's wealth, it is growing, and those new ships she has ordered are really making

BOOK TWO: BRAIDY

money. Who could know what the shipping business would do, she must know something about shipping.

Kenny and Marvin have a very shaky truce. They get along because they each have their own goals. They both desire Rose's Company and all the riches it holds. Marvin is always looking for something sweet to gobble down. He has a large development of real-estate on his front. Kenny isn't so plump; however, his middle is growing larger. Both these men are extremely lazy and haven't been to a Doctor in forever. Marvin looks like he may have some sort of liver disease and Kenny looks like a ghost. They wouldn't think of any kind of exercise and smoke and drink too much not really giving a damn.

At least when Barbra was feeding them, they were provided balanced meals but now what they eat is more like garbage.

Both these guys have alienated their families so much that no relative ever wants to claim that they know them. Kenny has a long criminal past including robberies, brake ins, and yes murders. Marvin has killed so many sailors on Rose's ships that the count is not known. These guys are rude crude and not very nice to say the least.

56

Barbra has for sure taken both boats, and she collects Rose's raft too. She hides the cabin cruiser in a secret cove that she thinks she only knows of. She gets some paint and changes the color on the run about. She likes the blue that woman Rose uses for her ships, but finally decides on black. She doesn't know why she has chosen black, she supposes it's something in her crazy brain that makes her do these things. She has grabbed a bunch of Kenny's money, he just left lying around in the library desk. She doesn't mind barrowing it, after all it can't be honest money. She doesn't even think Kenny will miss it, at least not for a while. She wants to refinish the bigger boat and is disgusted with its neglect. She thinks Kenny and Marvin must have something wrong with them to treat these fine boats so badly. She spends days cleaning up the inside of the bigger boat, it's not a bad boat. She knows boats well enough to know that her craft is seaworthy and needs mostly cosmetic help. The wheel house has peeling paint, and the brass looks dull but she will fix all that. She thinks the boat needs another name and calls her "True Wind." The name doesn't mean anything it just seems right to her. She doesn't know much about the Diesel engine; however, she finds information on the internet and studies hard. She has gotten a Smart Phone and is learning how to use it. She has a saddle lite connection that she pays way too much for, but it will have to do for now. She won't need this internet connection for long, she will move the boats to another place whenever she decides where. She hopes to use the bigger boat for fishing trips. She will hire out as a fishing guide, helping rich guys catch fish that they really don't deserve but can pay for. Barbra knows all about fishing, small fish and game fish too. She needs to buy bigger equipment used in ocean fishing and will have to make some sort of connection with people who can get her customers.

Barbra is very a where of Kenny and Marvin's coming back to the big house, she spies on them from a distance and the village people help her too. After the women in the village hear of how bad Marvin and Kenny are, they are very willing to keep an eye on the two bad guys. Barbra finds time to fish for her friends, they are very poor. She brings in her catch at night just in case the creeps are up and about. She need not worry; Kenny and Marvin aren't good at keeping guard. They just hang around that house drinking beer and eating those frozen dinners. She bets they miss her cooking, and smiles to herself, serves them right, she's nobody's fool

Barbra fishes nearly every day and learns where the best fishing spots are. She learned all about navigation from her father and is able to translate her knowledge to local waters. She has charts that she purchased from a marine store and is careful with her markings. She refers to these areas when she can't find new waters to fish. She is friendly with guys who sell her Diesel and gas for her boats. She doesn't want to make any enemies but at the same time she doesn't really want to be noticed. She likes men ok, she has to keep her head down while those two jerks are living on the island. If they know where she hangs out, surely, they will come and cause her trouble. More than that although, she doesn't want her friends at the little village to suffer because of her.

Barb wonders how that pretty woman that runs the shipping company is doing. The man was older not much it didn't look like. She thinks it be nice to be in love with a good guy like that Jones man. Barbra has had men in her life, well not including good old Kenny. Boy talk about a dud, he empties the Rum bottle that's for sure.

Barb thinks about those two people while the fish aren't biting and wonders what it would be like to be really loved by a good man.

57

Jones and Rose move back into their apartment in the headquarters building. The new helicopter is ready and Jones asks Rose if she wants to go with him and Braidy to get it? She thinks she will wait a while, nothing wrong with Jones's flying, it's the helicopters fault. Jones laughs at her.
    He brings her in close for a hug laughing too, "That was a bad attempt at sabotaging, and there's nothing to worry about."
    Rose hugging him back smiling into his eyes says, "He is probably right of course but she would rather wait."
    Jones just kisses her on her very pretty nose and admires how beautiful she looks.
    Rose with a knowing smile on her red lips demands, "What are you looking at Mr. Jones?"
    Jones looks away, pretending to be innocent, she knows better and swats his hard belly. Jones grabs her hands and pulls her onto his lap. She doesn't even try to resists him, she doesn't even want to try, she loves this man with everything she has. Jones nibbles her ear, and the rest of the evening is private.
    Jones and Braidy fly with the Cessna one eighty to pick up the helicopter. They will flip a coin to decide who will get to fly the new aircraft. Jones doesn't really care, it's just a game they play. After all, they will hopefully have this Jet Ranger as long as the old one was around. They both will end up with too many hours of flying in all the planes. Braidy wins the flight and Jones looks it over with him, it is a beauty, with avionics that are scary. This helicopter has everything and some of the new electronics surprises even Braidy. Jones doesn't worry, there will be plenty of time to find out all the secrets. Braidy takes off proud as he can be, and when he is airborne Jones follows

BOOK TWO: BRAIDY

him in the Cessna. The helicopter can fly faster than the old Jet Ranger, about the same knots as the Cessna. They are talking on the radio and will fly in formation, like a 2-ship flight.

They arrive back at the hanger and Jim and all the other mechanics are waiting there for this new helicopter. Braidy will provide rides for each and every mechanic, after all they need to know what it feels like to fly in this wonderful new craft. Braidy doesn't really wonder that, he wants them all to understand the feel of aircraft they work on. Jim and Braidy both believe that a flying mechanic is a good mechanic. It's just an old fashion belief that he has but still he uses it, so far it works.

Braidy wonders if it's good for pilots to be friendly with their mechanics, He wonders too, about that new guy Johnathan or as the rest call him Newbie. Jones says Jack watches the guy like a hawk and that means something to Jones, but Braidy isn't so sure. Maybe Jack doesn't like the guys smell or the way he looks. Who can know what runs through that silly mutt's mind? Braidy does think that Jack is smarter than most dogs, but he's not a genius, right!

Johnathan has been contacted by that Kenny fellow, and he has offered ten thousand dollars this time for bugging the new helicopter. Bugging any aircraft is next to impossible and Johnathan hasn't a clue as how to do the bugging. Kenny gives him a small box about the size of a cigar box and says for him to place it inside the power train of the helicopter. Johnathan doesn't ask what it is, he figures the less he knows the better. He is right, the box is from cigars, but it doesn't hold cigars any more. The box contains more explosive with a fuse that reacts to extreme heat changes. After the helicopter is good and hot the timer sets off the C4 and there goes another helicopter falling right out of the sky. Kenny can hardly wait until that new helicopter comes crashing down. Wouldn't it be nice if the bird crashed on the roof of the headquarters building? Man, oh man what a sight, maybe the entire building would just fall down. Johnathan doesn't like this part of being a criminal, it's terrifying for him, people are watching him all the time and that big black dog drives him silly. It looks to him like that dog wants to have him for breakfast and for not much reason.

Jack comes out to the hanger often, not on a schedule but very often and always unexpectedly.

Johnathan has been homeless much of his life, he got lucky when he was provided the opportunity to learn aircraft maintenance from a community college. He actually learned how to fix aircraft of all types. He was living under a blue tarp under a big shade tree. Fortunately, it was above freezing most of the time and he survived. He cannot remember any home life from his childhood, although there must have been something, after all he made it to adulthood somehow? He had a woman once, he lied so many times to her about his abilities that finally she couldn't stand it anymore and through him out. He just couldn't remember which lie he told her and when he mixed them all up, she became suspicious. Johnathan was supposed to help with monthly expenses and when he lied about that too she was really mad.

Johnathan lives on the top floor of a condemned building not wanting anyone to know of his checkered past. From time to time it became necessary to remove food items from stores without the benefit of paying anything to the stores. He doesn't consider himself a thief exactly, it's just that they have so much and he has so little. He thinks they should learn to share, its only fare.

Johnathan can be engagingly charming when he needs to be and that skill gets him far sometimes. When that Rose interviewed him, he was in fine form. He had her eating out of his grubby hand. The papers he made up were very impressive, for a while he was fooled himself by his own bologna. Rose is a sucker for sad stories and Johnathan is a fantastic liar story teller. He usually tells a story so well that he convinces himself as well.

When that guy Kenny offered him five big ones just for planting a little bug in the company helicopter, he jumped for it. Johnathan never had five thousand of anything before in his entire life. Five thousand dollars all at once was too much for him to resist.

Since Johnathan receives a pay check every two weeks, he decided to stash the five big ones away for a rainy day. He purchased a steel thermos and he stuff it all inside. Kenny paid him in cash and that made it easy for him to just hide it away. He rolled the bills tight and shoved them down into the bottle. The thermos bottle looks like any ordinary bottle and shouldn't draw attention to what's really in it. The thing that's funny, is that he keeps the silly thing in his locker at work. All that doe ray me right under their big fat noses

BOOK TWO: BRAIDY

Johnathan had a big scare the last time that black mutt was out at the hanger. For some reason he walked over to his locker sniffed than pawed on the door. Johnathan nearly shit a brick with fear. He ran out the back door of the hanger and the dog fortunately had to leave with that Jones guy. That dog has to go, and maybe one of these days Johnathan will help him along.

58

Barbra has a plan, she will change the way the cabin cruiser looks. She has studied Diesel engines and understands how they are supposed to work. She goes to shore to a Harbor freight store and buys herself lots of tools. She has to read up on things like socket wrenches and open-ended wrenches too, she gets screw drivers, nut drivers, hammers, vice grips, clamps and more. She buys about $500 worth and a really nice rolling around tool box. The box has 4-inch wheels and drawers enough for all her new tools. She doesn't want to ever have to ask anyone for help if she can help it. She isn't sure where she will start her new business but here isn't so bad. Barbra paints both her newly acquired boats black with red and blue trim, neither boat looks anything like it did before. She replaces warn parts on both engines and adds GPS too. She visits the village some times to catch up on what's happening on the island. The village people spy on Kenny and Marvin because they are able to move around unnoticed by the two creeps. Barbra has hidden her boats at another island, and she often stays there overnight. Barbra doesn't mind living alone, she can do what she wants. She just sleeps on the cabin cruiser and has made the inside comfortable for herself. She doesn't usually like frilly curtains and such but makes an exception. She can call this boat her home now and does. She knows fishing and practically lives off what the ocean provides her. Barb has found a merchant who buys her fish, and she can bring fish for sale nearly every day. She uses a different name, she is known to the fish buyer as Sandy. The fish buyer in turn sells the fish to fancy restaurants for much more than he pays Barbra.

Barbra sees the ships that belong to that pretty woman that she rescued all around. She wonders how things are going for her, and if they have had any more trouble from the creeps. She watches out for

BOOK TWO: BRAIDY

Kenny and Marvin, she isn't exactly afraid of them, not with her father's big gun. She just doesn't want to come near them. She does know they mostly take their little boat to shore for food and other supplies. She doesn't think of them any more than that. Whatever feeling she once had for Kenny is long gone.

Barbra gets lonely sometimes but gets busy doing some work. Barb wants to go back home and visit her family. She wonders if she can drive her boats all the way to Jamaica. It would take a lot of fuel and the open sea can be dangerous in a small boat like her cabin cruiser, and with the smaller boat in toe it might be worse.

Barbra has made the inside of her newly acquired cabin cruiser nice. She doesn't know a lot about curtains or carpeting but after reading up on decorating she thinks it looks good. She feels funny going in stores to purchase what she needs. She need not worry, in Seattle there are so many folks from so many places that a tiny accent isn't even notice by most merchants. They are glad for a sale; any sale. The sound of speech or color of skin means not a thing.

She takes her smaller boat to shore because it's faster and looks so different that she often forgets what it looks like herself. She has to really concentrate on what it looks like after the new paint job and other additions she has made.

In one store that sells parts for boats she meets a nice old man who reminds her of her father. He even talks with the people's accent, Jamaican of course. She delights in hearing the lilt and asks him too many questions.

He is kind to her and offers to take her out for dinner. Barb is so lonely and almost decides to go with him but at the last-minute changes her mind.

Barbra smiling big as her home islands, "Oh hey man, I gotta get back to work, but maybe next time I come ashore you'll let me take you out?"

The old man is turning red, he's not used to beautiful island girls paying attention to him.

59

Business at the Big Lift Salvage and Shipping company has gotten back to what they all hope is normal. Rose has ordered more container ships and is fading out the bulk carriers. The salvage business is decreasing as well, some of the oil companies have purchased their own tug boats. The lumber trade is booming, there are bigger demands for quality wood products. Nancy and her new guy are talking about getting married and everyone is happy for them. Carmen is enjoying living in her own apartment in headquarters building. Carmen Braidy or Jones are flying off visiting various parts of Rose's giant company. Rose, Jones, and Jack have settled down in the big apartment in headquarters building. Nancy borrows Jack often, she visits the hanger keeping an eye on Johnathan. They don't think he can do anything dangerous with people watching all the time, but still Nancy worries.

Joni is still sad over Don's death, she wants revenge. She lives in Brady's house, she insists on paying him rent, and she and Braidy drive to work together. Braidy and Joni are more like brother and sister and are considerate of each other's needs. Joni enjoys listening to books that are recorded. These books are done professionally and even Braidy listens to them with her. Joni is gradually recovering and has resumed her old job at the front desk. She is polite and knowledgeable and directs visitors to the right places. She has learned the entire building and knows where everyone who is anyone may be at any time. She does extra services to make sure that people are satisfied. Rose and Jones always stop at her desk to just say hello.

No one knows what happened to the mail lady, she has disappeared. There is a new guy who does the job now. He is Jerry and has a slight disability, although one would hardly notice. Jerry

BOOK TWO: BRAIDY

likes to kid and does with nearly everyone. Rose especially likes his wit and often visits with him. She doesn't think Jerry can be bought like the past mail person but experience has taught her to be careful.

Joe is back in the main office and greets people professionally and knows all the captains. Joe and Carmen are going out often and Carmen is almost her old bouncy self. Rose thinks that Joe is good for Carmen and encourages them.

Jack still has to visit the roof top facility for his necessaries and doesn't complain. He doesn't like flying anymore and rarely goes up. He has delicate ears that hurt when aircraft change altitudes, Braidy is right about that.

The police have exploded the bomb and it definitely was the real thing. They say that if the bomb had gone off inside the building, hundreds of employees may have been killed. They don't say what would have happened to the actual structure but probably the building would need to be torn down. The bomb could have been set off by an electronic trigger or some other type of fuse, they never did find the trigger. Jack knows what happened to the trigger, he just doesn't want to say, well he can't. Jack knows more than he can say, this language barrier is such a problem. He keeps a low profile however and moves about with ease. Jack had some implants inserted in his big block head when Jones was getting his unwanted work done. Jack is the same mostly, but still there are thoughts and impulses that haunt his mind.

Jack doesn't understand completely why he does what he does. He has come to really care about all of these new people especially Carmen. She is so special to him. He can always find her in the building, she has a unique smell that connect her to him. She is sweet and beautiful and Jack wants to be with her often. She talks to him in that special way, he knows of no one else who can communicate with him like she does. Even Jones can't speak to him like Carmen can. He and Jones are as close as any dog and man can be, and he would do anything for Jonesy. However, Carmen is special and probably always will be. She was nearly killed by that bad guy George. When Jack ran to find Rose, he smelled George and wanted to rip out his throat but when he got to where Rose was being held George was already gone. Jack knew that George was dead before Jones broke down the door. He can smell death sooner than other smells and he knew all about George being dead.

Jack admires that Nancy too. She is kind to him but she's too careless for Jack. She thinks that bad gun she carries will keep her safe but it's much more than that. You have to smell the bad guys so you can know where they are. When you know where they are you can sneak up on them and grab them before they know you are near.

Jack knows there's something in his head that causes him to run faster, be stronger, and detect smells, hear sounds and even see better than before. He doesn't know what those things are in his head, and sometimes they bother him. When he has to fly in one of those stupid airplanes the roaring of the engines nearly drives him mad. It is as if the sound is drilling into his skull causing pain that makes him want to howl.

60

Carmen is selected this time to brake the champagne bottle over the bow of Rose's newest ship. She practices braking bottles out at the hanger grounds. She isn't very big and has to really work at swinging the bottle just right. The mechanics like to watch her practicing and clap and cheer when she gets it right. Carmen thinks it's necessary to brake bottles over new ships because its tradition. She has a case of cheap bubbly and is batting around one thousand. She smiles big as she can, when the stupid bottle brakes. Sometimes she has given it several whacks, and each time gets more and more determined. After all she weighs only 100 pounds and is a slight woman. She says she will get this ship launched if it's the last thing she ever does.

Finally, the big day comes and Carmen, Rose, Jones, and Jack, travel to the ship yard where the newest container ship is to be launched. There are construction people, engineers and others to join in the fun. Rose always feeds everyone after words of course, they like fancy food too. Jones is still an old duffer, he thinks folks back home could eat for a month on what this giant meal costs. Rose waves her hand and tells him it's alright, they can afford it. Jones is surprised even still that Rose refers to him when talking about company moneys He isn't even her husband for instance but still she includes him in everything she does. She has granted him power of attorney just in case anything might happen to her. Jones is not comfortable with that much belief in him. What if, and of course he never finishes the what if's, what's the use. If anything happens to Rose, it will happen to him first, he will protect her with his very life if necessary. Jones and Jack are ever vigilant watching sniffing listening and noticing everything. They work closer and closer together, sometimes anticipating each other's ideas and movements. Jack looks into Jones's eyes and Jones knows that Jack understands what he is thinking. Jones supposes that Jack's implants could have something to do with their shared thoughts.

This time there isn't a live band to help launch this newest ship, only recorded music. That's ok, Rose doesn't care about a real live band, she is more interested in Carmen's performance. Carmen is on a platform at the bough of the ship and there is a drum roll. Finally, at just the right moment she swings the bottle down and first try smashes the bottle into tiny bits. She turns around with a big grin on her lovely face. Everyone else is looking at the ship in shock or surprise and finally laughter. The sham pain bottle was filled with red ink, and has stained the blue paint on the ship red, red, red. Carmen wonders what the problem is, she has done her job well she thinks. The rest come over to her and tell her what has happened?

Carmen with a trouble look on her pretty face wants to know, "Is that some kind of joke?"

Jones wonders too," What's up with the red stuff?"

The red is fading to gray and there is a bubbling in the paint on the surface of the ships outer skin. The spot on the hull grows larger and becomes more active, there is smoke coming off the ship where the red stain started. Jones gets a whiff of something acid like and understands what has happened. Jones grabs Carmen away from the ship, swinging her off the box and onto the dock with the others. He shoves everyone back away from the ship and tells them he believes that the bottle contained corrosive acid that will eat a big hole in the ship. The acid works more and there is a hole growing through the steel of the ship. The ships outer skin is thick and burning a hole through to the inside takes some doing. Jones doesn't like this one bit, he gets his people off the dock and back to the van. They are shaken and just stare at the ship in fear. Jack isn't with them, he has run off, somewhere besides the parking lot. Jack has a scent of something he recognizes and will follow it until he catches the nut responsible for today's nastiness.

Marvin is the guilty one this time, he has been researching on the internet looking for new ways to destroy ships. He finds this acid stuff and actually tried it out, and the metal just melted into a puddle. He finds some glass bottles that won't be bothered by acid. The bottle is just like the champagne bottles that Carmen is using. Kenny knows

BOOK TWO: BRAIDY

nothing of Marvin's latest actions and Marvin wants to keep it that way. Marvin can't resist, he wants to watch that tiny woman bust the bottle full of acid all over Rose's pretty blue ship. Man, oh man, did that stuff go to work, in a matter of minutes there was a big hole in the front of that pretty blue ship, too bad! Marvin is moving fast towards his rental car, he had to park it five blocks away from the launching. He walks fast not running, he doesn't want to draw attention to himself. He doesn't know why and probably never will know, he looks over his shoulder and theirs that big black dog of Jones's. Marvin didn't need to be told twice, he started hauling ass as fast as his big belly would let him. Jack gets a glimpse of him and Marvin knows that mutt has seen him. Marvin was never any kind of athlete but this time he really moves. He gets to the rental car pops the door open and leaps inside. Just as he gets in and shuts the door, a 180-pound dog hits the car. Marvin discovers later that there is a large dent in the rental's door. He loses his damage deposit and then some. He feels he has escaped with his very life. Marvin peals rubber leaving the scene and pore old Jack can't keep up with a roaring car and gives up. Jack comes back to the parking lot dragging his very tired but, his tongue is hanging out and he is thirsty. Jones gets out and goes over to his dog, he knows that Jack has been chasing the bad guy. He pets Jack on his noble head and finds some water for him. Jack laps up the water gratefully and sits back and looks up at Jones. Jones feels bad for Jack, he knows that his dog has done his very best. Jack isn't bothered long, he licks Jones's hand and decides to try for some sympathy from the girls. They grant him lots of pets and hugs telling him what a good boy he is, Jack doesn't deny it.

61

Joni loves her job, she enjoys whirring nice clothes, and especially dresses. She has a small collection of jewelry and she shows it off to her best advantage. Joni is 45 years' young with long light brown hair, and she has lost weight since Don was killed. She is getting to thin, her doctor tells her to fatten up a bit. Joni doesn't think she is too thin, she can still pinch an inch on her tummy, although it's becoming more difficult. She lives in Brady's house, renting a room and kitchen privileges. She and Braidy are like an old couple, wanting to stay home most evenings reading books and relaxing. Joni has been learning to use the computer from Carmen and Nancy. She has a screen reader she has installed on Brady's home computer and down loads books from the National Library Service. She doesn't completely understand how it works, she just follows directions with a little help from Braidy. Braidy tells her that he misses Jack and wonders how she feels about getting a dog. Joni wonders if she had a dog guide if it would have made any difference when she and Don were kidnapped. She has been around dog guides that belong to some of her blind friends and from what she noticed is that the only barked. She doesn't think those dogs are aggressive at all, they are trained to be very gentle. She can't say that about all dog guides of course, there are differences in all dogs. Joni wants revenge for Don's death and thinks about various ways of doing what she wants. She doesn't talk of wanting revenge with anyone, she knows she could very easily end up in prison. She doesn't care about prison, she just needs to kill the bad guy that took away her man. She can never forget that guy's voice, she will know that voice anywhere. She has to be careful with some of her questions. She asks Braidy about guns, he is reluctant to talk of guns, he says they scare him. Joni understands being scared of guns, they can be unpredictable. She still wants one and does a secret search on the computer when no one is near. She discovers that one can purchase a gun over the internet and everything needed with a gun. She wonders if somehow, she can get to a place where she practices using one. She can take a taxi anywhere whenever she likes. Thanks to Rose's generosity she has money for the extra's she needs. Braidy is always willing to simply drive her anywhere and anytime, but she doesn't want anyone to know what she is doing.

Joni finds a mail service that is more or less private and rents a big box. People can come and go anytime to check their mail. No one can know of her secret plan, she can be a no one if she likes.

Joni has some trouble ordering over the internet using a credit card, the form fields aren't easy to use. After several tries, she has done it, ordered a hand gun with bullets and a nice holster that fits in a purse. Thank goodness for being a woman, she can keep her gun hidden in a purse until she needs it. The more she thinks about it the more she is glad she purchases the gun. She doesn't ever want to be attacked again, if she had a gun, she could have just pulled it out and blasted the creeps into tomorrow. If she had had a gun no one would ever know that blind woman could or would use one. Would they be surprised when she shot them dead with her secret weapon? Maybe she could keep the gun in her purse and shoot the bad guys right through the side of her handbag. She thinks she could get at least the first one, after that she would need to be very quick in shooting the other one. Since she can't see anyway, she would need to use her ears to aim the gun. She believes she can do what she needs and maybe she could meet up with those guys one at a time.

Joni gets depressed some times and doesn't dare talk with anyone about how she feels. The cause of her blindness is unknown. What kind of diagnosis is that? Doctors put on airs. They don't know as much as they lead you to believe. She has been to the leading clinics all around the United States with the same result. They poke, prod, shine those nasty little lights in her eyes and come up with nothing.

Joni's family are scattered in many places and rarely write or call. She believes that they are afraid of her because of the blindness.

This new job she has with the shipping company feels right to her. There are several people she knows who have disabilities including Carmen. Joni has some usable vision, there are shapes, outlines of faces and with the help of special equipment she can read print. The practicality of her remaining residual vision isn't very useful in day to day living. She carries a white cane and actually uses it when she is somewhere uncertain or new. Most of the time she has been places before and remembers things.

Braidy like many others who work for the shipping company is kind and nice. He is a real gentleman. He has had experience being around blind persons probably because of Carmen. Anyway, it doesn't matter, all that she wants is to kill that nasty man Kenny. She has to stop herself from reliving the events leading up to Don's death. She can't change the past, he is dead. Changing the past is impossible for sure, but killing Kenny isn't. She isn't so concerned about the other bad guy, he was trying at one point to stop Kenny from hurting her with those lighted cigarettes. She still feels the burns the jerk caused.

Joni loves her job working for Rose. Rose is so thoughtful of others, she's like a breath of spring every day. Joni enjoys Rose visiting her along with Jones. These are good folks who care about their people. She looks forward to going to work and that is unusual. Working as a dispatcher at the cab company was interesting, however the management wasn't as fare or accommodating. Joni feels good about Rose's company and working with the others too. She feels like they are more like family than employers. She sometimes forgets about her sadness's and has to chuckle especially when that big mutt of Jones's comes lumbering along. The dog always stops for a short visit. He doesn't bark, he is so immense that she can simply feel his presents. It's like that dog fills the room with dog.

Joni is determined and will kill that Kenny. She pictures pulling the trigger often and that brings her a certain amount of satisfaction.

62

Rose's newest ship will be repaired, the hole in the hull is above the waterline and so the ship wouldn't have been in much danger if the attack had happened out at sea. The problem is more annoying than anything. The ship builders remove the plates with the burn hole and install new ones. The repair takes only a week and soon Rose's ship is quietly launched again. Carmen is really embarrassed, she thinks she should have noticed the difference in the way the bottle felt. Jones tells her that it wasn't her fault. He believes that someone switched the bottles out at the hanger where the sham pain was being kept. Carmen has a problem with blaming herself, she feels guilty about many situations that cannot possibly be her fault. Jones is patient with her, he knows about feeling guilty and spends time with her walking around. They walk to a nearby park and Carmen is traveling comfortably using her cane with ease. Jones really admires his friend and tells her he is so proud of her. Carmen is embarrassed and turns a bit red.

She tells Jones he is the best and he has saved her from a life time of failure. Jones has a problem taking any kind of compliment and just shrugs it off. They have walked all around a small lake in the park and Carmen can hear the ducks and geese. Jones tells her there is a couple of Swans swimming about looking lovely. Jack is walking around on his own, staying close to the people. He sniffs and lifts his leg like any dog does, but still is watchful. Jack stays close enough to Jones that he looks like he must be on a leash. Jones never uses a leash; Jack stays close on his own.

Suddenly Jack barks and launches off toward the trees. Jack is on a mission and surprised Jones. The dog actually tares up the sod when he takes off.

Carmen lets out a short scream and holds onto Jones with both hands," What's going on?"

Jones doesn't know, putting his right arm around her slim waste, "That Jack is after something or someone."

Jack is right, there is someone in the trees, and that someone is good old Marvin. This time Jack is quicker and grabs Marvin by the leg. Jack has big jaws and bites down past the material of Marvin's pants. Jack gets a good hold on Marvin's ankle and Marvin howls in pain. Carmen grabs Jones's hand and won't let go for anything. She doesn't want to be left behind. Jones knows that Jack will hold this guy until Jones tells him to release. He chuckles at Carmen's determination in holding on. She is small that's true but strong for her size. She will hold on and allow herself to be drug along if necessary.

When they get to Marvin, Jones sees that it is that Marvin, and he has a rifle lying beside him on the ground. Jones grabs Marvin by the neck and drags him to his feet.

Jones commands, "Jack release!"

Jack lets go, Jones can see blood in Jacks teeth and he licks his chops. Jones wonders if Jack would actually enjoy eating the bad guys some times. Jack comes over to Carmen and she holds his collar.

Jones pins Marvin up against a convenient tree and demands, "What in the hell are you doing?"

Marvin is terrified, he knows of this mad man's violence and fears for his life. Marvin can't explain the gun, he just can't talk, he is that scared. Jones cools down some, he doesn't need to kill this dude here and now. He wants answers and where they are isn't the best place for questions.

He says to Marvin, "You will come with us or I will tell my dog to finish having you for lunch."

Marvin looks over at Jack and shudders. Jack looks back and licks his lips. Marvin nearly wets himself, he doesn't like this big dog, and his ankle is throbbing and still bleeding. Jones takes Marvin's arm and heads for headquarters building. Carmen and Jack walk behind, Carmen ever mindful that Jack is alert and ready for action. She does have a cane with her and can travel on her own if she needs to.

When the four arrive back at headquarters, Jones tries to be discreet with his captive but still people notice. Marvin is practically dancing on his toes because Jones is applying so much pressure on his arm. Marvin doesn't like this one little bit; these guys could take

BOOK TWO: BRAIDY

the law into their own hands and hang him or worse. They all take the elevator to the top floor and Jones tells Joe to find Rose. Joe doesn't ask why, he simply goes about finding Rose. She comes breezing down from the roof. She has a small greenhouse growing lovely roses up there. The roof has always been somewhat baron and she wants to beautify it some. When Rose sees, Marvin being held by Jones she gets really mad.

Rose still holding her trowel waves it under Marvin's nose, "So you're the dirty bastard that has been destroying my ships?"

Marvin blinking his eyes rapidly wines, "I want a lawyer."

Rose smirks right into his ugly face saying, "I don't think so, you might get a trip out over the ocean in our new helicopter for a nice swim. You know the helicopter that you tried to wreck." She is so mad she sees red.

Fortunately for Marvin Rose's red isn't like Joneses red and he survives at least for the moment.

Marvin knows that his life hasn't been so good, there are so many crimes that he can't possibly remember them all. Not only Rose's ships and property but before those too. Marvin started out being bad and never did finish any kind of school. Even when they tried to send him to reform-school he escaped from there killing his roommate in the process. Marvin knows no other life than crime. He did learn all about Diesel engines some on his own and some from another criminal like himself. Marvin enjoys working on the huge engines on ships, and if he were to go straight that would be the way. However, he can stay working legitimately only for short periods of time. Before long unfortunately, he has to walk on the wild side. He believes the world owes him a nice living.

Marvin chances a look around at these angry faces and sees his miserable life flash before his eyes. Marvin knows he is a dead man and probably soon. The one person who appears pissed off the most is that Rose. How can someone so beautiful suddenly look so hostile? She looks like a different woman and the way she looks scares hi m more than that big ugly bastard of a dog.

Marvin would start praying if he believed that crap, instead he mutters under his breath.

The dog growls menacingly, Jones pierces him with a coldest stare ever and Rose gets even nastier looking if possible.

Kenny has been waiting for Marvin in another greasy spoon café, those little cafés are their favorites. Marvin doesn't answer his phone and has been gone for hours now. Kenny gets a bad feeling, he wonders if that stupid Marvin got into trouble with Jones. Say now, wouldn't that be something if Jones smashed good old Marvin into mush. Kenny is thrilled by the thought, he really doesn't like Marvin of course. Kenny secretly is afraid of Marvin, Marvin is at least 100 pounds heavier than Kenny.

Kenny gets up and forgets to pay his bill before leaving, and the boss guy comes flying out of the café after him. The man is wearing an apron that flaps all around him as he runs. He is holding a slip of paper, and yells at Kenny.

"You didn't pay me you creep, here is the bill, now pay me!"

Kenny pulls out a twenty and the man is satisfied, the money is more than the bill. The café owner doesn't offer any change and Kenny just keeps on walking. Kenny finally remembers that he isn't driving his old van anymore and finds the Crown Vick, with a parking ticket on the windshield. He tears it up like all the rest he has gotten, they don't know where he is living anyway. He doesn't know if the license plates are current or not, by the time it matters he will have another vehicle anyway.

At headquarters building Rose asks Joe to call Joni if she's not too busy. Joni comes up on the elevator and asks Joe what's up. Joe tells her he doesn't know but Rose would like to talk with her. Joni knocks at the office door and Jones lets her in and takes her hand.

Jones wanting to be understanding speaks softly to her, "Joni, I'm sorry if this may be difficult for you, we have one of the bad guys that captured you and Don.

Joni's heart skips a beat, could this be the one that killed her man? Joni is cool, she has gotten good at hiding her feelings. She tells Jones ok, where is the guy. Rose tells her that they have him over by Carmen's desk. Jack barks once, telling her at least she thinks that he is guarding Marvin. By this time, Marvin is resigned to his fate, he knows he is a dead man. When he sees, Joni coming over he knows that he is for sure. This is the broad they kidnapped and that stupid Kenny shot that guy Don. Marvin sags against the edge of the desk and Rose almost feels sorry for him. Not for long though, all she has to do is remember all of her ships and people that were destroyed by this mad man.

BOOK TWO: BRAIDY

Marvin is told to say something and he wants to know why, when he asks why Joni tells them that he definitely is one of them. She says that he's not the guy that shot Don, he was however the one who grabbed him in the first place.

Jones and Rose look at each other and wonder what's next. Jones knows that they could take Marvin here out to sea and launch him out of the helicopters open door. Rose and Jones both know that the police won't do much, there's not enough real evidence to convict Marvin that they know of. Marvin is really scared, he knows that the company people are capable of dumping bodies out to sea, and he starts to beg. Rose isn't affected by his pleas, she can't forget what happened to her people, they are all dead because of Marvin's attacks on her ships. Jones wonders too, about what they should do with Marvin.

Jones looking dangerous at Marvin asks, "Where is Kenny?"

Marvin tells him that Kenny was waiting for him at a café. He provides Jones where the café is and the name of it. None of them have ever eaten there, they like to think they have better taste than that. Jack sits back and stairs at Marvin never looking away, Jack can be scary at times like these. Carmen has wrapped a bandage around Marvin's ankle, she isn't gentle and Marvin yelps when she pulls it tight. She wraps tape around the entire bandage and doesn't clean out the wound first. She doesn't want to get Marvin's blood on Rose's carpet. Marvin figures his only chance now is to throw himself on their mercy. The company folks are so mad that Marvin's pleading for mercy has no affect. The problem is how to get rid of Marvin after they have finished with him. Rose isn't a murderer and has never killed anyone in her entire life. When she thinks of her people who died for nothing, she is changing her mind.

63

Kenny travels back to the island in the small boat, getting wet and not even caring. He doesn't like Marvin but misses his nasty presents. At least with Marvin there was someone to argue with if nothing else. Kenny misses Barbra too and wonders about her. He doesn't know who the boats belong to in the first place and doesn't think it matters. Probably drug dealers owned this house and the boats and those guys are long gone. They have either been killed by rival gangs or captured by the cops. Anyway, it doesn't matter at all to him, they are gone and he is here.

He heats some of those frozen dinners, he makes two forgetting for the moment that Marvin isn't there. He thinks oh well he'll just eat both dinners, they aren't that bad, not like Barbra's cooking but ok. Kenny wanders around not knowing what to do and finally decides to lay down and rest. Kenny is tired, more than he thinks and soon falls fast asleep.

Barbra sees Kenny come back by himself in the little boat and wonders where the other one is. She can't remember his name exactly maybe its Melvin or Morris or yeah, it's Marvin. She is trying to forget these nasty boys and has mostly succeeded. She has gotten in touch with people who can direct her toward charters. The men are fat and loud, and they always try to put their paws on her. She is good at avoiding their unwanted touches and grabs and remains bright and cheery. She always has plenty of their favorite beers in the cooler and offers them cold ones. They are so glad for the beer that most of the time they drink beer and leave her alone.

She has gotten to know the waters around the island and can always make sure that they catch some fish. She fixes lunch for them if they want to pay her extra and the big fat porkers chow it down hardly without breathing. Their fatness disgusts her and she wants to hang her head over the side and barf. She is good at what she does and puts up with their crap, she wants their money

Barb doesn't think of herself as being greedy only wanting to survive like anyone else. She has been welcomed at the small village on the back side of the island and enjoys living amongst them. She looks around for any and all eligible men but there aren't any. Most of the people are already attached and she respects that. They have a strange way of living, much different than what she has known. They have a leader, or chief, whatever he is somehow is important. Every decision that is made in the village has to go before the chief. He's an old duffer who smells like soured life and she is somewhat intimidated by his presents. He has never said anything to her to make her feel uncomfortable, it's just something that she can't describe.

Barb can get along with anyone and follows the rules like everyone else does. She enjoys her independence and doesn't take anything he says personally. She loved her father and he taught her much, but he didn't own her. She doesn't ever want to be owned by any man and secretly keeps her own council. She can be as nice as anyone and she believes that the villagers think she's wonderful. She does enjoy visiting with the women and exchange ideas and recipes.

Barb has been developing relationships with folks on shore who provide her with names of fat guys who want to catch big fish. She is becoming her own woman and feels good about that. She gets lonely sometimes, she was very influenced by that Rose and her man Jones. He looks so big and tough. She thinks he's very different than other men she has known and wonders why? Barb will get a good man one day she just knows it. Meanwhile, she keeps on working helping guys and occasionally gals catch the big ones.

64

Joni wants to ask questions of Marvin, she needs to know where the other guy is? Marvin tells them about the island, and Rose and Jones know nothing about what he is talking of. Joni doesn't give up at that, she wants Marvin to take them to the island. Jones looks at Joni in a different light. He sees that she is very determined wanting to do something. He lets her continue as much to find out more from Marvin but also to understand what Joni is after. Jones knows she is still angry over Don being killed but doesn't think it's any more than bitter feelings. He thinks, *'Who can blame her, after* all Don *was her man, and they have killed him.'* Apparently according to Joni, Marvin wasn't the one who pulled the trigger. Marvin is telling the truth Jones believes, he is terrified of Jack and none of the rest of the people look happy about Marvin's deeds either.

Marvin agrees to show them the island where he thinks Kenny is hiding out. Rose tells Joe to mind the store and he goes down to Joni's desk. He has all the calls transferred there, he will be in charge of the company for a short while. Rose likes Joe and trusts him to make good decisions. She gives him her phone number and tells him to call her if he needs anything. Joe is proud of his new power and takes his responsibility's seriously. Rose doesn't worry and they decide to call Braidy to fly over in the helicopter.

It's not far to Kenny's island but Rose wants to get this over with soonest. In a few minutes Braidy comes flying over and lands on the roof. Braidy is filled in and looks at Marvin with unveiled hatred.

He doesn't try to hide his displeasure for Marvin, "So this is the creep that blows up ships and sabotages our helicopters?"

Marvin thought that he was terrified with Jack and Jones but when he sees the look in Brady's eye, he trembles more. Marvin may not ever be killed by these guys, he may die of a heart attack instead. Could happen he thinks and decides that would be better. He thinks '*heart* attack as hard as he can, but his heart is good and he goes to the roof with the rest.

Jack is close to his sore ankle ready for some more Marvin. He doesn't doubt that Jack the dog could finish him off and doesn't like that way out for sure. The helicopter still smells new, it is cushy with soft leather seats and thick carpet on the floor. This new helicopter is incredibly quiet and everyone can talk in a normal voice. Braidy remembers an island and wonders if it might be the one that Marvin means. Braidy sees that it is, the island where Jim and he saw the lone woman fishing.

They land the helicopter on the front lawn and move over to the house. Jones and Braidy are both armed and have their guns up and out. They aren't taking any chances with Kenny. Kenny isn't there however, he has driven his boat around the island looking for Barbra.

Joni is ready with her purse gun to kill Kenny at first sound. She doesn't care what might happen to her, she just needs revenge.

The village people have noticed the helicopter landing of course it's not often that one lands on their island. Barbra has provided them with a radio to be used in case of an emergency and they believe this has to be one. They call Barbra, she is on her boat fishing with some more of those big fat guys with too much money and not enough brains. She gets the information and wonders what's up with all that. She looks at her party of fisherman and asks if they are done for the day? One man is, he is had good luck catching a nice big fish that he wants to get mounted. The second man isn't happy, he hasn't caught anything as large as his friend has. He is really trying and having no luck. Barbra uses her nicest voice with her best Jamaican accent and persuades the gentleman to try another day, she will take him out to a better place. He wants to know if she will charge him for another day.

She bubbles out with all her adorable charms, "No man, it's on me don't you know."

She is so charming and inviting that the pore guy just melts under her spell.

Barbra runs her boat faster than she should, she wants to know what's happening over on the island in the worse way. She takes her fisherman back to shore and waves them a cheery goodbye hardly allowing them time to get ashore. She runs her boat as fast as she can go back to the island. She doesn't even try for stealth, instead she drives her boat right up to the boat dock by the boathouse. She grabs her father's revolver on the way off her boat and moves over to the front porch. She stops and listens and hears the people from the shipping company coming out. Jones looks at her in surprise and Braidy says he has seen her around here before. He tells them that this woman is quite a fisher person. Barbra recognizes Rose and Jones from her rescue.

Marvin isn't happy to see Barbra either, he remembers the things he said and tried to do to her. Marvin thinks to himself, *this isn't his day.'*

Barbra hardly looks at Marvin she thinks he's nothing.

Barbra looking serious and challenging, "So where's that Kenny?"

Marvin says he has no idea, and Barbra can see that he is telling the truth. Barbra's radio beeps, then she excuses herself pretty as you please. She reminds Jones of a busy executive doing business as usual. Barbra goes out on the porch to answer the call. She finds out from the village people that Kenny is snooping around their side of the island. He doesn't come ashore but; looks all around. They tell her that they think he is looking for her. She tells them thanks and stay in touch please. She returns to the inside of the house and asks,

"So, what do we do with this garbage?"

Rose, smiles at that, nodding to Barbra and saying, "You got that right!"

Marvin is beyond fear now, he knows he will die this day, how doesn't really matter anymore, as long as it isn't that dog. Jack licks his chops again and not just a little lick but good and loud, he even allows a drip of drool to fall. Marvin shrinks back wanting to disappear but having to stay right there looking back at that bad dog. Jack is having some fun with Marvin, he isn't usually such a bad boy, but is enjoying Marvin's downfall. Barbra tells them that she has things to do and starts to leave.

Joni has been listening and says, "Stop!" she doesn't know this Barbra but is suspicious and wants to ask questions.

Barbra stops and looks at Joni, she can see that she is determined about something.

She looks amused and asks, Joni, "What's going on here?"

Joni doesn't want to say, she wants Kenny all to herself.

BOOK TWO: BRAIDY

Kenny moves off away from the back side of the island and when he rounds the end of the island sees the helicopter and Barbra's boat too. He isn't wanting any part of the company people if Jones is with them. He turns away heading out to sea. The day isn't too rough and he can make good time over the waves. Kenny doesn't know where he is going and decides to head for land. He turns in a big curve that eventually allows him to get to shore. Kenny isn't notice by most but, Barbra sees him and jumps in her boat pursuing him. Jones sees the chase and mentions it to Braidy.

Braidy looks over at the two racing boats and asks, "What should I do?"

Jones wonders too, and he looks for something to tie Marvin up with and decides that's not necessary. Jones tells Jack to guard, pointing at Marvin. Jack moves closer to Marvin within grabbing distance. Marvin settles down to the floor in the corner, he isn't moving for anything or anyone while that dog is there.

Jack understands what Jones has told him and stares intensely at Marvin. He can taste the creep's blood and some ancient dog in his past wants more blood. Jack is a civilized hound and refrains. He loves Jones and will obey him no matter what else may happen. Jack understands this bad guy has done something that makes his people unhappy and for now that's enough. Jack doesn't understand the meanings of their words, not always at least. He doesn't know about Kenny blowing up Rose's ships for instants. However, he does understand that this guy wanted to hurt Carmen and that can't ever happen. As long as Jack lives, Carmen will be protected and Rose too. Jack has been around Jones long enough to know that Jones is really strong and tough. He believes that he and Jones can do anything. Jack loves Jones as much as any dog can love any human. He has vague memories of a farm somewhere but the memories are growing dim. His life is here and now with these people and he will do his best to help in whatever way he can.

65

Kenny's boat is much faster than Barbra's and he soon leaves her in the lurch. Braidy has started the Helicopter and the two men are off after Kenny. Kenny looks up at the noise of the chopper and pushes harder on the throttle, but no more speed, the boat is flying cross the water flat out. Jones and Braidy are wondering what to do, they can't stop Kenny moving this fast. There are floats on this new helicopter, they could land on the water ahead of Kenny but he could just drive right around them. Jones wonders about just shooting the bastard and pulls out his gun. Braidy says they had better not, the coast Guard is near. There is a Coast Guard cutter moving through the water going in the same direction but apparently not pursuing him. Jones and Braidy are frustrated and can't do anything without the Coasties' knowing too much. They watch while Kenny continues to fly a crossed the ocean like he hasn't a care in the world. Kenny knows he is safe for the moment, he sees the Coast Guard too and for once is glad. The Coast Guard pay no attention to Kenny, they are however looking at the helicopter wondering why it is chasing Kenny's boat. Kenny gets to shore and waves them off, he is ok, they pull away ignoring the helicopter. Jones, looks at Braidy wondering what to do, he doesn't know, they fly back to the island.

Kenny is so lucky he can't believe it himself. He ties up the boat and finds his car, there is another parking ticket under the wiper blade. He gives the little slip of paper the usual treatment allowing the scraps to fall in the gutter. Kenny realizes that Marvin, must have been captured by the company people. Kenny snickers at what will probably happen to good old Marvin. Kenny wishes he could be there when they drop Marvin's fat but out of the helicopter, what a huge splash that fat boy will make.

BOOK TWO: BRAIDY

Kenny goes to his hide out, the one he has kept for just in case. He parks his Ford in the attached garage and finds some of those frozen dinners they have been eating lately. He thinks his cooking isn't that bad and decides to cook two of them. After all they are really small, hardly enough to feed a midget. Kenny doesn't think twice about Marvin he doesn't care, he just wants to stay out of sight for a while.

Kenny finds houses like the one he is in, he has always been lucky at finding what he wants. Other people search for months trying to find a nice place to live. Kenny finds them right away, he isn't particular as most people and so the first one that comes along will do. This house has mice and cracks in the plaster. The plumbing is leaky and he notices that the walls spark at him. How in the world can a wall spark at someone? The plumbing drips, leaks rattles and grown. The electric is blowing fuses often and Kenny fixes the problem with a dead fuse and a penny. He places the penny in the fuse holder first using an insulated screw driver than inserts the blown-out fuse on top of the copper. Sometimes the sparks come out of the fuse box making an interesting fire show. Kenny doesn't care about this house, after all its temporary. He can just leave whenever things get uncomfortable.

The mice are a different matter though. Kenny hates those little bastards. When he tries to sleep, they climb in bed with him, probably just to try and keep warm. Who in the hell cares why, the problem is they walk over his face driving him buggy with those tiny claws. When they squeak in his ear that wakes him up with a start. Finally, he decides to poison them all and buys a big box of mouse poison. The stuff is supposed to make the nasties bleed to death. Kenny thinks that people some time use this stuff to thin blood. So, what a way to kill someone, maybe the next time he has a prisoner like that black bitch, he should feed them some mouse poison. Apparently, the bleeding is inside the mouse, so no mess if he feeds it to one of his victims.

Kenny never wants to know any neighbors. People who are snoopy really piss him off. He usually turns around and walks away from their unwanted pleasantries.

He finally falls asleep in spite of the mouse populations and dreams of torturing that black woman all over again.

66

Barbra knows that she can never catch Kenny's boat, there is a 200-horse power engine on the back and that engine can out run her Diesel anytime. She sees the helicopter pursuing Kenny and then the Coast Guard too. She slows her boat and turns back toward the island. She will go around to the village and thank them in person for their help. She likes those folks and wants to protect them and keep them out of any trouble. Barbra doesn't worry about meeting up with company people, they are alright. She is concerned over that blind woman, she was hiding something in that purse she carries. If Barbra's guess is right, that girl has a big bad gun in there. She thinks Joni knows how to use it too. Just because she is blind doesn't mean she hasn't feelings and her blindness won't stop her from shooting the bad guys. Barbra likes that woman's Spirit and admires her determination. She wonders if one of those bad guys might have killed her man. Barbra would feel that way if someone killed her man, well that is if she had one.

Marvin is taken to his island and is provided some very nice MRE's to eat and a water purifier for drinking, and 100 of everyone's favorite books including several bibles. The bibles were Brady's idea, more as a joke than a demand. Who knows maybe Marvin will see the light whatever that means. Anyway, it doesn't matter, Marvin is there for life and won't ever be free.

Jones and Braidy finally tell Rose what they have done with Marvin. She burst into tears with relief and tells them she is so proud of them. Braidy gets embarrassed and looks away out the window over the harbor. Jones just takes her in his arms and tells her that she's ok. Rose doesn't like killing and has been worrying about Marvin. She wants him gone and thinks he needs to be punished but not killed.

BOOK TWO: BRAIDY

Jones says he understands how she feels and she is glad. Jones, does it for Rose, however, he actually believes that the rat needs killing like any other rat. He would have no problem just dropping Marvin out of the helicopter at 5000 feet or so, without a parachute of course. Braidy thinks that sounds good to him but they both respect Rose enough so that won't ever happen.

Marvin should be glad he's still alive. That big assed dog of Jones really wanted him for lunch. Kenny is getting off Scott free, when he is just as guilty. Marvin doesn't think the Big Lift folks are being fare. Than he remembers that the bad stuff he did was mostly on his own. Kenny did his own thing, and bad but probably not as bad as what Marvin did.

Marvin has always wondered what it would be like living on a tropical island and now he knows. The weather is nice, not much rain and plenty of sunshine. The days get hot that's for sure but the nights are pleasant. He can sit under some small trees near the top of the island and most days are ok. He is so sick of MRE's already. He looks through the supply of them and discovers their all the same. Marvin has always hated macaroni and cheese. The cheese must be there, however as hard as he looks, he just can't find any. Mac and some sort of phony bologna cheese and there are hundreds of them all the same. The water taste like plastic and is warm. Marvin can't help but feel sorry for himself. He is so sorry that he regrets what he has done to Rose's ships and to others over the years he has forgotten about.

Marvin settles into a routine and is sometimes surprised when someone from the shipping company shows up. He doesn't want to ever admit it, but he's actually glad for the company. Even Jones is better than nothing. Marvin thinks that maybe Jones isn't so bad, after all if he were Jones, he would probably feel the same way.

Marvin isn't much of a reader, and so reading books is difficult for him. He gets frustrated and throws several books away before he realizes that he's holding them upside down. He feels stupid for not noticing that earlier. After he turns books around in the proper direction, they begin to make sense.

Marvin will survive alright but he will be very unhappy and lonely too. He thinks if only he had a woman here that could make things different. He can see that Joni in his mind's eye. She is actually not bad looking, and who in the hell cares if she's blind. When you get right down to what's important who cares if a girl is blind or not.

Marvin loses weight, the meals Ready to Eat aren't too good. The diet is boring and much of the time Marvin isn't even hungry. He dreams of a juicy steak or even one of those greasy hamburgers from one of those café's they use to feed in. Marvin really loses it when he thinks of Barbra's wonderful baking and cooking. Now that girl was some kind of beautiful and could she cook!

Marvin grows a long beard and to his distress, it comes in gray. He never had gray hair before, must be the fault of that dog of Jones's.

67

Rose's new ship has been repaired and repainted, it looks good as new, well mostly because it is new. The ship-yard gang have replaced the entire plate that the acid was on. The work isn't as bad as Jones thought it might have been. These ship builders are good at building ships of course but also at repairing ships. Over the years, they have repaired many company ships and have earned a reputation for excellent work. Marvin is stored away and won't be a problem anymore and who knows where Kenny has gotten too. Jones tells Rose that he wants to go hunting for Kenny and she finally agrees, she says if it's the only way than ok. Jones reassures her and tells her that he will take Jack with him always. Besides he should be home almost every night. She hears the almost and isn't happy with that. Jones loves this woman and will rid her of Kenny and anyone else who causes her trouble. She is innocent and he hates people who attack others simply because they are greedy or worse than that, nuts!

Jones sets out hunting from the last sighting of Kenny and gets absolutely nowhere. Kenny is good at disappearing into the crowd or off the face of the earth. He checks out restaurants, cafes, rental stores and even bars. No one has any idea what he is talking about; Jack is with him always and guys step back at first, but good old Jack does his nice dog thing and most warm up to him. Jones travels to the island and the house is empty, he then goes around to the other side of the island. He sees the milk cows, black and white Holsteins, and that reminds him of his farm days. Jack too is looking, Jones can only wonder what Jack is thinking. Jones visits with the village people. At first, they are suspicious but warm up to him and Jack after Jack gets goofy. Jack sits up holding out his paw for shaking. After that he rolls on the ground and whimpers like a puppy. The village kids just love it and want to play on the ground with Jack. Jones is gentle asking easy questions in an easy manner. He wishes he had Carmen here to help him, she and Jones make a good team. Jones finds out that Barbra visits often and brings the people food and other needs. They think she is the best and look forward to having her back. Jones finds out that the village people have been spying for Barbra on the big house on the other side of the island. They tell him that those guys are bad men and kill the island cats.

There aren't that many cats, and each one is needed to keep the rats away. Jones tells them that the bad guys probably won't be back. He asks them who owns the big house and those boats that Barbra apparently owns now. They tell him that the people who used to live in the big house when away many years ago, and mostly the house has set empty.

Jones thinks about talking about his old life on the farm but decides not. He looks over their cows and wants to give them some advice. He can see that the cows are lacking in minerals. A simple mineral block could do wonders for those cows. Cows that produce milk need more minerals than cows who aren't. Cows that produce milk have to draw on every resource they have to make enough milk to be worthwhile. Jones remembers hearing something about the head guy, chief maybe, and decides to have a visit with whoever he may be.

Jones squatting down asks, "I wonder who is in charge of the dairy herd?"

Village people are startled by the question, "Oh hey, that's our chief." Pointing towards the small barn.

Jones isn't sure what to do and looks around for someone to ask. Finally, he slowly walks over to a gray-haired old man who looks as thin as a rail.

Jones waits to be noticed by the old gent. Finally, the old boy looks up smiling gently at Jones.

Jones moving slowly and trying not to look so big, "Hello, I am a friend of Barbra's. I am looking for her, it's nothing really that important."

Chief finally looking Jones in the eye, "Oh Barbra will be back soon, she is so good for us. She fishes and protects us against the bad men from the other side of the island."

Jones bending slightly looks all around, "How are your cows doing? I notice them grazing over there. They are hungry I guess."

Chief looking where Jones Is looking says, "I am worried about those cows, I try to take good care of them but still they aren't doing so good."

Jones settling down on the ground beside the old man, "Oh they don't need much, I use to milk cows and know all about dairy cows. They look mostly ok, I could suggest providing them some minerals."

Chief looking interested, "What do you mean minerals?"

Jones feeling his way along with this oldster, "You see Sir, when I milked cows, I put out a big block of minerals for them to lick on as they wanted. At first the block disappeared in a few days but as they got enough, they needed less."

Chief not understanding exactly what he is saying, "Where do these minerals come from? We don't have any big stores on this island. Where do we get mineral blocks?"

Jones understanding, "Well I'll tell Barbra and she will bring some for you, would that be alright?"

Chief nodding, "Ok, if Barbra says its good than it is. She is good to us, we trust her."

68

Kenny decides it's a good idea to beet it out of town. Before he goes, he needs to visit that blind woman Joni. She is the reason for his latest failure although he doesn't really understand exactly how or why? He feels that he should have killed the broad with her worthless boyfriend. He still gets mad over Don's tricking him with the zapper thing. Kenny knows a lot about Rose's Company, he has more spies inside the building and that Johnathan out at the air strip. Kenny knows that Joni is working at the front desk and that she goes home with Braidy each night. He finds out where Braidy lives and lays in wait for her. She is blind and will never know he is even near. He is cocky and doesn't even bother trying to hide himself.

Joni goes home with Braidy most nights, she rents a room from him. He enjoys having someone for company he is a sociable guy and likes people. He has been feeding her extra special meals trying to fatten her up. She has gotten slimmer since Dons death and her friends worry about her. Braidy gets them home and says he needs to go to the store and will be right back.

Joni settles into her favorite chair and turns on her latest book. She has a nice player that the National Library provides readers and she relaxes after working at Rose's Company. She is starting to look forward to Brady's delightful meals, he is a wonderful cook. She hears something at the back door and grabs her purse. She has not gotten past what has happened to her and is vigilant.

She goes to the kitchen and listens some more, whoever is out there isn't quiet or careful. She can hear him or maybe her, walking along the sidewalk. She steps into a small pantry and waits listening.

The creep just walks in like he owns the place, she wonders how he got the lock undone. She hasn't got time to think about that, her

BOOK TWO: BRAIDY

heart is beating a hundred miles a minute. The guy comes right on in, like he has a key, she waits. The guy, and she can tell he's a man, sneaks in loudly. She wonders at that thought for some reason. She has her gun out and is holding it with two hands. She lets the creep get past her and in a rush, springs out after him. She runs into his back hard enough to knock him around.

He exclaims, "What the hell?"

Joni recognizes Kenny's voice, she has the bastard that killed her Don. Kenny is really surprised and at first doesn't move.

Joni is mad and tough and says to him, "Don't move, not a bit."

Kenny feels the object in his back and knows it's a gun. How could this blind bitch get the drop on him so easy. Kenny doesn't move, he stands still. He has heard something in her voice that tells him she means business. For the first time in a while Kenny is terrified. Joni tells him that he killed her Don and now he's going to die. Kenny thinks of begging, but not from a blind bitch. Joni takes in a big lung of air and gets ready to kill this creep.

She has thought about this moment for so long and now it's here. She wants to kill Kenny but just can't, she's not a murderer, she begins to sob. Kenny starts to look around and she pushes the gun harder into his back, even though she is crying the gun is still against him.

Braidy comes up the driveway whistling some off-key tune. He comes in the same door that Kenny used and sees Joni holding a gun on Kenny.

Braidy looking amused smiling too announces, "Well now what do you know about that!"

Joni, starts to lower her gun and Kenny leaps away, but not fast enough, Braidy is armed too. Before Kenny can even think about getting away Braidy has him covered. Brady's aim is steady and he can see that. Kenny knows he is dead and doesn't move. Braidy tells him to turn around and ties his hands up with flex ties. Nancy has provided each of them with flex ties. Braidy makes Kenny lay on the floor and places is big foot on Kenny's back and ties his ankles with flex ties using one hand. Joni is over beside Kenny in an instant and holds her gun to his head. Kenny is done for and knows it.

69

Joni manages to call Rose using one hand speed dialing and Jones and all agree to come right out. Carmen is close to Rose and demands to be included, and of course Jack wouldn't miss it for the world. When they arrive at Braidy's house they find Joni still holding her gun on Kenny and Braidy munching a piece of ham wrapped up in lettuce. When Jones gets to Joni, she hands him her gun and moves back to the wall. She leans on the wall like it is her lifeline. She suddenly is very weary and needs the support of the wall.

Rose sighs in relief asking, "What do we do with this guy, he is worse than the other one, she means Marvin of course?"

Jones shakes his head at Joni, and asks her, "Were you going to shoot Kenny?"

Joni shaky draws in a giant breath before saying, "I have dreamed about killing this creep forever it seems but when it came time to pull the trigger I just couldn't."

Rose comes over to Joni and holds her close, "I understand that completely, I couldn't have killed Kenny either. Its ok honey you're alright now, this will pass, you'll see."

Joni is glad she hasn't killed anyone. Jones wishes he hadn't had to kill anyone either, but someone has too he guesses.

Rose looks at her two favorite men with trust and warmth and wants to know, "Is their room on that island for Kenny too?"

Jones thinks that is fitting, both of the bad guys on the same island to keep each other company.

BOOK TWO: BRAIDY

THE END

www.ingramcontent.com/pod-product-compliance
Lightning Source LLC
LaVergne TN
LVHW021810060526
838201LV00058B/3311